# The Co

J. Paul McDonald

Published by
POLYMAC BOOK PUBLISHING CO. in 2005

First published in the Republic of Ireland by:
POLYMAC BOOK PUBLISHING CO.

Printed and bound in Ireland by
Betaprint
Unit D1A, Bluebell Industrial Estate, Dublin 12.

ISBN 0-9551027-0-7
ISBN 978-0-9551027-0-7

POLYMAC BOOK PUBLISHING CO.
Carrowkeel House, Carrowkeel,
Clogher, Claremorris,
Co. Mayo, Ireland.

To my wife, Mary Virginia Monroe-McDonald,
Who everyone knows as Ginger,
My Love, My Heart

# Acknowledgements

I would like to thank the people of Loudoun County, Virginia, who have chosen to live in an historic and beautiful environment of gently rolling countryside that has provided the color and authentic backdrop for my story. I would also like to thank the judiciary and court administration staff of the 20th Judicial Circuit of Virginia who assisted me mightily when I was a young, struggling attorney in Leesburg attempting to learn my profession. It should be noted that in my tale the action takes place in the mythical 33rd Judicial Circuit of Virginia. I hope you feel I painted you and your efforts to administer justice in a fair and truthful light. You have my undying support and gratitude. Loudoun County has been blessed with outstanding jurists and court administrators. During my time as a defense attorney we had wonderful, fair and courageous judges. Carlton Penn and Thomas Horne were the Circuit Court judges. John Ryan was the judge in the Juvenile and Domestic Relations Court and Archibald Aiken was the judge in the General District Court. I would also cite three outstanding clerks of the Loudoun County Circuit Court as examples; the late Buddy Martz, Freddie Howard and Richard Kirk. I am sure the current office holders are equally good; it is just that they were not serving during my time.

Like most writers of fiction, I have taken a little poetic license along the way. For instance, the system of indigent representations in criminal cases was actually changed in the mid-eighties with the creation of an Office of Public Defenders. However, it suited my story to make, *The Counsellor*, Patrick J. Hurst, a more modern defense attorney, so I set my tale in the late nineties but utilized the old defense system of court appointed counsel. There are two other areas where I have purposely deviated from conventional court practice, particularly in a murder trial but to tell you now would give away the story and spoil it for you. Suffice it to say as an old defense counsel; sometimes it would be better if fiction indeed was fact. Brave action like depicted in my story might save innocent defendants and better portray justice to the public. Many lawyers believe in the legal system but the belief in justice is something different and very special.

For those readers who know Loudoun County, Virginia the setting will seem very real. This does not however transfer to any of the characters in the book who are totally fictional and are not based on any individuals either living or dead. Any similarity with a real person is totally coincidental.

I want to thank my dear wife, Ginger, who patiently input this manuscript on the computer and gave me encouragement to continue. Without her assistance, *The Counsellor*, would never have come to life. Her job was made harder by the fact the book was started in Ireland, continued in Bosnia-Herzegovina and completed in Spain.

Some will note that I have used the word counsellor with two l's in the title of this book. Probably both with one l or two l's are correct. However, I opted for two l's because this is the way it is used by the Virginia Board of Bar Examiners on their Certificates.

For my readers in Ireland and the United Kingdom please excuse the fact that I have used the American spelling of words as opposed to the English spelling. This was done consciously as I hope; 'The Counsellor' will be in bookstores throughout America shortly.

# One

PATRICK patted Kelly on her beautiful ass as a signal to disengage. He grabbed a tissue from his desk and started to swab himself off. He also handed two tissues to Kelly and she made a quick exist for his private bathroom. The situation with Kelly had started some three months previously after Patrick's wife of seven years, Cindy had filed for divorce. Cindy had volunteered her time to help a politician who was running for office for the third time after two unsuccessful outings. Cindy admired him and spent many hours working in his office in the Valley of Virginia. This had been going on for about one month prior to the ultimate breakdown of the marriage. Luckily, Patrick and Cindy had no children and their divorce at Virginia Law was speedy and rather uncomplicated.

Cindy had indicated she had fallen out of love with Patrick but claimed there was no one else. Patrick doubted this, as he was almost sure there was a relationship on-going between Cindy and her political candidate. Nevertheless, he hadn't used a private investigator to nail down with certainty his suspicions. He had done this many times for clients but couldn't bring himself to do it in regard to his own wife. He had taken the separation very badly. Patrick also knew it wasn't going to be great for his law practice. All types of rumors were on the street and many were developing legs. The nastiest rumor of all was that he had been very physical with Cindy and she left him because he was an abusive hot-head. This was totally untrue but nevertheless, once repeated frequently enough, it took on its own air of legitimacy. It was difficult to stop such rumors as Patrick never knew who to confront.

Patrick's mother and father had passed away some years prior and he wasn't too close to his only brother, Robert, who was working for an oil company somewhere out in the Caspian Sea off the shores of Baku, Azerbaijan. They talked via telephone infrequently but holidays, strangely, were not necessarily days they felt compelled to be in contact.

Kelly was Patrick's paralegal and she was damn good. She had graduated from a two year paralegal course at James Madison University in Harrisonburg, Virginia. When Patrick hired Kelly he was very impressed with her credentials. She was an absolute whiz at legal research and additionally had taken over many important duties in the practice without ever being asked. She acted as the law librarian and took care of all the pocket parts that arrived almost daily as supplements to the law library volumes. She also hovered over the date files regarding the statue of limitations on all necessary cases. Every morning, without fail, she referred to this file and put a list on Patrick's desk of a three months advance notice and another list of one month notice of the tolling of the statute in every operable personal injury or other appropriate case. She took responsibility for many other activities in the law practice which released Heather, the secretary, to simply hammer out briefs, pleadings, motions and petitions on the computer. Kelly was without a doubt a wonderful asset.

The first sexual encounter with Kelly had started rather innocently. Patrick had returned from a rather long trial in the Circuit Court of Loudoun County. It was late in the afternoon he had gone to the small refrigerator in the conference room and taken out a bottle of beer, then he went to his office and slumped in his large leather chair. He was tired and simply staring at some horse prints on the walls of the office when Kelly came in and started to massage his neck and shoulders. After a few minutes of this comforting stimulation, he recalled he had reached backwards and started to rub the calf of her leg. After a few minutes of this mutually satisfying massage, Kelly simply hiked up her skirt, pulled down her thong panties and bent provocatively over his desk. Patrick hadn't had sex in months and here it was being offered up to him on a silver platter. He could barely imagine his good luck as he had sworn he wouldn't go into local bars and night-clubs looking for women to pick-up. However, he was as randy as a man could get and his resolve on this issue was weakening daily.

After that first encounter, when Patrick wanted Kelly, all he did was simply call her to his office, lock his door, call Heather on the intercom telling her Kelly and he were working on an important case and shouldn't be disturbed.

Kelly always knew exactly what to do and there was never a problem or awkwardness about it. In fact, sometimes not a word was spoken between them until after their sexual tryst was successfully completed.

Kelly was single and now, unfortunately, so was Patrick. She didn't have, as far as he knew, a steady boyfriend, but seemed to date several people on and off. She never indicated any of these relationships were very serious. Patrick couldn't figure her out. She never asked for any special consideration in exchange for their lovemaking. He laughed to himself thinking if she ever left, would he have to write her sexual activities in the job description for the next paralegal. Kelly, however, showed no signs of wanting to leave. Rather, she seemed extremely happy in her work and Patrick wondered if her extra curricula exploits with him, were nothing more than a workplace romance. If so, he appreciated her efforts and had no intention of ever letting her go, although at some point he fully accepted one of them might find a steady partner and the locked door episodes would come to an end. He knew he had to sort out their relationship, if that was what it was, but he had too much on his plate to address it right now. Cindy was fresh in his mind and so was the hurt. Patrick knew one thing; Kelly was damn intelligent and very beautiful. She was loyal and very discrete. That was enough for now.

The brass plaque on the front door of the town house read, Patrick J. Hurst, Counsellor at Law. Patrick knew it was definitely re-evaluation time. He had graduated from William & Mary in Williamsburg, Virginia in June 1994. William and Mary was an excellent school, rated most competitive. It was founded in 1693 and was the second oldest university in the United States. Patrick's major at William and Mary had been American History. He was particularly interested in the history of the War Between the States, as Southerner's referred and the Civil War, as Northerner's viewed it; but he was a southerner through and through. Patrick was born in a small town in the valley of Virginia, named New Market and grew up on soil that had been fought over many times by the great armies of the North and South. In the Autumn of 1994, he started law school at the University of Virginia. Patrick was very pleased to have been accepted at UVA. Charlottesville was a lovely place in which to study and the University of Virginia was founded in 1819 and had history and prestige in the legal community. UVA was considered to be most competitive, across the board in almost every discipline and the law school was considered one of the ten best American Bar Association (ABA) approved law schools in American. He had graduated with honors from one of Virginia's great schools, William & Mary. He also had scored quite high on the LSAT examination. Patrick probably could have been accepted at many good law schools; nevertheless, he was very proud to have been accepted at UVA.

When graduation from law school of his class took place in June of 1997, many of his contemporaries were snapped up by some of the largest law firms in Washington, New York, Boston, Richmond and Atlanta. Alternatively, some were offered in-house legal counsel positions with some of America's largest and most powerful companies, including; Ford, GM, GE, IBM, Microsoft, Dell, Cisco, to name but a few. However, Patrick decided early on he wouldn't go down this road, in fact, he had decided on an extremely high-risk adventure. Without clerking for a prestigious judge or working in an established law firm, he wanted to be a solo-practitioner, calling his own shots and being his own man. Since his parents had died he had become extremely independent and wanted this independence to continue. Following his gut level feeling he didn't interview with any law firms. His fellow law students thought he was crazy, and he probably was, nevertheless, it was his life and he was determined to conduct it his way.

Luckily, Patrick had no problem passing the Virginia State Bar Examination. However, he remembered the day the letter arrived at his home in New Market from the Virginia State Board of Bar Examiners. He knew exactly what it was without opening it but he let it sit on the kitchen table for a full half-hour before addressing it again. Finally, with hands trembling, he opened the letter and read its contents. He had passed the bar examination the first time. He was absolutely thrilled. Patrick recalled vividly the bar examination procedures in Richmond a few weeks previously. He had checked into the hotel the day before the two-day examination was to commence. He had brought his briefcase with him stuffed with legal textbooks that he had studied in various law school classes. He took them to his room and kept repeating to himself, 'tomorrow is the most important day of my life, tomorrow is the most important day of my life". Finally, he thought about it for a few moments and knew that tomorrow really wasn't going to be the most important day of his life. He took the briefcase of books and slung them into a corner and turned on the television and watched the news on CNN. Patrick thought about one poor devil, one of his classmates, he had seen in the lobby wheeling in a dolly with the entire Code of Virginia, in its multitude of volumes. Patrick knew in his heart that it was too late for a massive review. He was either prepared or he wasn't and nobody and nothing could help him now. He was the master of his own fate. After all, he had graduated from a wonderful undergraduate school in William and Mary and completed his law degree at UVA ending up somewhere in the top one third of the class. He had taken the law review courses at Georgetown University in Washington, D.C. The review courses offered there were excellent. He had done everything he possibly could and now it was simply time to relax and get his attitude positively adjusted to the sixteen hours of testing that lay ahead. He hadn't been law review but he was solid nonetheless.

Patrick wanted to practice in Fairfax, Virginia because it was very close to Washington, almost depression proof, with many high paid government employees and in addition, had Reston, which was fast becoming the new Silicon Valley of the East. Of the thousands of counties in the U.S., Fairfax was one of the ten richest. This was a far cry from New Market. This is where he would make his stand, in densely populated Northern Virginia. The first day of the bar examination was taken up with a multiple choice format which tested students for the most part on non-existent common law. All the states had altered the English Common Law through Codified Statutes but the bar examiners needed a universal common denominator on which to test. The second day of testing involved essay type questions and concerned itself with the current law of the Commonwealth of Virginia. When the exam was finished, Patrick was quietly confident that he had done enough. At the end of the second day of testing, groups of students were discussing their answers on the margins and Patrick participated in this post-mortem for a short period but withdrew rather quickly as he knew such an exercise could do nothing but deteriorate his self-confidence. Now finally, he had made it. He was an Attorney and Counsellor at Law in the Commonwealth of Virginia, one of the original thirteen States. A state that had given America seven presidents. He was going to work his plan and he was going to succeed.

Cindy and Patrick had been sweethearts at William and Mary. Shortly after graduation they tied the knot. When Patrick started law school at UVA, Cindy found a job with a legal publishing house. Her employer was a large law book publisher who made their home in Richmond. Patrick felt very fortunate because Cindy could always wangle him a relevant law book to supplement his course textbooks. Every once in awhile, he even had her get him specialized publications for presentation to one or other of his law professors. He didn't know if such gifts helped him, they probably didn't, but he figured they couldn't hurt.

Cindy and Patrick lived off campus in a small one-bedroom garden style apartment, which rented for four hundred dollars per month. They were on the third floor. It was a walk-up apartment with old appliances that hadn't been updated for years but they at least all worked. The furniture was old and worn but it suited their lifestyle.

Patrick could study and dangle his feet over the chairs and sofa and prop his feet on the coffee table. If he fell asleep while studying he could nap on the sofa and there would be no kick from the landlord. In fact, the landlord was an absentee owner. He lived in Arlington, Virginia and worked for the Department of Interior. The apartment had been his parent's and when they passed away they left it to their only child, John, who kept it. John White wasn't greedy and four hundred a month suited him as long as no demands were made on him, the rent was promptly paid and the apartment not totally trashed. Four hundred was a good deal for Cindy and Patrick as similar sized apartments in the same and companion buildings routinely leased for six hundred per month.

Life wasn't too bad. Patrick had a little money left to him by his father. His mother, Susan, had passed away with liver cancer when he was in high school. She had gone very fast. She was diagnosed in October and before Christmas was gone. She died at age 49. She had been a librarian at the New Market Library. His father, Sam Hurst, had died young too. He was twelve years older than his mom and only outlived her by three years. He died at age 64 during the first semester of Patrick's junior year at William and Mary. Cindy had helped him through the hurt. His dad was a fireman. He had been on a crew that fought a very serious brush fire the day he died. He had inhaled quite a bit of smoke and that night he died in his easy chair of a heart attack while watching a football game on TV. He loved both his parents and their loss was soul destroying. On both occasions his concentration at school dipped and his grades suffered. Patrick was resilient though and came back. After his father's death, Cindy proved a great strength, without her Patrick would have been lost.

Patrick's dad wasn't a rich man but the New Market fire department had a good term-life insurance policy for its full-time employees. Many of the firemen were volunteers but Patrick's dad was different, he was one of only four full-time employees. The family had been very frugal. The house mortgage had long since been paid off and the on-going debts were small. In the end his dad left the house and one hundred fifty thousand dollars equally to both sons. Patrick's brother, Robert, had no interest in ever returning to New Market. He had left after high school and got hooked-up with a large oil company out of Houston. He had worked on oil rigs in the North Sea off Scotland and in Kazakhstan before ending up in Baku, Azerbaijan. The Caspian Sea has untold oil and gas reserves and Robert felt he would be in Baku for a long time. Two pipelines were planned from Baku; one going to the North through Chechnya all the way to Moscow. Another, to the Black Sea through Georgia. There were further plans for a pipeline all the way to Turkey if it could safely cross Armenia. Armenia and Azerbaijan had fought a dirty little war over Nagorno-Karabakh. Armenia had won after the Russians had weighed in on their side and they now occupied twenty-three percent of the landmass of Azerbaijan. However, in recent days the fighting had at least stopped and some stability was returning. The upshot of all this was Robert felt his chances of staying in Baku for a protracted period looked good and he liked Baku. The people were nice, the city safe, the beer cheap and the food good. New Market, Virginia was no longer on Robert's agenda. So Patrick had the family home in New Market appraised by the largest real estate firm in town at ninety-six thousand and purchased his brother's share for forty-eight thousand. The local banker knew Patrick was a junior at William and Mary and made the erroneous assumption that he would be out working at high wages within eighteen months, so giving Patrick a small mortgage looked a safe bet. Actually, it didn't matter too much as he now had sixty-six thousand equity in the family home and the mortgage repayment on thirty thousand was only two hundred and eight dollars a month. There were no secrets in small towns and the banker knew he had fifty-seven thousand still on deposit in his bank and probably everyone else knew too. It would be this fifty-seven thousand and Cindy's income that would eventually put Patrick through UVA. Later his home would be re-mortgaged to assist him to set-up his law practice if necessary. At least this was Patrick's long-term plan.

Cindy's parents were both alive and well. They lived in Greencastle, Pennsylvania, a small town not far from Waynesboro, Pa. and Hagerstown, Maryland. Cindy was the youngest of six children. Her father, William, owned the local hardware store and had no thought of retiring even though he was fast approaching sixty-five. Her mother, Rachel, was fifty-eight and very active in the community. She was a go-getter and highly respected for her charity and social work. Patrick felt they were lovely people and had really bonded with them because he no longer had parents of his own. They seemed to love him too and proved it when the divorce was in full swing. They stayed in touch with him and indicated they were sorry Cindy wanted to end the marriage. They had tried to convince her she was making a bad decision but had to back off as their position was driving a wedge between themselves and their youngest daughter. Patrick appreciated their courage. They were honest, hardworking, fair people and he was sorry to lose them too.

Cindy had been happy during the UVA years as a sales rep for her legal publisher. They gave her a new company car and she travelled extensively throughout Virginia, calling on attorneys, or if the firm was large, law librarians. She liked her work and had interesting information to share with Patrick. She described the office set-up of numerous law firms, told him about the customer service aspect of the receptionists she met and which attorneys were polite and which acted like, 'junk yard dogs'. She was learning a lot about law libraries and was certainly in a good position to help Patrick. She had many tales to tell and was the main breadwinner and proud of it. She often arrived home late so it wasn't so bad that Patrick had to study so hard and burn the midnight oil. Cindy paid for all the household expenses; rent, the mortgage on the house in New Market, electric, telephone, food, everything. Patrick paid all his law school expenses out of his decreasing legacy. They got on well and Cindy integrated well with Patrick's law school classmates, after all she was learning a lot about the law from the real world. They had to respect her and they did.

# Two

THE dream of practising in Fairfax County crashed and burned. At first everything looked like it was falling into place. Cindy's employer had agreed to allow her to move to Northern Virginian and keep her job. This was quite a concession because their top salesman, Ralph Perryman, had been stationed in populous Northern Virginia for years. He knew everyone in the legal community there and was very well liked. They had convinced Ralph that Northern Virginia was growing so rapidly that Cindy would take pressure off him and his income would not drop. In fact, they had put this guarantee to Ralph in writing. Ralph would continue to work in the areas he had developed so carefully; Arlington, Alexandria and Fairfax. Cindy would have as her territory the more distant areas of; Loudoun, Fauquier, Manassas, Manassas Park, etc. It sounded like a good arrangement for both. Ralph would cut his annual travel in half while making as much or more money and

Cindy, young and energetic, would sell in the emerging new areas and indulge in the punishing travel.

After Patrick passed the bar, Cindy and he travelled to Fairfax to survey the scene. They loved the area with its fast moving cosmopolitan atmosphere and numerous cultural opportunities. Unfortunately, the cost of office space and housing proved too costly. They looked for a rental house or apartment in; Reston, Herndon, Chantilly, Falls Church, Tyson's Corner; everything proved too expensive, office space was even worse. Appropriate buildings around the courthouse area, where many of the lawyers were housed, were non-existent and far out of reach of a new solo-practitioner, even if available. Sure many lawyers were located in swank office buildings throughout the county but Patrick had this dream of being a real litigator with a reputation for his trial tactics and success. In the United Kingdom and Ireland, both north and south, you had a formalized separation between barristers and solicitors. Solicitors handled all the normal office law functions, including most of the tedious paperwork. They seldom, however, made appearances in court, certainly not above the district court level. If a case needed serious litigation, solicitors would feed such work to their favorite barristers. In America the situation was entirely different. An attorney could handle any legal work they were competent in, or would take steps to become competent in, and this included litigation. However, in practice only ten percent of American lawyers went to court routinely enough to call themselves litigators or trial attorneys. Patrick wanted to join that ten percent. He wanted to be in some state or federal court every day.

Patrick asked Cindy where she thought they should try next since Fairfax was obviously now a dead letter. Cindy insisted she liked both Loudoun and Fauquier counties.

'Why have you selected these areas', Patrick inquired?

'Because they are in my new territory and both Leesburg and Warrenton look like potential office locations for you. Plus both counties still have some open space left where we might find a not too expensive rental.'

Patrick was impressed with her logic and agreed to commence a search in these areas.

'What about Clarke and Frederick Counties, he asked?'

'They are nice too she mused but let's concentrate closer to Washington. Loudoun has Dulles International Airport, you know'. As if they had any money to travel, they didn't.'

'Where should we stay while we look?, Patrick asked.'

'I think Warrenton has a Howard Johnson's Motor Inn', Cindy responded.

So they moved into Howard Johnson's and started their search.

Day one was spent in Warrenton, the county seat of Fauquier County. Both Cindy and Patrick loved it. The town center was nice. It had a real Virginia horse country atmosphere. The courthouse was very attractive and the main street had many nice shops, and some impressive bank buildings. The shopping was supplemented by more shops, restaurants and banks out on Route 29-211, where the Howard Johnson's was located. Patrick liked it because it was not overpowering and coming from New Market, it was a place and people he could identify with. Cindy liked it because it reminded her of Greencastle, her parents would approve and it was in her new sales territory. An overall view of the area was all they could accomplish the first day. Tomorrow they would contact a realtor or two and seek office space and housing.

About 8 p.m. they found a pizza parlor out on route 29-211 that looked clean and settled in for their favorite deep-dish pepperoni pizza and a pitcher of ice cold beer. They were both very excited about Warrenton. The people seemed friendly and there was a great laid-back horse country feeling about the place. They stayed in the restaurant a long time and another pitcher of ice cold beer was ordered. At eleven-thirty p.m. they tumbled out of the restaurant, left their car on the restaurant's parking lot and walked the short distance back to the Howard Johnson's Motor Inn. Patrick theorized it would be a very shabby introduction to Warrenton if the newest lawyer in town was brought up on DWI charges before he had even gone back to Richmond to receive his license in a mass induction type ceremony addressed by the Chief Justice of Virginia's Supreme Court.

Back in the room both Cindy and Patrick felt amorous. All their short married life, motels had been conducive spots for sex. Cindy went into the bathroom and when she returned she was totally naked. She spent the next ten minutes walking around the room hanging up clothes, laying out other clothes for tomorrow and stretching and bending as the various tasks demanded. Patrick watched her from his location on the bed. Cindy had a beautiful body. She was slim, weighing one hundred twelve pounds and her skin was firm and toned. She had a very athletic form and with a thirty-four c bra size she was well proportioned to say the least. Even more importantly she had a beautiful face, long brown hair and beautiful dark brown eyes, her lips were full and a little pouty. Her skin was without blemish and Patrick felt she was absolutely gorgeous. Many other men must have too because she was a real head-turner. He too got undressed and they went to bed. They turned on the T.V. and started to watch a late movie cuddling beneath the sheets. The cuddling turned into rubbing and massaging and the massaging turned into full blown foreplay. When Patrick finally entered her he counted no less than six separate positions until she finally came in one glorious orgasm with him right behind. Both very satisfied, they turned off the movie, which they had never really gotten involved in anyway and slept a sound and beautiful sleep.

They were awakened by the usual motel noises as the maids went about their daily routine. The travelling salesmen and tourists were already gone, it was nine-forty-five a.m. and checkout time was twelve noon but they didn't have to worry about this as they intended to move on to Leesburg in Loudoun County tomorrow morning, hopefully earlier than they had gotten up today. They ate a good breakfast at the Howard Johnson's restaurant next door and then walked to their car, which was safe and sound at the back of the pizza parlor lot.

Real estate agents were plentiful along route 29-211. This location was obviously the place where their importance could be seen by everyone leaving or entering town either from the North or South. They selected Horse and Bridle Real Estate simply because of the cache of the name. The receptionist referred them to a sales agent who was in the office, Sharon Baldwin. Sharon was; young, pretty, highly motivated and very pleasant. She made some small talk to put them at ease and it wasn't long before Cindy and Patrick were telling her why they were in Warrenton and what they were looking for in both housing and office accommodation. Sharon was very congratulatory to Patrick concerning his passing the Virginia Bar the first time. Sharon had an older brother, Randy, who was an attorney in Maryland and he had passed the bar exam the first time just as Patrick had. Sharon recalled the family's joy with his success. Randy had told her how happy he was and how he knew quite a few law school acquaintances who took multiple times to pass. Each time they failed their confidence and self-belief was crushed. Self-doubt about everything crept in. They questioned their choice of law schools, the lectures of their professors, their study habits, their choice of a study group, their use of too many Horn books, their reading habits, and their legal research ability, literally everything. Randy had said that ten percent of law school graduates in America never pass a bar examination in any jurisdiction. Patrick concurred that Randy had it right, taking the bar examination was something to be done once and he knew that Cindy and he had been spared a horrible personal burden of pressure, stress and self-doubt.

Sharon went to the computer and through the multiple listings checked out all the rental properties in and around Warrenton as well as office space. There were four properties which were for rent under seven hundred dollars per month. One was a garret apartment over one of the banks. It was a one bedroom at six hundred fifty per month. The location was total but as Sharon explained the walk-up wasn't desirable. The second option was a garden one-bedroom apartment about one mile from downtown; it was six hundred ninety-five per month and in ok condition, freshly painted. The third possibility was the upstairs of an old rundown house ten miles north of Warrenton. It had two bedrooms but Sharon observed it needed a lot of work, which the owner refused to do. It was six hundred twenty-five per month, take it or leave it, as is. The last property was a one bedroom apartment over a three car garage located six miles south of Warrenton. The apartment was fine but the family included six children who were very active and quite loud. They were sports crazy and a basketball net on the garage got a workout day and night. Sharon wondered if Patrick could stand the noise while attempting to write briefs. True, it was only six hundred per month but would they ever have any privacy. Sharon couldn't guarantee they would. It wasn't the start they had hoped for.

Cindy and Patrick decided over breakfast that it was best to look at office space prior to viewing any further potential house or apartment rentals. Their reasoning was if no proper office space was available there was no sense in spending time looking at possible housing. They therefore asked Sharon to check again on the multiple listing service for available office space. Sharon came up with three possibilities; the first one was in old downtown Warrenton and was in a small accumulation of shops and offices at the end of the main shopping street just before the built-up area gave-way into the countryside. There was some parking available in front of the shops and offices. The office, which was available, included; a reception area, one small room and a second larger room and one bathroom. The asking price was fourteen hundred dollars per month. The second possibility was a walk-up office on 29-211 over an insurance broker's premises. Again, there was ample parking and the office had the advantage of a sign which could be hung out near the street which would have indeed caught the eye of passers-by. This office was a little larger and had a reception area, three large rooms and a bathroom in the hallway at the top of the stairs. The rental for this office was two thousand dollars per month. The last possibility was located in a mixed area of residential and commercial. It was off the road leading from route 29-211 to the center of old Warrenton. According to Sharon, the area was convenient and tasteful, as some larger houses had simply been turned into offices for doctors, dentists and lawyers. The only difference between other residences in the area was the small professional signs hanging out front and the fact that the bulk of the lawn had been hard surfaced for parking. Otherwise Sharon felt they were not offensive. The office on offer was a walk-up on the second floor in a substantial brick building. The asking price was two thousand five hundred per month but included; a reception area, a large room that could be used as a conference room and three separate offices that would suit either an attorney and/or paralegal each. The largest room was obviously the master bedroom in another incarnation and had a separate bathroom. Another bathroom was on the landing as you arrived at the top of the stairs. Cindy and Patrick thought the price of this office space was far too large and expensive for Patrick's limited budget, however they agreed to look at all three properties with Sharon. Sharon had a large new station wagon and knew the town intimately. As they drove around she was able to tell them many antidotes about Warrenton and some of its illustrious residents. After viewing each option Patrick felt that the first office at fourteen hundred dollars was the most attuned to his meagre budget. It had the advantage of being in walking distance of the courthouse and he felt it would be very advantageous being seen continually on the street as he made his way to and from court or the clerk's office. The thought of his professional sign hanging on 29-211 was a temptation but even an extra six hundred dollars per month was out of the question for a new lawyer with no client base. Cindy and Patrick thanked Sharon and told her they would contact her soon in regard to their decision. Sharon dropped them back at the office where they had left their car and they returned to Howard Johnson's.

# Three

IT was two o'clock and Patrick decided to call their house in New Market to see if there were any messages. The first call on the answering device was from one of his best friends at law school, Jonathan Pritchard.

Pritch started by saying, 'hello counsellor, this is Pritch calling from Charlottesville. I want to ask you to do me a favor. A girl I use to date from George Mason University lives in Reston and needs some legal assistance. I told her you were going to open in Fairfax and I hope you don't mind but I gave her your mobile phone number. She will probably contact you this afternoon or evening. Help her if you can, she is a nice person. Her name is Sarah Foster'.

There were two other calls on the answering machine but they were of no consequence. Cindy and Patrick went to lunch and then decided to take a long drive out in the countryside around Warrenton. They enjoyed this, as their previous lifestyle had not allowed for such leisurely pursuits together. They arrived back at the motel at seven p.m. They were watching television together when the mobile rang. It was Sarah Foster. She indicated she was a friend of Pritch's and she needed some assistance in drafting a will. Patrick said he would be delighted to assist her in writing her will but he hadn't located office space yet, could he call her back in a week or two and she could come to his new office for consultation. Sarah sounded agitated,

'No, I can't wait for a week or two.'

'Why not, it isn't so long and getting a will ready will take only a few days Patrick suggested.'

'I can't wait, I have taken a massive overdose of sleeping pills and in an hour I will be dead.'

'Oh my God, what did you do that for Sarah?'

'Oh, it's not so important now, what is important is you instruct me on how to make a legal handwritten will that will stand up in court.'

'I can do that and that's easy enough but there is one huge problem. For your will to be legal it must be witnessed by two individuals who actually are present when you sign the will and hear you declare it is indeed your last will and testament. If you tell me where you live, Cindy, my wife and I will drive to Reston immediately and assist you.'

'No, I can't do that Patrick, because I know you will call an ambulance and have me taken to hospital where they will pump my stomach and attempt to save me and I don't want to be saved.'

'Look, Sarah, we won't do that. Cindy and I will just rush to Reston and give you the witnessing assistance you require.'

'I don't believe you Patrick, Pritch told me you were a really nice guy and very caring.'

'Look Sarah, think about it logically, if you don't tell me where you live, then you are not going to be able to execute a legal will and you will die without full-filling your goal. Sarah, why do you need a will anyway, most young people our age don't have a hell of a lot to give anybody?'

'You know Patrick, I would tell you all these things but I am becoming kind of sleepy.'

'Jesus Sarah, just give me your address and some directions and I will find you and help you.'

'But you don't understand Patrick, I don't want to be found and as for why I need the will, I am going to give away thirty million dollars.'

'Thirty million dollars, that's one hell of a lot of money. What bank did you rob to get that?'

'I didn't have to rob a bank Patrick, my father was J. Walter Foster, the financial wizard and he left my mother six hundred million and each child, there are six of us, thirty million each. I am a rich girl Patrick but I have a lot of problems and I just don't want to live any longer.'

'God Sarah, don't talk like that, Pritch said you were very nice and quite beautiful, don't give up on yourself. Give me the damn address.'

'If I give you directions Patrick, you probably won't be able to reach me in time anyway. Where are you now?'

'I am in Warrenton, but don't worry where I am, just give me your address.'

'Well, Patrick, I am within two blocks of the Reston Town Center, and I am in a large brick apartment complex at the corner of Bouregard Street and Maple Avenue.'

'What is your apartment number, Sarah?'

'I'm in apartment eight hundred.'

'What floor is it on Sarah?'

'It's the penthouse, Patrick.'

'Now, promise me you won't call the emergency services. If you do Patrick, I will hate you and Pritch forever.'

'Look Sarah, I am just going to do what I told you, I am coming there with Cindy to help you with your will.'

'Ok Patrick, but if you get here and I am still not with you, I hope you feel badly you didn't help me like I wanted because you will have created one hell of a legal mess and there are always vultures circling when thirty million is at stake. I am going to write a good-bye note and give the Virginia State Bar Association your name. Maybe they'll disbar you before you start to practice.'

'Gee thanks Sarah and Pritch said you were nice, wait till I tell him this. I'm on my way, keep awake, walk around and don't sit down.'

Cindy and Patrick rushed to the car. He was yelling instructions to Cindy. 'Call emergency services, have them send an ambulance, ask them what hospital they will take her to and get them to give us directions to the hospital from Warrenton.' Cindy did exactly as she was ordered. 'They are on their way', she announced. 'They will take her to Fairfax Hospital', Cindy screamed. 'I have the directions, just drive and don't let us crash'. Patrick was driving very fast, often over one hundred mph. He took one corner on two wheels. Cindy was terrified, that was when she peed her pants, which would have been embarrassing under other circumstances, but now it didn't seem to matter. She didn't want to but she couldn't hold it. At first it made her crotch hot but then it turned cold and felt very uncomfortable. Luckily, not too much came out and it was August and still very hot. Hopefully, it would dry by the time they reached the Fairfax Hospital as long as Patrick didn't crash first. If he did, she knew this time her bladder would be practically empty.

When they arrived at Fairfax Hospital they had no problem finding emergency. Patrick followed an ambulance the last few blocks. They jumped out of the car and ran breathless into reception. Patrick blurted;

'Do you have Sarah Foster, I'm her attorney.'

A nurse behind the desk said she arrived twenty minutes ago and the doctors were currently with her. They couldn't see her now so they should just sit and wait. She would tell them when they could see her. Cindy rushed to the ladies room, removed her still somewhat moist panties and stuffed them in her purse. She dried herself off and cursed quietly to herself. She couldn't take too much of this high drama. She had notoriously weak kidneys, a sneeze could release a dribble but this kind of excitement could release a torrent. She hoped nothing else would happen. She had no panties now and if so it would run down her legs and fill her shoes. Not a happy thought, Cindy mused. She wasn't a happy camper and Patrick had empathy for her situation but he told Cindy he wasn't going to leave the hospital no matter how long it took without seeing Sarah. Sarah wasn't officially his client but she sure had given him one huge fright and he wasn't simply going to drop the matter without finding out more about what had driven a young, beautiful woman to the brink of suicide.

Cindy and Patrick waited on a hard bench for three hours. Cindy was complaining that her jeans were cutting her crotch. He believed her and had sympathy but the best he could suggest was she go to the ladies room again and stuff her pants with toilet paper to cushion her crotch. She did this but indicated she was worried the toilet paper would fall out down her pants leg. He told her not to worry, if anyone saw it they would just think she had a hole in her pocket and a tissue fell out. This seemed to satisfy her and the wait continued. Many people came and went from the waiting room. No one looked happy.

At eleven-o-five p.m., a doctor who looked absolutely exhausted walked towards them. He asked if we were waiting for news concerning Sarah Foster. Patrick introduced himself as her attorney and then introduced him to Cindy. The doctor introduced himself as Dr. Oliver Newcomb. He indicated that Sarah was ok and resting comfortably. He said they pumped her stomach. He congratulated Patrick on saving her life. He said they pumped out enough sleeping pills to have killed ten women. How she survived the ordeal he didn't know. Patrick asked if they could see her. Dr. Newcomb indicated they could but didn't hold out much hope for a coherent conversation.

Patrick and Cindy walked into Sarah's room which was a private one. A nurse was at her bedside and moved away slowly but indicated not to stay too long. Sarah looked very pale and quite spent. However, even in this state she was obviously very beautiful. She was blonde with long hair and very delicate facial features. She had a very pretty nose and full lips. She opened her eyes slowly to reveal eyes that were turquoise in color. Patrick couldn't evaluate her height very well as she was covered with a sheet and blanket right up to her chin but judging from her delicate features he guessed she weighed about one hundred ten pounds and was approximately five foot six. She smiled and asked, 'why did you do it Patrick?' He told her because he wanted her to have a valid will. In fairness, under the circumstances, this was a stupid answer but he didn't know what else to say. He quickly introduced her to Cindy to move the subject away from his betrayal. They smiled at each other and Cindy kissed her on the cheek. They could see that she was exhausted so they told her they would see her in the morning, realizing nothing further could be accomplished now. It was almost midnight and they drove back to Warrenton much slower on the return trip. They discussed the drama of the last five hours. Cindy said, 'you did save her life you know!' Patrick told Cindy she was an equal partner to that saving and she seemed very proud of this fact which of course totally true. Cindy said if Patrick's law practice was going to involve cases like Sarah's, it was going to be interesting, stressful and full of drama. He told her drawing up wills was normally pretty mundane stuff and he certainly didn't expect this sort of thing to ever happen again. Finally, they got around to discussing the thirty million dollars.

'Do you believe her Patrick?'

Strangely, for some unexplained reason, he did. He pointed out to Cindy that there wasn't one scintilla of bragging concerning her statement about the money. It was simply put in a matter of fact way.

'Well Patrick, if she is telling the truth your first client may be one that most attorney's search a lifetime for and never find.'

Patrick told Cindy he wasn't sure she was his client or ever would be now, particularly, since he had betrayed her trust.

'We will see tomorrow Patrick!'

'You are right', he said as he swung the car into what was becoming his favorite parking space at Howard Johnson's Motor Inn. There would be no playtime tonight.

# Four

LEESBURG would have to wait. They were up at seven a.m. and had completed breakfast and checkout out by eight. Cindy waved good-bye to Howard Johnson's Motor Inn and then waved good-bye to Warrenton too.

'Good-bye beautiful Warrenton', she said and meant it, Patrick's sentiments too. This time the car edged towards Fairfax at a very reasonable speed at least ten mph below the speed limit at all times. Patrick realized that in attempting to save Sarah's life last night he might have cost Cindy and him theirs. This thought had a sobering affect on him and he questioned if he had done the right thing in driving so fast. In the end he had no answer. It was true, they arrived at the hospital only to sit and wait for three hours, but what if the doctors had needed him to give them a time sequence as to exactly what time Sarah had taken the overdose. Evidently, in the end they didn't and applied the stomach pump on the basis of Sarah's condition upon entry and Cindy's good description of what had transpired. The rescue squad must have gotten to her fast. They made a mental note to ask Sarah if she was conscious when they arrived. Had she been able or willing to open the door or had the building security supplied a master key in a rush to save her? All important details to be teased out to arrive at the truth of what happened. What actual drug or drugs had she taken? Patrick had a thousand questions that called out for answers.

They arrived at Fairfax Hospital at eight forty-five. They figured the trip took twice as long as last night. Patrick should have been picked-up for speeding and under the circumstances was lucky he wasn't. Most police officers would take a dim view of putting many lives at risk even if it was to save one. Particularly, since Sarah's life had rightly been turned over to the only professionals who could really help her. Patrick could hear them telling him, 'when you called for emergency assistance that was good but when you endangered others, that was wrong,' they would be right of course.

When they asked to see Sarah the receptionist indicated it was breakfast time and no one was allowed on the wards before nine a.m. unless of course it was an emergency. So Cindy and Patrick took their places again on the hard benches and waited. When nine a.m. arrived Patrick looked at the receptionist and she gave them the ok sign. As they walked down the hall to Sarah's room he prepared himself for what he guessed was going to be the worst telling off of his life. He even imagined that she would use her millions to get him disbarred. He thought he might be a landmark case.

The only Virginia attorney ever disbarred before he started practice. Virginia's only legal fraternity's still-birth!

Strangely enough it didn't happen that way at all. When they entered Sarah's room she seemed truly happy to see them. She said hello to Patrick and also addressed Cindy by name. He was amazed as he had thought last night when he introduced Cindy to her that she was almost totally out. After the pleasant greeting, Sarah made a big fist and shook it at Patrick, but she kept smiling and that took the sting out of the gesture. She seemed very happy and surprised both of them. Patrick decided to attempt to get Sarah to fill in the blanks by asking a few open-end questions. He started by asking Sarah what happened, she was bubbly and in a mood to talk.

'I am glad you and Cindy saved me Patrick. I was very depressed and decided to end it but I have been thinking about it and want to live after all.'

'What brought you to such a desperate point Sarah?'

'Well, it's a long story but the bare bones of it are that I fell in love with a fellow student at George Mason University. I became pregnant and was extremely happy. He didn't want the baby and pushed me into an abortion which I didn't want. I had the abortion because he insisted and he told me that when we finished university we would marry and we could have as many children as we wanted. I pleaded with him that I had all the money in the world and that he didn't have to work and could continue his studies but he told me if I didn't do as he said he would end our relationship. I couldn't face that but I knew as soon as the abortion was over I had made a big mistake. About two weeks after the abortion he dumped me and told me he had fallen in love with someone else. I just cracked and after three days of being alone and not eating, I decided to end it all.'

'What a cad,' Cindy said.

'Yes, he is a cad and this morning I decided I really do want to live. However, I do want a will Patrick, but this time I will come to your office and there won't be a big rush.'

'Well Sarah, most college students are on parental dole or educating themselves with loans and don't have much to leave to anyone but you are different. I will contact you as soon as I get office space and you should come in. In fact, if I can't find space quickly I will come to you and you can tell me about your wishes regarding your estate. I don't need fancy office space to write a will for you.'

'Thanks Patrick that would be great'.

'How long will they keep you in hospital?' Cindy asked.

'Oh, not very long, Dr. Newcomb was by this morning on his rounds and said if all went well today, I might be able to leave tomorrow at eleven a.m., of course assuming there are no complications.'

'Did he think there might be complications?' Patrick asked

'No, after examining me this morning he said I looked fine. He just wanted to keep me one extra day to make sure everything is ok, so where will you practice Patrick?'

'I really don't know, I had hoped to practice in Fairfax but have now ruled that out. I am considering Warrenton and Leesburg. Winchester is also a possibility but it's further from the lucrative Northern Virginia market.'

'You sound like a marketing man instead of an attorney.'

'Well, Sarah, location is critical to success and I want to at least be able to pay my bills.'

'I am sure you will be able to do that and more, I don't know too many poor attorneys.'

'I don't know Sarah, attorneys are pretty good actors but not all make a pile. Probably five percent make ninety-five percent of the fees. Little country attorneys like me probably are in the ninety-five percent that only make five percent of the fees.'

Cindy re-entered the conversation. 'He had better make money; after all someday I want to be a lady of leisure.'

Patrick took Sarah's address and telephone number again and this time preserved them in his little address book. He told her he would contact her when he got settled or alternatively she could reach him on his mobile. He wrote his name and mobile number on the back of the pizza parlor card from Warrenton and gave it to her.

'I see you eat at the best places!'

'Yes, of course', Patrick replied. They took their leave and everything seemed reasonably ok. He didn't get an opportunity to ask all the questions he wanted but felt there would be another time. Often in life complete stories take time to tell. By ten thirty they were out on route 7 headed toward Leesburg.

When they got in the car Cindy was very agitated.

'Can you imagine that dirty cad forcing her to have an abortion she didn't want and then dumping her? I believe in a woman's right to abortion but that is assuming the decision is hers and that she isn't doing it under coercion or duress, men can be such dirty bastards.'

Patrick didn't reply but he agreed what had been done to Sarah was horrible. It deprived her of two loves and ended in her almost taking her own life. As they went by Broad Run Farms, Cindy again blurted out, 'dirty bastard.'

# Five

LEESBURG was all they had hoped for. Growth had obviously hit it and wasn't going to stop anytime soon. Still, there was a beautiful historic center of town that looked imposing. The old courthouse with its white pillars and the large bronze statue of a confederate soldier in front spoke of its past. The General District Court and the Juvenile and Domestic Relations Courts were both very close by as was the jail and the various Clerk of Court's offices. The Circuit Court was housed in the historic building described above. Leesburg was the County seat of Loudoun County. There were about ninety attorneys in town according to a source they checked with. The rest of Loudoun County only had a few attorneys housed outside Leesburg. Middleburg had about five or six attorneys obviously hoping to cash in on lucrative real estate conveyances and possible litigation among the rich and famous. Alternatively, a few attorneys were probably born there and didn't want to give up the life they had known and grown to love. If Warrenton was horse country and home to the Gold Cup then Middleburg was also the total personification of the hunt country. There was real wealth in and around Middleburg. The stud farms were large, all featuring manicured fields enclosed by black four board fences and of course the occasional white four board fence which also looked completely in place. Many of the homes and stables were magnificent. There was no mistaking; the horse was king in Middleburg. Time really did stand still there. The locals told them there were more upmarket shops in town than ever before but the countryside preserved by large holdings hadn't changed too much in years. Middleburg happily remained untouchable to the large land developers. Wealth evidently tolerating few encroachments.

Their research discovered that a few attorneys operated in Eastern Loudoun. It was here that the development had spilled over from Fairfax County and continued to do so. Additionally, a few attorneys operated out of Purcellville in Western Loudoun but for the most part ninety percent of Loudoun's legal fraternity clustered around the courthouse in Leesburg, the county seat.

Cindy liked the atmosphere in Leesburg; she put it right up there with Warrenton. Both towns were growing rapidly but Leesburg she thought even faster than Warrenton. Patrick also liked Leesburg and if he was going to practice in Loudoun this was where he wanted to be.

The first day they simply drove around Loudoun County; North to Lucketts and Lovettsville, South to Aldie and Middleburg and West to Hamilton, Purcellville, Round Hill, Hillsboro and Bluemont. Cindy was delighted to learn the county, as this was part of her new sales patch. They decided not to stay at one of the new motels just outside town and happily opted to stay the night at a historic inn right in the center of the old town. This proved a winner and after a lovely candlelight dinner at the inn they walked around town. It became quickly apparent that the real center of town was where Market Street (route seven) which goes east and west crosses King Street (route fifteen) which goes north and south. The court system was in this district as were some of the banks and nicest restaurants and shops. Window shopping was fun and it hit Cindy and Patrick that they had been deprived of this simple pleasure during the law school days. They happily returned to the inn determined to make-up for the lost night. Soon Cindy was astride, giving what she called her best hunt country jockey imitation. Patrick loved it but reminded her never to call him an old nag either in public or private because he would know her secret meaning.

At breakfast Cindy and Patrick discussed a new strategy. So far they had concentrated on accommodation, both office and home. Now they thought it best to concentrate on the market potential first. The idea was that if the market for a new attorney wasn't there they should move on and look elsewhere. It was agreed the best way to do this was to talk to attorneys already operating in Leesburg and see how they were getting along, particularly financially. They discussed the reality that no attorney was going to open his books for inspection and often they would have to read between the lines regarding what they said. They also discussed the real possibility that competition among attorneys was keen and probably none would be too encouraging not wanting to create more competition than would arrive through natural growth.

They made two command decisions. First, Cindy would not accompany Patrick on these visits but would only attempt to help him make sense of what was said in a debriefing discussion. Cindy of course would meet these attorneys eventually in her own work but thought it better that take place separate from Patrick's initial contact in case the meetings went badly. Second, they would look in the yellow pages and select six attorneys; three with firms and three solo-practitioners. Patrick didn't expect to be able to find all six in, or for that matter, six that would talk to him. If he could meet with three or four that might prove enough. They looked in the yellow pages and selected the six moving down the alphabetical listings at random; solo-practitioners – Roland Alberts, John Castor, and Ralph Lanagan; firms – Deland, Fullerton and Dunbar; Roberts, Planelli and Goss; and Sullivan, O'Brien and Kelly.

Patrick started out and the first office on their selected list which he came to on King Street was Sullivan, O'Brien & Kelly. The outer office looked smart and the receptionist was attractive and pleasant. Patrick asked to see Mr. Sullivan but she said he was in court; Mr. Kelly was filing in the clerk's office, the only partner in was Mr. Liam O'Brien. She indicated Patrick was an attorney and surprisingly she didn't enquire as to his business and buzzed Mr. O'Brien. 'I wonder if you could see Patrick Hurst, Esq.?' Liam O'Brien must have said yes because he was promptly shown into his well appointed office. With a name like O'Brien he was obviously an Irish-American. Patrick looked around quickly to see if he could note anything Irish in his office. Two items stood out; on one wall was a photograph of Liam with Senator Teddy Kennedy in what Patrick guessed was Teddy's Washington office. The second was small American and Irish flags which were imbedded in a black granite block on Liam's desk. Liam O'Brien greeted Patrick in a most friendly fashion and put him immediately at ease. Patrick told him quickly the nature of his business and emphasized he would be brief. Liam didn't seem to be in a rush and offered coffee or tea. He indicated tea, thinking it might be Liam's own preference. Liam buzzed someone and soon tea was delivered but not by the receptionist Patrick originally met. Liam introduced his secretary, Joan Collins, to Patrick and she also offered a warm smile. Patrick asked Liam if he thought there was room for another new solo-practitioner in Leesburg. He said he thought there was and offered the advice to keep his expenses very low the first couple of years until Patrick could build his practice. Liam indicated that he and his partners were all Irish-Americans who were classmates at Georgetown Law School. Patrick told him he had taken the law review classes at Georgetown in preparation for the bar examination and this seemed to please him. Liam indicated they had started their law firm eight years ago in Leesburg. Things had gone well for them but again he cautioned that it probably took five years to properly establish a law firm. He asked if Patrick was married and when he said yes, he asked if his wife worked. Patrick told him yes and Liam said he would probably need a little financial backstopping in the beginning. A 'laying hen' was the way he referred to Cindy; although Patrick vowed never to tell her where that phrase came from for fear she would instantly dislike Liam. They chatted on and Liam seemed in no rush to push Patrick out. When Patrick left Liam's office he was very pleased with the reception he had received and even more pleased with the message. Liam O'Brien thought he could make it if he used financial caution. Patrick liked Liam and thought Liam liked him. The first meeting was a good result to report to Cindy. The offices of Ralph Lanagan, Attorney at Law, were located next further up King Street. Unfortunately, Mr. Lanagan was in the General District Court this morning on a DWI (driving while intoxicated) case. Afterwards he was going to meet with a client in Berryville and the secretary didn't expect him back today. Mr. Lanagan's office wasn't as plush as that of the Irish group but it had a well worn comfortable look. The chairs in the waiting room were deeply cushioned; there was good reading material available, particularly for the field and stream outdoor's crowd.

Patrick walked down King Street in the opposite direction and came upon the offices of Deland, Fullerton and Dunbar, Attorneys at Law. Upon entry he noted the waiting room was crowded. The receptionist looked very busy, even a little harassed. He asked if any of the attorneys were in and she immediately asked if he had an appointment. When she learned he didn't she almost waved him out of the office. She had the schoolmarm of yesteryear appearance, glasses down on the nose, hair in a tight bun. She wasn't young but thin and well groomed. She asked if he wanted to make an appointment but he told her he was only in town for two days and tomorrow was taken. This was only a half-truth but he thought he and Cindy would be looking at property with real estate agents. She said to call for an appointment when he had more time and handed him a business card. Patrick had no business card to exchange so he was a little embarrassed and retreated quickly. So far his hit rate was only one out of three and some of his early confidence gained after his visit with the Irish group was flagging.

Patrick decided to try his luck on East and West Market Street. The first brass plaque he noted was that of Roland Alberts, Attorney at Law. Mr. Alberts' law offices were on the second floor. Patrick walked up and entered. The receptionist's chair was empty but a man stood in front of it opening and reading mail. Patrick asked if Mr. Alberts was in and he said he was Mr. Alberts. Patrick introduced himself and told him the general nature of his business. Roland said if he was looking for a job he was not currently hiring any associates. Patrick told him he was not job hunting, which seemed to set Roland at ease. Roland invited Patrick into his inner office and offered him a chair. Roland Alberts was a big man; he was about six foot four tall but was almost as wide. Patrick estimated his weight at close to three hundred and twenty pounds. Patrick quickly told him his purpose. Before he could ask his first question, Roland asked, 'who have you seen already?' Patrick responded he had only been successful in actually meeting with Liam O'Brien and indicated two other visits did not yield personal meetings. 'So you have met with the 'Irish Mafia', Alberts said. Roland explained they were called that locally behind their backs although no disrespect was really meant. Roland guessed the connotation came from the long history of troubles in Northern Ireland and the fact that their office did the bulk of the paid criminal work in the county. He went on to say that if Patrick opened in Leesburg he should put his name on the list of public defenders in indigent cases with the clerks' of all three courts. He indicated Patrick would be paid by the Commonwealth and the fees generated, although meagre in nature, might assist a new solo-practitioner like him. Roland had done this when he started but stopped once fee paying clients arrived in sufficient numbers. Patrick asked Roland if he conducted a general practice and he replied he did but emphasized he did a lot of divorce. Roland said many of the more successful attorneys no longer wanted to handle divorce cases as they were viewed as messy and created enemies often among the opposing sides' extended families. As more attorneys rejected cases his family law practice grew. Today, it was eighty percent of his entire practice. Roland made another suggestion of real value. He suggested Patrick quickly learn how to do real estate settlements. He said in the beginning cash flow would be his biggest problem and at least he could deduct his fee as part of the settlement costs ensuring speedy payment. He was just explaining that personal injury cases were good but had a long fuse in regard to receiving a pay-day when his door burst open and a large man in farm-type clothing appeared brandishing a pistol.

'I am going to kill your fucking ass Roland, you two bit gangster. I am not going to pay my wife any alimony even if I did leave her. She's fucked every man in Aldie and probably in Middleburg too.'

At this point he walked right-up to Roland's desk and pointed the gun at his head. In so doing he stepped on Patrick's left foot with his right boot and continued to stand on it with his full weight.

'Who's this dizzy little shit, your assistant in fucking the ordinary citizen?'

'No, Roland said, this is Mr. Patrick Hurst, a young lawyer considering opening his practice in Leesburg.'

Patrick was confident that in a moment or two Roland Alberts would be blown away and so would he. He was absolutely paralyzed with fear. What would Cindy do when he didn't return to the inn? She didn't know one person in town to help her or give her comfort and support. Suddenly, Roland Alberts stood up, all six foot four and three hundred twenty pounds of him and glared at the intruder.

'Give me that pistol Billy Joe and fucking sit down before I have your ass hauled away to jail.'

The dynamic changed almost immediately. Billy Joe started to cry and collapsed in the chair next to Patrick, the gun in his lap.

'Give me that damned gun now,' yelled Roland.

When Billy Joe collapsed in the chair the weight on Patrick's left foot was lifted but his foot felt broken. Billy Joe slowly handed Roland the gun. Roland grabbed it and threw it in the bottom drawer of his desk so hard Patrick thought for sure it would discharge. Patrick jumped up but crumpled back into his chair. Billy Joe continued to cry but Roland was now on the offensive.

'Damn it Billy Joe, you know your wife has the right to an attorney just as you do. If it wasn't me it would be someone else who wouldn't treat you as fairly. Now you're not getting that fucking gun back until your divorce is final and all issues are settled. Just remember, Jean may not be perfect, not one of us is, but she has rights and I am here to preserve them for her.'

Then Roland did an amazing thing, he walked over to a small under counter type refrigerator, took out three cans of beer and slung one at Billy Joe and another at Patrick. Billy Joe babbled on but started to drink his beer and was obviously calming down. Patrick drank the beer too and hoped it would lessen the pain in his foot. Roland now shifted the conversation to farming and got Billy Joe to respond to a few simple questions. When the beer was finished Roland stood up and extended his hand to Billy Joe. They shook hands warmly and Billy Joe left as if nothing had ever happened.

Patrick asked Roland, 'aren't you going to call the sheriff and have him picked-up?'

Roland said, 'heavens no, I went to high school with that boy, hell I've known him all my life. Besides he's right, Jean isn't acting the way she should, I must talk to her about not inflaming him. I have his gun; he will be all right now. He wouldn't hurt me, we go back too far, besides, I never had a cross word with him in my life before today.'

'Wow, Patrick said, they never taught us this aspect of the law at UVA.'

'No, I don't suppose they did but understand this is a once off, these types of things don't happen everyday.'

Patrick thanked Roland for his time and limped out. Roland's parting comment was, 'and remember that injury didn't take place in my office.'

Patrick didn't know if he could continue but since Cindy was shopping, and generally looking around and they had agreed to meet at the inn at five o'clock. He decided to walk around the block and see if he could shake off the injury. Slowly, the pain subsided and the foot became more manoeuvrable. He decided he could continue even though he wanted to find Cindy and tell her immediately what had transpired. Still he figured the story would tell just as good tonight.

The afternoon proved an anti-climax to Patrick's late morning visit with Roland Alberts. He did meet Mr. John Castor, Attorney at Law, who indicated he was seventy-six and really came to work everyday out of the habit of a lifetime, to serve a few old clients and have lunch with his legal pals at Jackson's Restaurant. He didn't really know if there was room for one more lawyer in town but he mused soon Patrick could take his place as he didn't know how long he could last. Patrick made a mental note that Mr. John Castor was an old style Virginia gentleman; very kindly and polite and would make a hell of a good mentor for a young attorney if he would agree. Patrick imagined John Castor had forgotten more about the law than most modern attorneys would ever know. Just as Patrick was getting up to leave his office John Castor went to his file cabinet and showed him a photo of the house he was born in outside Fredericksburg, Virginia. It was a magnificent antebellum mansion. Mr. John Castor was not only a Virginia gentleman he was a blue blooded aristocrat. Patrick realized he hadn't shown him the photograph to brag but just out of nostalgia. It reinforced in Patrick's mind that John Castor was the product of a gentler, slower, more elegant time in Virginia history. He left his company with great regret and hoped he could invent some reasons to necessitate future visits. He did give Patrick one important tip.

'Never lose your temper in court, judges and juries don't like their hero's out of control.'

Patrick thanked him and told him he would try to follow his advice and John Castor gave him a wide smile.

The last office visit was a wash-out. Patrick found the offices of Roberts, Planelli and Goss, Attorneys at Law, without difficulty. They had a large building on West Market Street. Mr. Planelli was in hospital with a hernia, Mr. Roberts was playing golf with some executives of a company he represented and Mr. Goss was in Winchester on a mandatory continuing legal education course.

Patrick had a little time left so he wandered across the street to the clerk of the circuit court's office. He stood at the counter and an assistant clerk asked if he could help him. Patrick introduced himself as a new attorney who just passed the Virginia State Bar examination. Patrick told him he was considering practising in Loudoun County and the assistant clerk said, 'good choice, nice place this.' Patrick asked him about the personnel in the commonwealth attorney's office, 'well, Mr. John Brandywell, who was recently re-elected for his third term is the commonwealth attorney and he has five assistants. Two assistants are women, Ms. Grace Adams and Mrs. Evelyn Caldwell. Ms. Adams handles a lot of the juvenile offences, Mrs. Caldwell and Mr. Roger Groves handle most of the workload in the General District Court. Finally, Mr. Eugene Harrison and Mr. Bruce Rodgers handle most of the workload in the Circuit Court. Mr. Brandywell often tries the most high profile cases assisted usually by Mr. Rodgers, Mr. Harrison, or both.' Patrick had stepped back from the counter but then remembered to ask Mr. Aldice, the assistant clerk about the judges. 'Well', he said, 'we are really growing fast'. 'We have two judges now in the General District Court. Judge Alice Lee and Judge Benedict Valentine, one judge in the Juvenile and Domestic Court, Judge Ryan Gossett and two Circuit Court Judges, Judge Philip Draper and Judge Herbert Fleming.'

'Have they been here long?' Patrick asked.

'Oh my yes, years, he said, all except Judge Lee, she has been here for only two years.'

Patrick thanked the assistant clerk and asked who the clerk was, he said, Mr. Sinclair Munro. Patrick thanked him and walked slowly back to the inn.

Cindy was already in the room freshening-up for dinner. Patrick told her he had big news for her but decided to leave it for the conversation over dinner. They decided to drive to Middleburg for dinner as they had spotted what looked to be some very up-market and interesting restaurants on their previous drive through town. They parked and then walked around town peeking in windows and reading posted menus. They made their decision, a small but ornate restaurant that featured a wide and varied menu. Patrick decided wine was in order and after they both had decided on a meat dish he ordered a lovely Spanish wine, Tarragona, Gran Reserve. Cindy told him about her day, the window shopping, how nice the shops and people were, etc. She neglected to tell him about the new suit she had bought but it wasn't much of a secret as she was wearing it and lovely it was too, as was the girl in it.

Finally, Patrick started his tale commencing with his meeting with Mr. Liam O'Brien of the 'Irish Mafia'. He went on to describe his meeting with the courtly John Castor and last talked about his visit with the big man, Mr. Roland Alberts. True, the sequence was out of order but he decided to leave the most shocking details until last. When he told Cindy about the gun and when Billy Joe asked, 'who's this dizzy little shit?' Cindy grew pale. At the end of the tale she seemed genuinely upset. When they were driving back to Leesburg she said two or three times, 'what a fool, how could he do that, he should be locked-up.' There was a benefit to his day though, as that night Cindy pressed her naked body against his tightly and affectionately told him he was lucky to be alive and she couldn't live without him.

# Six

BASED on their dinner discussion they had decided that Leesburg definitely held potential promise for them and based on this they contacted a real estate agent to start their investigation. They selected a firm in downtown Leesburg, their sales agent was Tom Harrington. Tom came from an old Leesburg family and understood fully Patrick's desire to be very close to the courthouse square, preferably in a street level space not a walk-up. Tom explained that what Patrick was looking for would be difficult to find and expensive. At the present time only one such office space was available anywhere near the courthouse. It was on North King Street in an older building that had been recently renovated. The office space available consisted of only two rooms, a reception area with a larger office behind it. The bathroom was in the hallway and was also used by the other first floor tenants that included an insurance broker, accountant and surveyor. The bathroom was unisex, meaning who ever got there first and locked the door, had possession. Tom indicated visitors to the firms could also use the facilities which meant that twenty to thirty persons per day would be using this bathroom which was not ideal. The cost was a big shock. The landlord, a Mr. Harry Dean, wanted $1800 per month. This was out of the question but Tom called the owner and hatched a plan for a three year graduated lease. Patrick would pay one thousand per month the first year, fifteen hundred the second year and twenty-nine hundred the third year. Tom theorized this would help Patrick get properly established. Patrick had two huge concerns; first the third years' rent at twenty-nine hundred per month could prove to be his undoing, second, if he had to leave for any reason, paying off the balance of the lease could prove impossible and force him into bankruptcy. Patrick asked Tom to call Harry Dean again and offer him this arrangement. If he had the privilege of leaving at anytime for whatever reason, Patrick would agree to pay the following penalties; ten thousand if he left during the first year, seven thousand five hundred the second year and five thousand if he left during the third year. These caps to be written into the lease in lieu of the entire balance falling due upon his departure. Patrick was pretty sure Harry Dean would never accept this, particularly his right to leave for whatever reason. However, he explained to Tom the vagaries of what might happen. He could find it difficult to make it and be forced to go to work as an associate for some other firm. Alternatively, he could prove successful and need extra space. He could suffer ill health. He could be forced to leave the law entirely. Hell, he could be disbarred. The possibilities mandating change were almost limitless. Tom was sceptical but agreed to roll

Patrick's proposal past Harry Dean. Harry didn't like the offer but Tom reminded him how he had arrived in Leesburg twelve years earlier in an old beaten up pick-up truck with literally nothing, but had made good. This was the one thing Harry understood. He was a self-made man and Leesburg and life had been kind to him. He had worked hard, fought off every adversity, lost everything he had amassed twice, been reduced to sleeping in his truck, but, he had made it. Tom had hit a nerve and Harry accepted after a few choice words to Tom, which Patrick gathered revolved around the threat that Tom would never get another listing out of him if this went sour.

Cindy had remained fairly quiet during the negotiations. Now that the deal was agreed she seemed pleased but cautioned that she didn't think Patrick could pay a secretary and the rent too. She was actually right and Patrick wondered how on earth he would solve that problem. Nevertheless, their biggest problem now was to find a place to live. Tom made a suggestion. He had an uncle Ralph who had a farm in Western Loudoun, past Hillsboro, in a place called Neersville on the road to Harper's Ferry, West Virginia. Ralph and his family lived in the main house on the property but there was a little guest house snuggled in behind the farm house. Ralph had never rented it but he didn't seem to have many guests either. Maybe, just maybe, he might let it out. Tom felt if he agreed the cost wouldn't be too much. Tom called him and reached him at home as he was just ready to sit down to his main meal at one p.m. The discussion went on for quite a time but finally Tom told him to go eat his dinner before Eleanor, Ralph's wife, got mad at them. So the deal was struck, three hundred dollars per month and they pay the utilities.

Tom indicated if they left immediately they could be in Neersville before Ralph returned to work. So they left post-haste. Tom had to stop at the General Store in Hillsboro but that only took a minute. Cindy sprang for the cokes and they proceeded. All the time Tom giving them a running description of the area and people. Tom asked if they liked horse racing. They said they really didn't know as they had never been to a race track. He said they wouldn't be too far from the track at Charlestown, West Virginia. Tom promised to take them one night and Cindy and Patrick both agreed that they would really look forward to that.

When they arrived at Ralph's farm both Eleanor and Ralph were both still in the kitchen. Ralph was a large powerful man with hands as big as ham hocks and as hard as galvanized steel. Eleanor on the other hand was petite and very slim. Both seemed friendly and very relaxed. Patrick often wondered why petite women were attracted to tall powerfully built men? Maybe it was a throwback to earlier days when women needed physical protection. On the other hand why were tall strong men attracted to small petite women? Did they bring out some need in them to play out the protection role? Or was it simply as one man told him, 'my wife is a shrimp but I am a seafood lover.' Never mind they seemed very happy and long may it be so regardless of their inner motivations.

Ralph took them to the cottage. He apologized that the lawn had grown-up around it in contrast to his own lawn which was manicured, said he only really cleaned it up if they were expecting guests. Said if they liked it he would clean it up once for them and then Patrick could take over but he would lend him his lawn mowing equipment, strimmers, etc. When they entered there was a surprising amount of space. The kitchen and living room were done up in an open plan with a big island work center separating the rooms. Patrick glanced at Cindy and could tell she liked it. It had one large bedroom with adjoining bathroom and a half bath off the entrance hall. Amazingly it had central heat and air-conditioning with all the utilities neatly packed into a utility room off the bedroom. The furnishings were very up-market and Cindy complimented Ralph on this fact. Ralph took no credit but indicated that Eleanor had been an interior decorator as an earlier career.

Patrick looked at Cindy and said, 'your call,' before he could get it out Cindy said, 'I'll take it; I mean we'll take it!' It was only fair; Patrick had really rented the office space and now Cindy the house. Tom drove them back to Leesburg pointing out more roads and sites along the way. They got back to Leesburg about four fifteen and decided to return to the inn to freshen-up for dinner. Tom said he would type up the leases and they could sign them and get the keys tomorrow. He reminded them two deposits were due; one for one thousand on the office and the other for three hundred on the house. Cindy and Patrick crashed on the bed and discussed their good fortune for over an hour. They were both thrilled. Cindy kept saying, 'what a master stroke, what a master stroke!'

# Seven

THEY went to dinner still on a high. After dinner Patrick called Pritch with all their news. When he reached him he said, 'hello counsellor', which made Patrick feel good. He told him about the office, the house and of course about Sarah Foster. Pritch was shocked about her attempted suicide but Patrick decided not to tell Pritch about the abortion or her wealth. Those were private communications that she could tell him herself if she so desired. The suicide attempt on the other hand had been all over the airwaves and anyone with a scanner was able to listen in. Patrick felt no client attorney privilege was violated here as the information was already in the public domain. Plus, Pritch was her friend and quite concerned about her.

Pritch had some good news of his own. He had been interviewing with large firms in Richmond, Norfolk and Roanoke and things had gone pretty well. He was waiting for word when a friend in the office of the Attorney General of Virginia had contacted him and suggested he come in.

He had met the Attorney General and other lead attorneys in his office. The discussions were very informal, not real interviews but the next day he had been offered a position. He was told in the beginning he would be assigned to monitor industrial compliance with new legislation. Pritch was thrilled as he had long-term political ambitions and he felt he was now strategically placed to learn and beef-up his resume at the same time. Patrick was very pleased for his best law school friend and wished him the very best as he was scheduled to start almost immediately. The UVA law class of 1997 was beginning to weave its way into the establishment.

Cindy and Patrick met with Tom Harrington the next day at eleven a.m. Patrick signed the office lease and Cindy and Patrick signed the house lease. Patrick had gone to the bank an hour earlier and opened a law office account and an escrow account. The bank agreed to open the escrow account without funds on the supposition he would soon place it in use. Patrick wrote the deposit on the law office on a starter kit check on his new law office account. Cindy and he also opened a joint household account and fueled it with funds from their New Market account. They figured that they now had to look and act like Loudoun County people. Tom gave them the keys and thanked them for their business. Cindy kissed Tom on the cheek and they both thanked him profusely for his assistance. Tom's parting shot was 'don't forget me counsellor when you're rich and famous, ok.' Patrick smiled and said he wouldn't.

Cindy and Patrick walked to the office and started measuring for office furniture and drapes. He knew it would take a little time, maybe a week to outfit the office. He decided to call Sarah Foster and tell her where he landed. Sarah picked-up the phone on the third ring and again sounded bright and bubbly.

'Hi ya Patrick, how are you?'

'Fine Sarah, I just thought I would call you and let you know we found office space and a house too.'

'Great Patrick, where are you located.'

'Well the office is in Leesburg, North King Street in a newly renovated building, The Dean Building, and the house is in a place called Neersville, out past Hillsboro in Western Loudoun.'

'I know Leesburg and Western Loudoun; you certainly made a good choice.'

'Yes, I think so, Cindy loves the house and while the office is small it is right across from Courthouse Square. When can you come down? I should be operational in about a week.'

'Ok Patrick, well, about Thursday of next week at eleven a.m.'

'Fine Sarah, you are my first client so you can have any hour of the day you want.'

'I am at 29 North King Street, don't forget, Dean Building.'

'Oh, Patrick, I'm sure it won't stay small too long, you will be a big shot soon.'

'There will always be time for you Sarah and he meant that most sincerely.'

'Yes, I will have to stay close to the man who saved my life.'

'When Cindy and I get settled in the house we want you to come out for dinner and maybe go to the races in Charlestown, West Virginia.'

'Ok Patrick, that sounds like fun.'

'Maybe Pritch could come up and join us.'

'That would be fine by me, that Jonathan Pritchard is a hunk.'

'Pritch has some good news but I will let him tell you, see you Thursday.'

'Bye, bye, Patrick, love you.'

When the furniture, drapes and computer arrived on Tuesday of the following week Cindy had a wonderful surprise for Patrick. With her last commission check she had purchased at cost a set of the Code of Virginia and several other volumes including the latest edition of Black's Law Dictionary, two volumes of necessary Virginia legal forms, a reference book on family law and a volume of model jury instructions. Things were really falling in place fast. The telephone was installed including a great little fax machine they purchased at Wal-Mart. Only one huge problem loomed; Patrick had no secretary.

Cindy and Patrick discussed the secretarial problem. Cindy felt he couldn't afford a full-time secretary but agreed he couldn't operate without some assistance. She suggested he advertise for a part-time legal secretary willing to work now for twenty hours per week and later additional hours as the practice took off. Patrick thought this might work as he recalled when he went to Roland Alberts' office there was no secretary present but Roland handled his visit personally without difficulty. Patrick could ask the new secretary to leave her desk a little cluttered when she wasn't there so it would appear she had just stepped out to run an errand to the bank or clerk's office, etc.

So Patrick put his ad in the local newspaper:

---

<u>Wanted:</u> Experienced legal secretary part-time for new law practice in Leesburg. Please call for an interview time. Patrick J. Hurst, Esq. Tel. no., etc.

---

Five calls were received. Two individuals eliminated themselves when Patrick reiterated the position was only part-time to start with. Of the three remaining all sounded sharp and business like. Patrick set-up all three interviews on the same day. He thought this would better facilitate a head to head comparison. The first interview was with Mrs. Heather Thompson. She was attractive, quite tall, about five foot eight and wore an immaculate blue business suit. She was thirty-three years old. Heather told him she had worked for nine years for a large law firm in Arlington, Virginia and only left when her first child arrived. Her little girl was now in school and Heather thought she would like to ease back into work. Part-time would suit her perfectly to start but she had no aversion to increasing her hours as the practice expanded. She was very experienced in trial practice, conveyancing and general practice matters. Patrick liked her immediately and knew she would be a great asset to a neophyte solo-practitioner. He would have hired her then but he felt he had to complete the interviews and then fairly make his decision. The second candidate was Ms. Linda Early. Linda was twenty-three, had worked four years for another attorney in town but had decided to take a year out to travel around Europe. She was just back and needed to commence work quickly to start paying off a travel loan. He liked Linda and her local knowledge would certainly help him but she really did need money to pay off her debts and hence pushed him for a firm time schedule as to when he could increase her hours. When he couldn't provide this she seemed to lose some interest. He understood her need. Finally, they parted friends but with Linda resolved to look elsewhere. The last interview was with a Ms. Kelly Madison. Kelly was twenty-one years old and a real stunner. She had graduated and received her certificate from a two year paralegal course at James Madison University in Harrisonburg, Virginia. Patrick told Kelly he was looking for a part-time secretary and there was no way he could entertain the thought of a full-time paralegal. He was new and had no client base and funds were almost non-existent but Kelly was very determined and told him she really needed to gain practical work experience and she would work full-time for nothing until he could afford to pay her. Then if he hit a big pay day, he could give her a bonus to help compensate for her efforts. Patrick told Kelly he was leaning toward hiring an individual who he had interviewed earlier in the day for twenty hours per week and he would have to pay her. It would be unfair to have her working in the same office sitting next to a legal secretary who was being paid. Kelly didn't seem to be deterred. 'You'll pay me too it's just that my pay day will be deferred, that's all.' She indicated that if he would supply her with a desk and chair she was ready to go to work. It was then Patrick did an insane act. He picked up the telephone and ordered another desk and chair from the supply house. 'Thanks boss,' she said and gave him the most beautiful smile he had ever seen. What on earth would he tell Cindy, that he had gotten two for the price of one? She was hardly going to believe that. Still, his legal assistance problems were solved even if his money flow would be small, at least to begin with. When Kelly left he telephoned Heather and told her she could start immediately from nine a.m. to one p.m. daily. She was pleased, Kelly was pleased and Patrick was delighted if a little apprehensive as to how it was all going to work out.

But it did work out and that was the simple fact of it. Heather and Kelly got on brilliantly and soon fell into a pattern of work that complimented each other. They became great friends and back-stopped each other with fantastic efficiency. They were like the three musketeers, each pulling their own weight and yet each pulling for the other two. Patrick wasn't really a solo-practitioner as much as the team leader of a group of legal professionals. That's not to imply success came early, it didn't. The first few weeks he sat in his office becoming better acquainted with the Code of Virginia and the other legal volumes Cindy had bought him. He had completed Sarah's will and she had paid him his very first legal fee. One day he was sitting at his desk looking out over North King Street, about ready to resort to flying paper airplanes out his window hoping to hit somebody in the head with the message, come to attorney Patrick J. Hurst when he saw a remarkable site. Roland Alberts was plowing up North King Street with a small bunch of flowers in one meaty hand. It looked to him as if he was steadily strangling them into submission. When

Roland arrived, Heather and Kelly greeted him and he surrendered his victims to them. 'I thought I would come by and wish you well counsellor on the opening of your office.' Patrick was impressed; Roland didn't have to do that. It was a real ice breaker, Patrick knew then he had his first real legal friend in Roland Alberts and hopefully he could add Liam O'Brien to that category soon too. Roland sat down but was barely able to squeeze into the chair. Patrick made a mental note that when he was successful he would order a special extra-large chair big enough for Roland. Roland didn't just come with flowers, he came with an invitation to join him next Wednesday to go to the monthly meeting of the local bar association; said he would introduce Patrick around.

The gap had been breached. Patrick was a functioning attorney with his own humble law offices and a great legal team behind him. He had kept his promise to himself; he was a functioning solo-practitioner. His classmates still thought he was crazy! Pritch kept him informed where each had landed and some had been offered and accepted great positions. He wasn't jealous and to prove it he walked out with Roland and talked to him on the street for awhile then grabbed a local pharmacist he had met and entreated him in conversation. Cars rolled by. Patrick thought the passengers don't know who I am now but one day soon they would say, 'that's Patrick Hurst' and he would know them and wave back. The street would be his advertising space. Patrick was just where he wanted to be.

# Eight

THE practice didn't exactly take off with a bang but steadily it grew. Patrick went to the three courts and got on their list of attorneys willing to represent indigent clients. Selection was on a rotation basis. The money from the commonwealth was small but the cases helped to fill time and teach him his profession. All representations were criminal cases so the clients in almost all cases were incarcerated in the jail. They couldn't come to Patrick's office so he had to go to the jail to interview them. They would be sent up by the jailer to a room with a cage-type divider and here the interviewing would take place. Sometimes, the rooms would be in use, so he would ask the jailer if he could visit them in their cells. Patrick spent a lot of time in the jail that first year. Sometimes Kelly accompanied him. He figured in a few years he would have spent more time in jail than most criminals but at least they let him out at six o'clock.

Rumor was around that this system of rotation of court appointed representations in indigent cases was soon going to end and be replaced by a formalized office of public defense lawyers overlaying the prosecutors. Both groupings would be employees of the commonwealth, but for now Patrick did his best to represent his jailed clients. One of the biggest eye openers for Patrick was once an individual was in custody nothing happened for them in an extraordinary way unless their attorney got one of the judges to sign an order. Even if a prisoner's parent died he couldn't attend the funeral without the judge signing an order. The same for any special medical care the prisoner demanded that the jail doctor didn't provide. Patrick was fast turning into the mother and father to his prisoner flock. The biggest shock of all was many of the prisoners were really quite nice people; many had just gotten off on the wrong track.

The practice grew in other ways too. They did their share of; wills, collections, divorces, DWI's, planning representations and personal injury cases. The real estate settlements took a little longer to develop because realtors normally favored their friends and long-term attorney relationships. However, purchasers, sellers and realtors too started to come his way. The realtors were critically important because they pointed purchasers new to the area to attorneys they thought highly of. Slowly, slowly, they were making their way. The bills were getting paid and the team was busy and happy. Heather was up to thirty hours per week and a full work week wasn't far away. Kelly was getting paid sporadically. Time happily passed.

The criminal representations came in various forms. There were a lot of; burglaries, assaults, domestic violence, sodomy, drugs, property damage, etc. but so far he hadn't handled a rape or murder case.

Cindy seemed happy in the house in Neersville. Ralph and Eleanor Harrington turned out to be lovely people. They would lend them anything they had. In the summer they were the recipients of all kinds of fresh vegetables from the Harrington's garden. In the winter all types of jams and preserves arrived. Occasionally, Ralph and Patrick would have a few beers together and talk about baseball, football or basketball according to the season. Cindy was doing well in her work. She had learned her patch well and made many friends in law offices across her district. Her publisher seemed delighted with her progress.

Tom Harrington kept his promise and introduced them to horse racing in nearby Charlestown, West Virginia. Now they were addicted. Most of the racing was at night which suited their work schedules. Sarah Foster had been out to the house for dinner on several occasions and Pritch had joined her on as many occasions as possible. They had commenced dating steadily and Pritch was very protective of Sarah. She loved all the attention. She not only had her hunk but someone who really cared. Plus, she had money and he had position. Cindy and Patrick called them the Fab II.

Everything was going so well and then what later could be rightfully called disaster struck. It started innocently enough. Patrick was in the office early on a Friday morning and Heather announced a call from Judge Draper of the Circuit Court. He asked if Patrick could come over and meet him in chambers at eleven thirty a.m. Patrick said 'of course your honor, I'll be there.' He said, 'it's important' and said goodbye. 'Goodbye your honor.' For the next two hours Patrick was very perplexed and a little fearful. Had he done something wrong? Was he going to be put in his place in a humiliating way? He fretted on but couldn't divine what on earth was afoot.

At eleven twenty-five a.m. Patrick left his office and walked across North King Street to the court. The judge's office was to the right of the bench. It was a large room and well appointed with law books. Judge Philip Draper greeted him. He was not wearing his black gown but rather was in his pinstriped business suit. He was a natty dresser and sported a beautiful blue tie with yellow specs, a blue striped shirt and a matching handkerchief which cascaded out of his pocket in a most elegant manner. Judge Draper was tall; he looked about six two and had retained a very athletic looking form even though his hair had turned white. Patrick hadn't inquired specifically about his age but guessed he was in his early sixties. He had practiced in Loudoun County before his elevation to judge and was the senior partner in a five man law firm. He was reputed to have been one of Loudoun County's best ever attorneys and a real money-maker. He evidently really deserved his appointment. He had a strict no nonsense authoritarian presence that he had undoubtedly developed over a long period of trial practice and then as a judge. He was the Senior Circuit Court judge in the 33rd Circuit of Loudoun County having served on the bench for twelve years.

Judge Draper started with small talk. He inquired how Patrick's law practice was going, was he enjoying himself and had he made many friends in the legal fraternity? Patrick answered each question as comprehensively as he could. He thought it was very kind of him in inquire about his progress. It showed a human side of him Patrick hadn't been privy to before. Finally, he said,

'I want to get to the point; we have had a murder here in Loudoun County which fortunately is a very rare occurrence. A man who I know here in town has been arrested and is now in custody. He is a good family man but would not be able to pay for legal representation. He and his wife have five children and rent their house. While he has a job he can just barely support his family I stand ready to qualify him as indigent, particularly with him facing a murder trial.'

'I see your honor.'

'Now I want to see him have proper representation from the very first minute. I will be very honest with you; I have previously contacted two local attorneys to ask them to take this case. On both occasions I was turned down for valid reasons which I fully understand. So you can see that you were not my first choice, no disrespect meant.'

'No insult taken your honor.'

'I think you can handle this case properly . but you understand this case is entirely too important to allow a defense attorney to be selected off the clerk's list by the normal rotation system.'

'I see your honor.'

'Now, before I ask you whether you will accept this case I want to tell you what you might expect in remuneration from the commonwealth. The normal fee is five thousand dollars. I know that's a small amount and I have discretion to up that amount to eight thousand dollars, which I am perfectly willing to do. You also can affiliate co-counsel to help you out, which I highly recommend by the way, and they too would receive five thousand dollars. That's the limit of what you will receive'

'I see your honor.'

'Finally, you would have to agree to start your representation immediately. What do you think about taking this case?'

'Well your honor, I am honored that you would think me competent to handle a murder trial even if I was not your first choice, which I can accept. I don't know if I am ready yet for such a major trial.'

'None of us ever knows if we are ready for a murder trial. I don't know that even after twelve years as a judge I am ready for a murder trial. This will only be my third thankfully. However, the decision is yours.'

'I understand your honor.'

'Again, I want to be honest with you. A high profile murder trial will give you great exposure and notoriety. It probably will help your practice in years to come. The downside is it will preoccupy your every waking moment from now until the very end of the trial.'

'Well, your honor, can I think it over and give you my answer in one hour?'

'Yes, that's not an unreasonable request but I really must have your answer as soon as possible.'

'Fine your honor.'

'All right Patrick, I will be in this office awaiting your telephone call.'

Patrick hurried back to the office and called Heather and Kelly into his office, 'what's up boss?' Kelly asked.

'I have just been offered a murder trial defense by Judge Draper. If I take it you both almost certainly will be hugely affected. We will all have to work much longer hours at probably no extra pay. It will be an exhausting and frustrating experience. Judge Draper is awaiting my answer within the hour but I didn't want to accept without your agreement.'

Kelly asked, 'how do you feel about doing it boss?'

'I am leaning towards taking it on but if either of you don't want to do it, I won't accept. It's all or nothing.'

'Who murdered who? Kelly asked.'

Heather spoke up, 'I was just going to tell you when Patrick returned. When I was at the bank a few minutes ago, I heard that Frank Appleby killed a man that interfered with his nine year old son.'

'Well that's more than Judge Draper told me, Patrick said, but I am sure he didn't want to discuss the details of the case. What else did you hear Heather and who is Frank Appleby?'

'Frank Appleby is a gardener who lives out Route 15 North about a mile past the Union Cemetery. He rents the old Davidson place. He basically does gardening in the summer and odd jobs in the winter. I doubt he makes much money though.'

'That's what Judge Draper said, that is why the judge is willing to qualify him as an indigent' Patrick said. 'Decision time, what should we do?'

'I am for it boss,' Kelly said.

Heather agreed, 'I guess I am too, I am not afraid of the extra work and it's your big chance to get well known, Patrick.'

'OK, it's settled, I will telephone Judge Draper and formally accept. Then the real work will start. I will go to the jail and meet Frank Appleby. Heather, you call Mrs. Appleby; tell her I have been appointed to represent her husband. Tell her I would like to come out to the house late this afternoon if that is OK with her. Kelly you snoop around and gather all the news, see what information the sheriff's office is releasing, contact the local newspaper to see what they know, check your sources at the hospital. Find out what you can about the little boy and his treatment, contact the morgue and see if the county pathologist will reveal any information yet about the dead man. Find out everything you can about the dead man; who is he, how long has he lived here, what did he do for a living, etc.? Oh, and find out if he was married and had children.'

'OK boss, I'll get right on it.'

'Heather, if anyone contacts the office looking for information tell them I'm out and you don't know anything about the case.'

'OK Patrick, I'll handle that.'

Now, I had better call Judge Draper. I promised him an answer within an hour.

'Judge Draper, Patrick Hurst.'

'Oh yes, Patrick, thanks for calling me as we agreed. Do you have an answer for me?'

'Yes your honor, I have talked the matter over with my office staff and am pleased to report I will accept this court appointment.'

'Wonderful Patrick, I am very pleased, now let me put you in the picture of exactly where we are in the process. The Grand Jury is already empanelled. They were empanelled on June 1 and will serve for a three month period. They started with a heavy workload. The Commonwealth Attorney has already presented quite a few cases to them and will want to present the preliminary evidence in this case to them as soon as possible. It would be my guess that will be on Friday of next week. Normally, the Grand Jury reacts swiftly to the cases put before them as you know. If they return a true bill and indict Mr. Appleby for murder next week then I will place it on the next roster day which is the first Monday in August. Now one other matter is quite important Patrick, I will try to deal with the defense as fairly and humanly possible but out of a need to be impartial I can't help you beyond approving your court appointment. Oh, one other thing, once you start your representation I will not replace you unless the circumstances are extremely compelling. Do you understand Patrick?'

'Yes, your honor, I do.'

'Fine, then commence your representation and good luck and don't forget what I told you about co-counsel.'

'I won't your honor.'

Patrick ended his telephone call to Judge Draper with great excitement and more than a little apprehension. He decided to go to lunch and then return to his office and see if Kelly had returned. He wanted to take her with him to meet Frank Appleby. This would be a procedure he would use continually as she would be his second recorder of facts and his sounding board for all strategies. Patrick also thought he had better call Cindy and put her in the picture before she heard the news from another source. He dashed into Earl's Café for soup and a sandwich as he knew he would need all his energy for the afternoon.

When Patrick arrived back at the office there was a local reporter and one from the Washington Post waiting for him. He was shocked at the speed of their arrival but shouldn't have been because he was learning there were no secrets in small towns. Patrick was pretty confident Judge Draper hadn't released the information regarding his appointment but the Judge had a secretary and two court bailiffs who were milling around outside his chambers in the empty courtroom. He made a mental note that there was a leak somewhere and if that source told once they would probably leak other important information as well. This was an area to definitely watch.

The reporters were full of questions.

'Has the court appointed you to represent Frank Appleby?'

'Yes, Judge Draper appointed me earlier today.'

'Have you met with your client yet?'

'No, I haven't, that should take place later today.'

'Is your client guilty?'

'That is a matter for the jury if the case goes that far, which it might not. Remember, my client has not been indicted for any crime as of yet.'

'But certainly he will be indicted?'

'No, that may not occur. That is a matter for the Grand Jury gentlemen and we will not be privy to their deliberations. I think you will have to wait and see if they return a true bill and they may not.'

'Aren't you young to be handling a murder trial?'

'I am a young attorney but not without some criminal law experience. I will represent Mr. Frank Appleby to the best of my ability. Now, I really must get on with my work gentlemen. Give me time to meet with my client and start my investigation before you ask me any additional questions.'

'OK, but this is a big story and you have to understand we have a job to do and our readers demand to know what's going on in this case.'

'Gentlemen, I will keep you informed within the limits of what I can tell you, just give me time to ascertain the facts.'

'Ok, Ok, we'll be back with you later.'

Patrick rushed to his desk and telephoned Cindy's mobile. She picked-up immediately. He had reached her in her car between appointments and she pulled-over away from traffic and they had about a thirty minute conversation. He quickly told her everything. Cindy was concerned that a murder trial would take up too much of his time and arrest his financial progress. She was confident he would do a good job but thought that the money on offer was so small that he would rue the day he had every heard of Frank Appleby. Patrick accused Cindy of pre-judging matters but in his heart of hearts thought she was probably right. When they ended the conversation he felt like an impetuous fool. What he didn't know at the time was that thought would be a re-occurring one that would haunt him on a daily basis from then on.

During his conversation with Cindy, Kelly had returned to the office. Patrick called her in and told her to tell him everything she had learned.

'Well, boss, the dead man is named Wilbur Cosgrove. He is married with two adult children, a boy, Wilbur, Jr. 29 and a girl, Selma, 25; both now live away from the county. He was 55 years old and lived with his wife, Marion, on the old Waterford Road Northwest of town. He has lived in Leesburg all his life and seemed to be well respected. He and his wife were active in their church and his hobbies were golf and fishing up on the Shenandoah River. He was an accountant by profession and by all reports a pretty good one.'

'How did he die?'

'One shot gun blast to the chest at close range. I understand he was fairly out of shape with a pot belly and the shotgun blast really caused quite a mess. The pictures will look pretty gruesome to any jury.'

'What about the little Appleby boy?'

'Well, he is nine years old and was fondled, buggered and otherwise abused. His intestines were pretty badly torn and there were other internal injuries too. He is being treated at the local hospital. He is out of danger but they will not release him for a couple weeks or more. A child psychiatrist is working with him daily. I don't know the results of those discussions which are on-going.'

'What more do we know about Frank Appleby?'

'He's forty-eight and has five children; four are girls and the one son, Frank, Jr. who is the rape victim. Two of the sisters are older than Frank, Jr., fourteen and twelve and two are younger, seven and five. The wife doesn't work.'

'Do the police have the murder weapon?'

'Yes, I think so; they have a shotgun which they found in a creek behind Wilbur Cosgrove's back garden they think is the murder weapon. Fingerprints and ballistic tests are not yet completed. They can't positively attribute the shotgun to Frank Appleby yet.'

'Does Wilbur Cosgrove have any history of paedaphilia?'

'No record but the police obtained a search warrant for his home and office. My source says they found child pornography on the computer and some downloaded images of children in a locked room in his basement. The police are not ready to release this information. They don't want to prior to the grand jury hearing for fear it might prejudice the grand jury in Frank Appleby's favor and of course Wilbur Cosgrove is dead so he can't be prosecuted.'

'And our esteemed commonwealth attorney wouldn't want that fact in the public domain.'

'Right boss,'

'That's our job to see that this information is made public prior to the grand jury hearing. Since it will never be formally released somehow the rumor mill and newspapers must get this info.'

'Right boss.'

'I don't like to fight dirty but withholding critical information from the grand jury is wrongful. We can't let that happen. Let me think about how we can progress this issue.'

'Right boss.'

'Where did the shooting take place?'

'Wilbur Cosgrove was shot in an outbuilding in his back garden. Evidently, neighbors heard raised voices before hearing the shotgun blast. He was taken to the local hospital but pronounced dead on arrival.'

'What does his house look like?'

'He had a very nice house as you might expect of a successful accountant. The back garden was large with some heated outbuildings too good to be called sheds. He had all kinds of small animals; birds, rabbits, hamsters, dogs, cats, a real magnet for children.'

'Kelly, did I ever tell you, you are wonderful!'

'A few times boss.'

'Well, let me tell you one more time, you are wonderful.'

'Thanks boss, that makes all the hard work worthwhile.'

'I wonder upon what information the sheriff obtained a search warrant for Wilbur Cosgrove's house. I am glad they did but this is very strange, Cosgrove being the victim? We need to follow-up on that Kelly. Try and find out what they suspected, who was their source, what are the linkages, etc.?'

'Right boss, I'll try.'

'Ok, Kelly, it's time we meet our client. Please come with me and take notes as I interview Mr. Appleby, write down any questions he asks on a separate list.'

Walking over to the jail Patrick asked Kelly. 'How did you get that sensitive police information?'

'Well boss, you have to remember I was born in this county. My next door neighbor and best pal when I was growing up was Wayne Broomfield.'

'And let me guess, Mr. Wayne Broomfield is now a deputy sheriff?'

'Right.'

'I hope he doesn't clam-up when he finds out you work for me.'

'Oh, he knows boss, told me that was the only reason he was telling me was he heard today Judge Draper had appointed you to represent Frank Appleby.'

'You don't say, well we do have friends in high places.'

# Nine

THEY arrived at the jail and phoned downstairs to the head jailer from a small lobby telephone. They were told to use the room on the right and the prisoner would be brought up in a few minutes. They entered the room and sat down. About ten minutes later the door behind the heavy wire mesh opened and Frank Appleby entered. He was in a prison orange jump suit. He looked to be about six feet tall and very powerfully built. He had brown hair and eyes and a very pleasant looking face. His skin looked tanned and weather-beaten. He was quite handsome for a man of his age and Patrick made a mental note that he would look well in court with a suit on. Patrick introduced himself and Kelly.

'Mr. Appleby, I am Patrick Hurst and this is my paralegal Ms. Kelly Madison. Judge Draper appointed me today as your lawyer.'

'I don't have any money to pay you, Mr. Hurst.'

'Call me Patrick and don't worry about any money, I am court appointed and will be paid by the Commonwealth of Virginia.'

'That's good, I know I need help and I sure appreciate you helping me Patrick.'

'I want to ask you a few questions Frank and hope you don't mind Kelly will be taking some notes for me?'

'That's fine.'

'Oh, one other important thing Frank, I would like very much to meet your wife and children. I hope you don't mind if Kelly and I go out to your house tonight and meet with them. We can tell them we met with you and you are alright.'

'Yes, please go see them. They must be worried sick about me by now so I know they will appreciate the visit. The boy won't be there Patrick, he's in the hospital.'

'I know Frank, Kelly was at the hospital today checking on him. He's out of danger but it's going to take some time for him to completely heal.'

'Yes, I knew it would because he was hurt real bad Patrick.'

'Frank, one other thing you need to know. Kelly found out they have a child psychiatrist working with Frank, Jr. to try and help him come to terms with what happened. I believe he will visit Frank, Jr. daily but I can't tell you how long the visits will continue, I am not sure they know themselves at this point in time.'

'That's good Patrick; I am real worried about the boy. Please tell me any news you have about him when you visit me.'

'I will Frank, now there are some things I need to know.'

'Before you start Patrick, can you tell me what's going to happen to me next?'

'Yes Frank, the grand jury will hear the evidence in your case as put forth by the commonwealth attorney. I would think due to the seriousness of this case that Mr. John Brandywell will handle the presentation of the evidence himself. He will undoubtedly call the sheriff and possibly some deputy sheriffs also someone from the state forensic laboratory and the county pathologist to testify, maybe others. The grand jury holds their hearings in secret so we may never learn about all the testimony although some information often leaks out from some source.'

'Will they find me guilty?'

'No, the grand jury has very wide powers to investigate and to indict. If you are indicted they will return what is called a, 'true bill,' meaning there is enough evidence to hold you for trial. If they don't find enough evidence to hold you for trial, they will return 'not a true bill' and you will be a free man. I would hope the grand jury would do a lot of investigation but my experience tells me they won't. The grand jury will probably act only on the evidence placed before it. In my experience there are investigating grand juries and charging grand juries. This will probably be a charging one.'

'And if they return a 'true bill', then what happens to me?'

'You will be bound over to the circuit court for the thirty-third circuit of Virginia, that's our local circuit court for trial.'

'And who will the judge be?'

'Judge Philip Draper is the senior judge and he will handle your case. We will of course ask for a trial by jury. This will entail a long process of jury selection.'

'Ok, I understand Patrick, now what would you like to know?'

'When were you arrested Frank?'

'Sheriff Dunn came to my house last Wednesday evening and again on Thursday morning, said he was investigating the injuries to Frankie and the murder of Wilbur Cosgrove. He wanted to know everything about the injuries to Frankie. My wife and I told him everything we knew. Then Thursday night he returned with two deputies and arrested me.'

'Did he read you your rights?'

'Yes, he did, just like on T.V.'

'Tell me about the injuries to Frankie.'

'Frankie came home about two p.m. last Wednesday and collapsed. My wife said he was crying and very upset before he collapsed, said Mr. Cosgrove hurt him. He was bleeding badly from the rectum. My wife called the doctor who called the ambulance immediately and she went to the hospital with Frankie. She knew I was working that day for the Granger's so she kept trying to call me there. The Granger's had been away all day but luckily they had returned by three thirty p.m. when the call came in. I rushed to the hospital and we stayed with Frankie until ten thirty or so. The doctor told us to go home, there was nothing else we could do, said the nurse would telephone us if there was a turn for the worse. When we arrived home the sheriff was waiting for us.'

'Did the sheriff tell you that Mr. Wilbur Cosgrove had been shot?'

'Yes, he told us Wednesday evening, we were shocked. We were both angry regarding what Mr. Cosgrove had done to Frankie, but I didn't shoot him.'

'Did Sheriff Dunn ask if you had gone to the Cosgrove home on Wednesday last?'

'Yes, he asked but I told him I hadn't been to Cosgrove's house, I was working all day for the Granger's.'

'You realize Frank; it doesn't look good for you. The police have a body. You had a motive and probably the opportunity plus they feel certain they have the murder weapon?'

'Yes, I know.'

'Kelly, has the time of death been established?'

'Pretty much boss, neighbors heard loud argumentative voices followed by a shotgun blast at about two-twenty p.m. last Wednesday. Mrs. Cosgrove found her husband a few minutes later in one of the outbuildings, lying on the floor with a gun shot wound to the chest. She called an ambulance but he was pronounced dead at the local hospital at two fifty four p.m. according to my notes.'

'I think you can see the problem Frank, your son arrives home at approximately two p.m. indicating Mr. Cosgrove hurt him and then collapses. About twenty minutes later someone confronts Cosgrove and kills him. The prosecution is probably going to contend that you went home for lunch, learned of the unnatural sexual abuse of your son and immediately went to Mr. Cosgrove's house, confronted him and killed him and then returned to your work at the Granger's house and were there when the Granger's returned home about three thirty p.m.'

'That would be physically possible Patrick, but I normally don't go home for lunch. My wife packs my lunch and last Wednesday I never left my work at the Granger's until they received the emergency call from my wife.'

'The Granger's were away all day until about three-thirty p.m. Is there anyone who saw you working or eating lunch at the Granger's, Frank?'

'No, I don't think so. I started work at nine in the morning as usual and never left the back garden where I was working all day. The back garden is enclosed with a high stone wall and there are a lot of large trees that sort of shelter the place.'

'Could anyone have heard you working, Frank?'

'I doubt it, I wasn't running any equipment. Last Monday I had mowed the lawn so that was done. The hedges were well clipped; I had done those earlier in the week too. I spent last Wednesday weeding, transplanting some shrubs and flowers and watering.'

'Um, not so good for our side.' Do you own a shotgun Frank?'

'Yes, I do Patrick.'

'And where is it now Frank?'

'Well that's another problem Patrick. The sheriff asked me about that too but when I went to my bedroom to show the sheriff where I kept it, well, it was gone.'

'Gone?'

'Yes, my wife and I searched everywhere in the house but we couldn't find it.'

'Kelly, tell Frank about what you learned regarding the potential murder weapon.'

'Well, the sheriff's department found a shotgun in the creek behind the Cosgrove's residence. They don't think it had been in the water very long because it was in good condition. They have sent it to the State Police Forensic Laboratory in Richmond, where they are attempting to find fingerprints. They will probably also do ballistic tests.'

'Frank, could that shotgun be yours?'

'Maybe, Patrick, but if it is it must have been stolen. I never confronted Mr. Cosgrove and I certainly didn't shoot him. He did a horrible thing to my boy but I am a Christian and I forgive him. He needed help, not killing.'

'Frank, I believe you but we are going to have to prove that you are telling the truth and the circumstantial evidence strongly implicates you.'

'Yes, I can see that Patrick. Can you help me?'

'I am going to try my best Frank, Kelly too. Well that's probably all we can do for this first visit Frank but please try to think of someone who might be able to corroborate your story that you were working all day at the Granger's and never left the premises until your wife telephoned. We will see you tomorrow Frank.'

'All right Patrick. Oh, there is one thing in my favor. I drive an old pick-up truck and it was parked at the Granger's house all day.'

'Was it visible to the public?'

'No, the Granger's driveway sweeps out back behind their house so the house blocks the view from the street.'

But no one could have seen me drive it around the time of Mr. Cosgrove's death.'

'That's true, Kelly, inquire if anyone saw Frank's pick-up around the Cosgrove's house. I don't think they will and this will help to confirm Frank's story.'

'Ok boss.'

'Frank, could you tell me; the color, make, year, license number, etc.'

'Well, it's old; 1990, green, Chevrolet, license number AV93748.'

'That's fine Frank, we will visit again soon. Keep positive.'

'Ok, Patrick.'

As we walked back to the office Kelly said, 'he didn't do it boss, I believe him.'

'I believe him too Kelly but now we have to find a way to prove he is telling the truth and to do that we are going to have to find the person who killed Wilbur Cosgrove.'

'How are we going to do that boss?'

'I am not sure yet Kelly, but what we need to do is find one or more other suspects who would have a motive and opportunity to kill Wilbur Cosgrove, right now everything points to Frank Appleby, most of all the timing. It looks as if Frank Appleby acted swiftly in a rage over the sexual abuse of his son. Additionally, we have to pray that they can't find any forensics that further implicate Frank.'

'Why would a man like Wilbur Cosgrove risk everything to sexually abuse a local child?'

'I don't know exactly, I'm no psychiatrist but my guess is his own sexual development was somehow arrested during his youth and he was drawn to children as a preference even though he had a wife and two children of his own. He may have been abused himself as a child. His compulsion may have become so strong that he finally, in a desperate moment put caution to the wind and sexually abused a local child who he drew to him through his little animal farm. The child pornography he had on his computer may have excited him and pushed him over the edge.'

'Boss, these paedophiles are evil people.'

'They certainly do evil things Kelly; I think we should look into how deep Wilbur Cosgrove was into child pornography. Was he simply downloading images from the internet, which is bad enough, or alternatively, was he a player in a child pornography ring, trading images and photographing children in unnatural sex acts which is even more evil? See what you can find out about this issue, Kelly.'

'Ok boss, I'm making a note to look into that as soon as possible.'

'Fine, let's return to the office first then drive out to Frank Appleby's house and meet his wife and children. I'll telephone Cindy before we leave.

'Cindy I'm going to be late tonight. Kelly and I visited with Frank Appleby at the jail this afternoon. Now we are on our way to his house to meet his wife and the other Appleby children.'

'Oh boy, now it starts, I guess I won't be seeing much of you until this trial is over.'

'Well, let's hope it's not as bad as you expect.'

'How is the little boy?'

'He is out of danger but it will take time for him to completely heal. A child psychiatrist is visiting him daily.'

'Poor baby, they ought to burn all those damn paedophiles.'

'Yes, I know how you feel. I have good news for you; Frank Appleby is an innocent man.'

'Good, well then you will have to work doubly hard and make sure he walks free.'

'I intend to Cindy, I intend to, see you late tonight, don't wait up.'

'Ok, Patrick, love you.'

'Love you too.'

# Ten

PATRICK was reasonably happy. He was sure Frank Appleby was innocent. The fact that Kelly also thought so gave him added confidence. He thought the shotgun found in the creek bed was probably Frank's. He figured it had been stolen from Frank's bedroom and used to implicate him. Patrick was fairly confident the sheriff had already made a positive connection between Frank's shotgun and the one found near the crime scene. He could see how this was the basis for Frank's arrest, plus of course he had a motive and the opportunity. However, Patrick was hoping there would not be any additional forensics linking Frank to Wilbur Cosgrove's murder. He wanted to verify with Mrs. Appleby what Frank was wearing last Wednesday and find out whether she had washed his clothes. Had the sheriff taken any clothing items away? Could she verify that Frank didn't come home for lunch that day and that she normally packed his lunch? Did she feel that Frank had only learned of Frankie's injuries when he arrived at the hospital in response to her call to the Granger's? There were a lot of important questions to be asked.

About half-way out to the Appleby house Patrick received a phone call from Pritch.

'Well, well, counsellor you're in the big time now, your first murder trial.'

'Pritch, how did you learn about my appointment?'

'Oh, counsellor, news travels fast in Virginia. Actually, I heard from one of my colleagues who was in a meeting with Delegate Jeremy Ricketts who represents your area in the House of Delegates.'

'Yes, I know Delegate Ricketts, good man, very popular up this way. We're going to make him governor one day.'

'He will have to cosy up to the south-side boys to accomplish that, but yes, I think he's in there with a chance.'

'What's happening with you?

'Things are going well. I have met a lot of new people and I am starting to get stuck into my work of monitoring compliance of industry with the latest laws. There are a few real corporate scamps out there. I'll tell you more about them when I see you next.'

'More importantly, how are you doing?'

'Great, I am happy with the appointment and feel pretty confident after meeting with my client.'

'Will he be indicted?'

'Yes, in fairness there is strong circumstantial evidence, enough probably to convince the grand jury to indict him.'

'Ok, counsellor, got to go but we'll be watching you down here in Richmond.'

When they arrived at the old Davidson place, Patrick and Kelly were a little shocked. They had expected a beautiful lawn with magnificent flower gardens and orchards befitting a master gardener. True, the place wasn't overgrown or anything like that but it wasn't beautifully manicured either. It was obvious Frank Sr. had to work too many hours to make a living for his large family to have time to create the beauty for himself that he created for others. There were signs of hard work though. There was a shed chocked full of fire wood. Additionally, there was a rather large well cared for vegetable garden to the left of the house. A small child was swinging in an orange plastic tire fashioned to mimic the real ones. It was hung from a large oak tree in front of the house.

Kelly and Patrick got out of the car and walked up to a large front porch with much of the paint long since worn off. The house was a two story, quite weather-beaten and definitely in need of repairs. The front door was open but an outer screen door was closed. Patrick called through the screen for Mrs. Appleby. A child who looked to be fourteen or fifteen ran to the door. Momma is out back in the kitchen garden. Kelly and Patrick walked around the side of the house and saw a woman bending over cutting some herbs. 'Mrs. Appleby, it's Patrick Hurst, your husband's attorney.' She stood slowly and walked toward them. She was a slight woman of about five foot six. She had brown hair and eyes and stood extremely erect. Her face was pleasant and she greeted them with a wide smile. Patrick introduced Kelly. 'This is my paralegal, Ms. Kelly Madison; she will be assisting me with your husband's case.' Mrs. Appleby asked them in and they entered the house from the back screened door. It was early July now and the weather was extremely warm.

Patrick was in a short sleeve shirt. Kelly was wearing a short sleeve white blouse and Mrs. Appleby was in a short sleeve printed cotton dress typical of those worn by farm family wives.

Once inside Patrick thought it best to put Mrs. Appleby at ease. He told her of their visit to her husband that afternoon and that they found him well, under the circumstances. He indicated that after their conversation both Kelly and he thought he was innocent and Patrick promised her they would work hard to make sure he was found innocent of the murder of Wilbur Cosgrove. She seemed pleased but looked very worried.

'Mr. Hurst, we can't pay you, we don't have much money and I don't know how I'll make ends meet with Frank unable to work.'

'Mrs. Appleby, please call me Patrick. Don't worry about the attorney's fees, Judge Draper appointed me and I will be paid by the Commonwealth of Virginia to represent Frank.'

This seemed to settle her a little and some of the worry left her face. Patrick then gently started his questioning. They found out that from the Appleby's location on Route 15 North, Frankie could walk across some open fields behind the house cross a small creek and come to the back garden of the Cosgrove's house on the Old Waterford Road. Mrs. Appleby felt the distance was about a mile and only took Frankie about fifteen to twenty minutes to cover. Frankie had told her about Mr. Cosgrove and all his animals and birds. Mr. Cosgrove seemed friendly towards Frankie and let him drop by on the weekends and other days that he wasn't at his office. He even let Frankie help him feed the animals and birds. She saw nothing wrong with this and it helped Frankie pass some of his idle summer time. She never imagined that Mr. Cosgrove presented a danger to her son. She verified that Frank had left for the Granger's house in Leesburg at about eight forty-five a.m. Wednesday morning and she had packed his lunch in the usual manner. No, Frank never came home for lunch; felt she had enough to do to take care of the children and liked to stay on the job anyway as it saved gasoline. She confirmed the three visits of Sheriff Dunn; once on Wednesday evening and again on Thursday morning and evening. Frank had telephoned the Granger's and told them he couldn't work on Thursday as they planned to return to the hospital to visit Frankie. She explained how Frankie had arrived home on Wednesday at about two p.m. in a terrible state with blood all over the seat of his shorts. He told her Mr. Cosgrove had pulled his pants down and hurt him and when he finished Frankie had bolted out of one of the back garden buildings and run all the way home. His legs were badly torn by briars and were all bloody. When she took his pants down there was a lot of blood and what she thought was semen oozing from his rectum. Frankie fainted and she called their family doctor who told her to get him to the emergency room as soon as possible. The doctor was the one that actually called the ambulance. She went to the hospital in the ambulance with Frankie and after Frankie was being cared for she called the Granger's house looking for Frank and finally reached him about three-thirty p.m. He came to the hospital immediately. So far, everything Frank had told them was being corroborated.

Finally, Patrick decided it was time to ask about the shotgun. She said Frank kept it under their bed and fully loaded at all times. He kept other ammunition with it. Frank had it there under the bed in case someone broke into the house in the middle of the night. The children weren't told where the gun was kept and had been warned by Frank never to touch any gun. She wasn't too happy about the location of the gun and she had discussed this with Frank but they couldn't figure out where else to put it so it could be used in the middle of a night-time break-in. Sheriff Dunn had asked Frank if he had a shotgun and Frank had said yes. When he went to get it they couldn't find it or the ammunition anywhere. The Sheriff did take away a booklet on the shotgun; it was a Remington pump action as far as she could remember. Frank had purchased it at Sears and Roebuck some months ago. As far as she knew it had never been fired as Frank didn't hunt or anything like that.

Patrick then asked about the clothes Frank had been wearing on Wednesday. She took them to the bedroom and showed them Frank's coveralls lying over a chair. There was a work shirt and coveralls. Kelly and Patrick inspected them. There weren't any stains on them except grass stains and smudges from soil. She explained Frank had worn better clothes when he went to the hospital with her on Thursday. No, she hadn't washed them yet. When Sheriff Dunn came by Wednesday evening Frank was wearing his coveralls.

Sheriff Dunn looked at him carefully but not seeing anything suspicious, hadn't asked for the clothes. Patrick thought they could have them tested by an independent laboratory and then use them as evidence at the trial. He felt if the prosecution demonstrated through professional testimony that Wilbur Cosgrove had been shot at close range that the coveralls couldn't help but be splattered with blood if Frank was the murderer. Patrick instructed Mrs. Appleby to put the clothes in a plastic bag. Then she should hide them until Kelly collected them Monday morning, taking them with a signed and time noted receipt. Kelly could then rush them to the laboratory again getting a time noted receipt when she turned them over for analysis. It was Patrick's hope that this would satisfy any challenge that there was a break in the chain of custody while the evidence was in their possession. He felt the court would want to be seen to apply the same chain of custody rule to their physical evidence that it applied to the physical evidence held by the sheriff's department. Mrs. Appleby was totally confused but Patrick assured her they had a motive in their madness.

Patrick and Kelly left Mrs. Appleby after being the recipients of coffee and apple pie. The pie was the best Patrick had eaten since his grandmother's apple pies recalled from his youth. When they swung out onto Route 15 North and headed back into Leesburg, a black Lincoln pulled out from the margin behind them and followed them into Leesburg. They went directly to the office. Patrick walked Kelly to her car on the parking lot behind the Dean Building and noticed that the black Lincoln was parked about a half block away on a side street. He told Kelly to spend her Saturday collecting information and to make sure she touched base with her buddy, Deputy Sheriff Wayne Broomfield. He also asked her to go by Mrs. Appleby's house on her way to work Monday morning and collect the work clothes and then head directly to the independent laboratory in Fairfax. Patrick asked her to call him Sunday at home and he would give her all the information about the lab's location and dictate how he wanted the time receipt set up. Kelly had a computer at home so the receipt would be made to look professional. Patrick had learned one rule in his short career; people tend to believe things in writing, the more formal the better.

Patrick went up to his office and called Heather at home. It was ten forty-five p.m.

'Heather, I hope I haven't disturbed you calling so late.'

'No, Brad and I were just watching t.v., Rachel is in bed.'

'I want to ask you to do me a favor; are you still going to that antiques fair tomorrow?'

'I guess so, why?'

'Could you look around and see if there are any reasonably priced sofas? I would like to get one for my office; I think I may have to sleep over some nights.'

'In the office?'

'Well, yes.'

'Wow, you are taking this case seriously. I hope Cindy knows what you're about to do?'

'She doesn't yet, but I will have to tell her.'

'You had better.'

'Oh, by the way, don't pay too much. Give them a small deposit if you find one. I will reimburse you and pay the balance when they deliver.'

'OK, Patrick, it's your life.'

'Sorry to trouble you, tell Brad hello for me. Goodnight.'

Patrick went home to Neersville and the black Lincoln followed him. Cindy was still up and he told her all about their visit with Mrs. Appleby right down to the apple pie. Two things he left out, he didn't tell her about the black Lincoln, and he didn't tell her about the sofa either.

# Eleven

SATURDAY morning Patrick arrived at the office about eight a.m., a little earlier than usual. Kelly and Heather normally had the weekends off and he usually worked only a half day and then went to lunch locally. Basically, he liked to be seen around town and to see who he could meet. He called this his P.R. exercise. Cindy normally cleaned the house Saturday mornings and spent a little time completing her weekly report. The late afternoon and evening they could plan activities together. This weekend was different. Kelly was out gathering information and Heather was scouring the antiques fair looking for a low priced but not too shabby sofa for Patrick's office. His job was to plan their next series of moves in their effort to save Frank Appleby. Most local people thought he had indeed killed Wilbur Cosgrove although they were quite sympathetic concerning the injuries to Frankie. Two distinct camps were forming; those who had been friends or clients of Wilbur Cosgrove normally defended him and his family. Patrick could understand this as Wilbur Cosgrove had saved a lot of client's considerable money and they knew an entirely different side to him. In most cases they were still in a state of denial regarding his wrong doing. The other camp was made up of those who saw Wilbur Cosgrove as an evil paedophile, a predator stalking young children. Many were afraid for their own children feeling Wilbur Cosgrove was just the tip of the iceberg and there were others lurking in the shadows ready to strike other innocents. This camp was generally agitated and angry demanding Sheriff Dunn face up to this emerging threat and protect them and their families. In fairness, the Sheriff understood these concerns and had made a public statement that any paedophile ring on his patch would be systematically crushed. He was sincere in his determination but Patrick was not so sure these paedophiles would be crushed so easily.

Around eleven a.m. Liam O'Brien paid a visit to the office. He was carrying a funny looking stick that looked like a wooden hatchet. Patrick asked Liam what on earth that was and he indicated it was his camán or hurley stick. He said it was that time of year for Craobh na h'Éireann or the All Ireland Gaelic football and hurling championships. The purpose of his visit was to invite Cindy and Patrick to a Céilí; a session of Irish dancing and music which would take place a week from this Sunday. First of course they would watch the Gaelic football semi-final from Croke Park in Dublin via satellite. Liam thought it would be a great introduction for Patrick to the local Irish community and to learn a little about Irish culture. Patrick quickly accepted. He asked Liam if his partners would also attend and he said, 'of course.'

Liam then inquired as to Patrick's progress on the Appleby case. Patrick told him he had only been appointed yesterday morning by Judge Draper but he had met with his client and his client's wife. Additionally, he had already been invaded by the press. Patrick indicated that in his opinion, Frank was an innocent man, wrongly accused, and he intended to prove that fact if Mr Appleby was indeed indicted. Patrick then took the opportunity to tell Liam that Judge Draper thought it prudent he attempt to locate co-counsel to work on the case with him. He also reviewed the financial arrangements with Liam including his own remuneration. He felt these were standard fees probably published somewhere in a Commonwealth of Virginia journal or report and hence Patrick was not revealing confidential information. Liam indicated what he already knew, that the fees were very meagre. He was building up to ask Liam to serve as co-counsel and he thought Liam anticipated what was coming. Nevertheless, Patrick rattled on for a few minutes about the time and nature of the death of Wilbur Cosgrove. He asked Liam if he had ever represented any members of the Cosgrove family but he indicated he hadn't. He then asked Liam to join him as co-counsel.

Liam thought the proposal over for what seemed a long minute and then responded.

'Our firm, as you know, does a lot of criminal law but only on a private fee basis. When we started the practice eight years ago, all of us accepted court appointed cases much as you have been doing over the past year. We found it useful as a starting point as I am confident you too are finding. However, as the practice grew, the partners decided not to accept any additional court appointed criminal cases. That's where we are now.'

'Yes, I know that, I think you told me that when we first met. Surely, a murder trial however is a whole different issue.'

'Yes, you are right; they don't come along too often in this area at least.'

'Liam, wouldn't working on a high profile murder case interest you?'

'It does interest me Patrick but I don't think I could devote all my time to it.'

'Liam, I want to make you a proposal. What if I said I needed your expertise and to get it I would be respective of your other caseload and time constraints?'

'Well, Patrick, here is about what I could do. I would be willing to attend all strategy sessions and offer my best opinion. I would also agree to be present with you at the defense table throughout the trial. I would handle some of the examinations and cross-examinations as assigned but I can't become bogged down with the day-to-day operations of the case. Furthermore, the center of all defense matters must remain in your office and with your office staff, not mine. '

'That would be agreeable to me.'

'All right, I will clear this with my partners and have an answer for you Monday or Tuesday.'

'If all goes well with your partners, I will contact Judge Draper and have you formally appointed as co-counsel.'

'Fine, well I must get back, I have a little catching up to do today.'

After Liam left Patrick noticed he had forgotten the hurley stick which was propped up in a corner of the reception area. Patrick picked it up and noticed there was a steel band around the top of the hurley for what purpose he didn't know. It was also very heavily taped on what obviously was the handle and there was additional tape just below the mallet top. What was it Liam had said, something about the 'clash of the ash'. Very strange apparatus altogether, Patrick thought, placing it back in the corner. It looked like an axe leaning there.

The next two hours were spent thinking about the various ways the defense team might find out more about Wilbur Cosgrove's involvement with other paedophiles. Kelly could dig out some information, particularly by staying close to Deputy Sheriff Wayne Broomfield. However, busting a major paedophile ring dealing in child pornography with possible international links might prove to be beyond the team's reach without assistance. If indeed Cosgrove was involved in one, a riddle still to be solved, the question was soon to be answered. The telephone rang and it was Kelly.

'Boss, I had another meeting with Wayne Broomfield and guess what I found? Wilbur Cosgrove was part of an international paedophile ring dealing in child pornography. The sheriff's department had him under surveillance for weeks and were about to close in when he was murdered. They theorized he was pretty high up in the illegal organization. They even had the search warrant prepared and signed by the judge prior to his death and were going to raid his house on the day he was murdered. After the murder they decided to go ahead with their plan.'

'Did Wilbur Cosgrove know they were closing in on him?'

'No, Wayne at least said the sheriff didn't think so. But here's the amazing news; evidently the FBI informed the sheriff's department that there was a lot of turmoil in the child pornography ring and certain people were being weeded out because they had been too lax on security. Evidently, the headquarters of the ring is in Amsterdam and they weren't too happy the way things were going and set about attempting to eliminate the weak sisters.'

'Eliminate, as in murder?'

'Maybe, yes, maybe no, Wayne didn't seem to know that information.'

'Wow, I think you may be on to something, a possible other person or persons who wanted to see Wilbur Cosgrove dead. Stay close to this lead and let me know where it takes you. By the way, I have good news for you. I offered Liam O'Brien the co-counsel's job and I think he will accept. He wanted to roll it by his partners first before he responds.'

'Boss, that is good news, Liam O'Brien is a heavyweight and I heard Draper loves him.'

'By the way, Kelly, do you know anyone locally who drives a black Lincoln?'

'Oh sure, old man Dodd has one. He lives out on route 15 south. He doesn't drive much though, he's about 75.'

'Anyone else?'

'No, not that I can think of, why do you ask?'

'Well, remember when we left the Appleby house last night, a black Lincoln followed us into town and then followed me home to Neersville.'

'Have you seen it today?'

'No, it's probably just a coincidence, don't worry about it.'

'Listen boss, don't take any chances if that car continues following you, call the sheriff's department or if you don't want to go formal, let me know and I'll have Wayne check it out quietly.'

'Kelly, what would you think, if I hired a private detective to check into this child pornography ring?'

'Can we afford one? He might have to travel a lot in Europe to start digging and that would cost you a bundle.'

'Well, let's say I could find the money. Who would you recommend?'

'Well, there's a guy in Fairfax, named Jim Brogan, who they say is real good. He's an ex FBI agent, retired. He has worked a little in Loudoun on high profile divorce cases.'

'Right, Ok, maybe I will telephone him and set up a conference. Thanks Kelly.'

'No problem boss be talking to you.'

Patrick looked in the yellow pages and found James J. Brogan, private investigator. He telephoned him but got a recording. He identified himself and left his home number in Neersville as well as the office number. About an hour later Jim Brogan returned his call reaching Patrick at the office. Patrick outlined the situation briefly indicating he was court appointed counsel in a murder case and asked

Jim if he would be interested in meeting with him next Wednesday. Jim Brogan agreed to meet Patrick at eleven a.m. on Wednesday at Patrick's office. Patrick purposely made the appointment for Wednesday hoping Liam would be aboard by then and could join in the discussion. Patrick was happy; he thought the team was moving in the right direction as fast as reasonably could be expected.

Patrick next telephoned Roland Alberts at his office. He asked Roland if he could support him in the Appleby case by attending some strategy meetings. Roland again reiterated he was basically a divorce attorney and not an expert in criminal law. Patrick countered with the fact that he had a very good legal mind as well as a logical approach to situations. He reminded him how he had diffused the Billy Joe gun affair at their first meeting. Roland was worried he wouldn't be able to contribute much and his reluctance seemed to grow when Patrick told him Liam O'Brien was considering coming aboard as co-counsel. Patrick kept attempting to convince Roland that he didn't have to be a great criminal lawyer to offer the type of assistance the team needed. Finally, Patrick told Roland it was like putting together a corporate board of directors, where each member brought different experiences and skills to the table. This seemed to satisfy Roland somewhat and he eventually gave Patrick a qualified yes. He agreed to assist and attend as many meetings as possible within the limits of his time and schedule constraints. Patrick told him he couldn't ask for more commitment than that after all Patrick felt his practice was probably going to be ruined; he couldn't ask Roland to ruin his too. Patrick did take the opportunity though to press him into rather immediate service. He asked Roland if he could come to his office next Wednesday at eleven a.m. for the meeting with Jim Brogan. This seemed to really interest Roland as he had never met Jim Brogan but knew of him by reputation. Roland indicated he might have need for Jim Brogan's services at some point and would like to get a line on his fee structure. Patrick told Roland, 'see this is not totally a one-way street, you might also get some benefit from the experience.' Now Roland seemed more engaged and promised to be at Patrick's office on Wednesday.

Patrick thought it had been a pretty productive Saturday and decided he would leave the office for Neersville. He had missed the usual Saturday lunch with the legal fraternity but was content with his progress. On the way home, he looked carefully to see if the black Lincoln was tailing him. It was, at a good distance back but it was there alright.

# Twelve

CINDY was happy to see Patrick. She had finished her weekly report, had cleaned the house and had coffee with Eleanor Harrington. Now she was looking forward to their weekend to begin. Patrick found her on the sun lounge topping up her tan. He told her about their invitation to the 'Irish night' from Liam O'Brien a week from Sunday. She seemed quite pleased, social invitations represented to Cindy an opportunity to meet local people and become more immersed in the community. Of course she was right and it was good for Patrick's business too.

They decided to go to the races at Charlestown that evening. Neither Pritch nor Sarah would be along on this occasion. Patrick told Cindy he would take her to dinner in the club house. She wore a white sun dress and looked absolutely smashing with the white against her tanned skin. They had a really good night and worked their newfound betting scheme. They each bet two dollars on each race on the nine race card. They always selected a horse to win, no other options. They figured their total exposure was hence thirty six dollars. The dinner, they theorized, was no more or less than going to dinner at any local restaurant. The price of admission, well they figured this was equivalent to what one could be expected to pay at other sporting events. Anyway, they won a total of two hundred thirty two dollars that night. Subtracting the thirty six dollars they still cleared one hundred ninety six. This was more than enough to pay for admission, plus dinner with two bottles of wine. They arrived home in a very festive mood. Patrick opened a bottle of champagne and Cindy and he sat in the semi-darkened living room sipping their drinks and reviewing Cindy's progress in her job and Patrick's progress with the Appleby case.

Patrick told Cindy that to win at trial they needed to mount a concerted team effort. He had been attempting to organize a winning defense team. He felt if all went well they would end up with Liam O'Brien as co-counsel, Roland Alberts as legal expert ex-officio, Jim Brogan as their private investigator and of course his stalwarts, Kelly and Heather. Cindy thought the team approach sounded logical but she felt the employment of Jim Brogan might prove Patrick's undoing. She guessed that Jim Brogan's hourly fee might be as much or almost as much as his own. She opined that if he turned Jim loose without direction and a fee cap that he could bankrupt Patrick in short order. Additionally, she cautioned that foreign travel would be extremely costly. The airline tickets were just the beginning, then there would be hotel bills, internal transportation, per diem for food and incidentals. If he could get by with Jim

Brogan agreeing a reasonable daily fee, Cindy's suggestion was to start Jim out gently committing for only a week or two of work in the first instance to be completed in the local area. Her idea was to monitor his results and see how useful the information he turned up would prove. As usual her thinking was impeccably sound. Patrick decided to adopt her approach in full.

It was three fifteen a.m. when they finally retired. They went to bed quite tired with no thoughts of sex. Sunday morning they slept late and didn't surface until eleven a.m. Patrick drove into Hillsboro to buy a Washington Post at the general store. Not too many people were stirring in town but Hillsboro looked like a glistening jewel in the morning sun with its fine stone houses facing towards route nine from both north and south of the highway. Hillsboro was Loudoun's and Virginia's smallest incorporated town and as such maintained its own mayor and council. It had its own water commissioner and other functionaries but operated in a quaint unbureaucratic manner. Hillsboro was the nearest town to them and gave Patrick great delight to drive through. When he got to Hillsboro he knew he was close to home. Patrick made it a point to always buy all his gasoline at the Hillsboro General Store.

Sunday afternoon Patrick and Cindy read all the news unfit to print. Unfortunately, there was misery world-wide; floods, droughts, earthquakes, serious storms and plenty of dirty little wars almost one for everyone in the reading audience. Besides, you could almost divine the news yourself. Trouble in Northern Ireland, killing in the Middle East, friction between India and Pakistan over Kashmir, economic woes in Russia, starvation in Africa, etc. Finally, out of total exasperation, Patrick turned to the sports page; at least there one could read about man's accomplishments rather than their darker sides. About three p.m. the telephone rang and it was Heather. She reported she had picked-up a nice sofa-bed, very clean, for one hundred ninety-five dollars. She had put forty-five dollars down and the balance of one hundred fifty dollars would be due upon delivery which she had scheduled for the following Thursday morning at nine a.m. Heather indicated he would like it as it was a beautiful lemon yellow. Patrick thanked her for her efforts. Kelly too, telephoned about four p.m. and Patrick gave her the co-ordinates of the independent forensic laboratory in Fairfax. He also dictated how he wanted the receipts to be set-up. Kelly said she would work them up on her home computer and be at Mrs. Appleby's house early Monday morning as agreed and then drive directly to the independent forensic laboratory in Fairfax. Patrick realized he was one lucky attorney to have such loyal people around him. He couldn't wait for next week to begin so he could round out the team's so called board of directors.

The rest of Sunday afternoon and evening went by in an unremarkable manner. Patrick had watched the University of Virginia's opening basketball game on t.v. against great rivals, University of Maryland. The Cavaliers of UVA won by six points, 98 to 92. This put Patrick in great form and set him up for a wonderful evening. Cindy however brought him back to reality when she inquired how he was doing with the balance of his clients. He was afraid to tell her the truth, that since he had accepted the court appointment in the Appleby murder case he hadn't billed one hour to another client. Additionally, he had been very dilatory in answering his calls other than those specifically related to the Appleby case. Judge Draper's warning rang in his ears. Basically, he had said he would gain notoriety which would help him in his future practice but the downside would be at the expense of his current client base, how right he was. Patrick resolved to try harder not to let that happen.

At seven p.m. the telephone rang again. This time it was the two reporters on a conference call that had confronted Patrick earlier. They demanded to know what he had learned from his visit with his client and Mrs. Appleby. Patrick told them conversations with his client and his family had to remain confidential. He indicated however that it was clear to him that Frank Appleby was innocent and he intended to prove that if he was indeed indicted. Patrick asked them what they had been able to learn about the victim and they acted surprised. What was there about the victim that they needed to know that they didn't know already? He was dead. Patrick indicated they should look into the background of the victim for a real story. He told them that he wouldn't say anything more but they should immediately cast their attention in that direction if they wanted a huge story. They thanked him for the tip but cautioned that they hoped he wasn't sending them on a wild goose chase to deflect them gathering information about his client. Patrick told them if they did their investigative journalism correctly they would uncover a major story. They seemed satisfied he was serious and indicated they would check it out immediately and get back to him. Patrick wished them good luck and told them the story was there for them if they persisted. He hoped privately that they could expose the paeodphile ring and publish details prior to the grand jury hearing next Friday.

# Thirteen

THE new week started encouragingly. On Monday morning Patrick actually met with two new clients. One wanted advice concerning their rights in an easement dispute. Right-of-way disagreements often caused problems between neighbors and were tricky to defuse. The second case had to do with an interpretation of the legal meaning of certain clauses in a set of recorded restrictive covenants which ran with the land. So both new clients had presented Patrick with real property questions. Patrick was feeling quite good that he not only could offer them immediate assistance and sound advice but also that he was keeping his commitment to himself and Cindy indirectly, that he was not ignoring his normal client base by devoting all his time to the Appleby case.

The afternoon also started well. Another new client who owned a small electrical appliance shop that featured major appliances brought Patrick a group of twenty-six bad debts which he wanted collected. Patrick worked collections on a percentage not a flat fee basis. He looked at the twenty-six delinquent accounts individually. He divided them into two piles; those delinquent for one year or less and those delinquent for over one year. He told the client he would work on the cases delinquent for one year or less for thirty-three and one third percent. However, he would charge him forty-five percent of any amounts collected from delinquent accounts due over one year. Patrick told him that it had been his experience the older debts were quite stale and hence far more difficult to collect. For instance, one customer had not made a payment in over three years. These type accounts were very work intensive to collect. The debtors normally had been experiencing financial problems over a protracted period and had become surprisingly resistant to dunning letters even from attorneys. Patrick's client evidently had been attempting to collect these accounts himself and knew the truthfulness of his comments. He readily accepted and signed Patrick's standard percentage fee agreement without a whimper. Patrick figured he had been driven crazy by these accounts and was extremely happy to dump them on him. Then he would have only one point of contact. He could call Patrick and question him as to how he was doing with his collections.

Patrick altered a collection form letter to be sent in the first instance to all twenty-six delinquent accounts informing them he had officially entered the fray. He turned the accounts and letter over to Heather for processing. A few debtors would be intimidated by an attorney's letter and pay up. Many more would string matters out, not even flinching until court proceedings were threatened with exact filing dates stipulated. The final group would resist all his attempts and generally thumb their nose at him throughout the whole process. One thing Patrick had learned in his short practice was that a minority of people really enjoyed beating attorneys out of money and this went for his own bad debts as well. These types seemed to know that most attorneys found it shabby practice to sue their clients as it was obviously bad public relations.

Monday afternoon also yielded other good news. Liam O'Brien telephoned to indicate his partners had no objection to him serving as co-counsel on the Appleby case. However, he thought it was important to memorialize their oral agreement regarding his duties and responsibilities in the case. Patrick told him he had no objection and that Liam should draft such an agreement and he would sign it. However, he cautioned that as court appointed co-counsel to defend Frank Appleby, the court would hold Liam to a standard of professional dedication and competence. Liam said he understood that completely and his draft agreement would address matters such as the use of office staff and such that would please his partners. Patrick indicated he would telephone Judge Draper immediately and request his appointment. Finally, he told Liam how genuinely pleased he was to have him aboard as he could cover his inefficiencies and keep him out of trouble.

Patrick immediately telephoned Judge Draper. He was in court so Patrick left a message. Before he hung up Kelly appeared. She told Patrick she had followed his instructions and surrendered to him the two signed and time dated receipts for Frank Appleby's work clothes. Patrick told her she was always faithful and meant it. She beamed; it was obvious Kelly was not motivated by money alone. She was driven to be the best damn paralegal in existence and Patrick was becoming increasingly convinced she would make it. Kelly told him the forensic laboratory would render them a written analysis report in about ten days and of course Patrick would be invoiced for the analysis and report which they felt would be somewhere between five hundred and seven hundred fifty dollars depending on how many separate tests proved necessary.

Around five p.m. Judge Draper returned Patrick's call When Patrick told him of Liam O'Brien's agreement to serve as co-counsel on the Appleby case, Judge Draper seemed extremely pleased and praised Patrick's good judgement. He said he would sign a motion to that effect as soon as he received it. Patrick prepared the appropriate motion immediately and first thing Tuesday morning Kelly delivered it on his behalf to the Judge's chambers.

At about eleven a.m. Patrick and Kelly made their second visit to his client. Frank seemed a little depressed during the visit. An outdoors man, it was obvious, he was beginning to suffer from lack of working in the gardens and his loss of freedom. Patrick thought it best to attempt to lift his spirits with all the new developments in the case. He told him about the appointment by Judge Draper of Liam O'Brien as co-counsel. He told him how experienced Liam was and how fortunate they were to have him aboard. He told him how their visit with Mrs. Appleby had gone well and how Kelly had taken his work clothes to the forensic laboratory in Fairfax for analysis. He told him that Roland Alberts, another local attorney, had agreed to assist the defense team at strategy meetings. Frank seemed to perk-up and thanked them for all the work they had done on his behalf. He told them that testing his work clothes was fine, that no blood or DNA matter from Wilbur Cosgrove would be found on his clothing because he never met Mr. Cosgrove.

Finally, Patrick thought it prudent to discuss the possibility with Frank that they might employ a private investigator to help with the case. He told him they were meeting with one candidate to explore matters as early as tomorrow. If they found the right private investigator it could impact their preparation very positively. He cautioned, however, the Commonwealth of Virginia did not provide funds for this explicit purpose and hence any investigator hired would have to be paid out of his fee. Still, he wanted to assure Frank that every attempt on their part would be made to provide necessary professional services to properly defend him. If Frank was depressed when they arrived he was greatly impressed with the speed of progress on their part. His depression lifted, his face became more expressive and his actions became increasingly animated.

There were three matters left to discuss. Patrick asked Frank had he been able to think of anyone who might have seen him working all day at Granger's on the day of the murder. Frank had racked his brain but unfortunately no one came to mind. He again explained to Patrick and Kelly the layout of the Granger's lot and reiterated he worked all day in the high walled back garden out of view of anyone passing the Granger's residence. The second topic of discussion was the information on Frank's shotgun that had been given to Sheriff Dunn. Patrick asked Frank what type of documents or brochures had been given to the sheriff. As far as Frank could recall there was the receipt for the purchase of the gun from Sears and Roebuck. Frank was unsure if the serial number of the shotgun was shown on the receipt. He did recall he had also given Sheriff Dunn the gun's guarantee and a color brochure describing in detail the care and operation of the gun as well as the gun's safety features. Frank thought the gun could be pretty fully identified utilizing the information he had given the sheriff. He also knew that his finger prints would obviously be all over the gun. Patrick told Frank he was pretty sure his gun was the one found in the creek bed behind the Cosgrove's house. His guess was that this was the one positive link that the prosecution would attempt to use to place Frank at the murder scene. Barring the gun, Patrick felt they had no other physical evidence and certainly no eyewitnesses. He was in doubt if finger prints would be washed off if a gun was in the water overnight and asked Kelly to contact their independent forensic laboratory and ask their professional educated guess. Then they discussed how and when the gun was stolen from the Appleby house. Again, Frank had no idea as he hadn't looked at the gun for at least a month previously.

Wednesday morning the team assembled in Patrick's office a little before eleven a.m. All members of the team were present. Roland looked a little uncomfortable with his huge frame draped over a chair made for an ordinary mortal. Liam was as bouncy and gregarious as ever. Kelly and Heather were busy making coffee and tea and organising some donuts and sweet rolls that Kelly had purchased on the way to work. Kelly and Heather were marvellous and thought of everything. The team settled and quickly outlined their needs from Jim Brogan. They needed a benign daily rate, some ability to work with all the relevant police bodies including international ones to dig out information on paedophiles and the child pornography ring. Finally, some basic but sound police work locally to see if they could turn up any witnesses to the fact that Frank Appleby had indeed worked all day at the Granger's house while they were away and of course any witnesses to the murder if indeed any existed. There probably was a whole host of other things they should be looking at and they were hopeful Jim Brogan would help educate them as to the direction the investigation should take.

Jim Brogan arrived promptly at eleven a.m. and Heather showed him in. Patrick introduced him to everyone and spent a few minutes explaining their team approach. Jim Brogan was a soft spoken, laid back type individual, he was about five feet eleven inches in height and looked to weigh approximately one hundred eighty pounds. He had sandy colored hair and wore very modern metal framed glasses with lightly tinted lenses. Patrick took the opportunity to brief him concerning the Appleby case. He told him he thought Frank Appleby was an innocent man but probably would be indicted Friday based in great part on the fact that his shotgun was found in a creek directly behind the victim's house. Jim then offered up some new information. He said in preparation for the meeting he had called a friend in the state police that was working with the local sheriff's department on the case. His source confirmed Frank's shotgun was the gun found near the murder scene. In addition they had two witnesses who heard the murderer and Wilbur Cosgrove arguing. The words paedophile and child porn were yelled out during the argument. They were all set back as they now realized for the very first time that the prosecution had more than simply the shotgun to present to the grand jury. They were certain the prosecution would use those witnesses to convince the grand jury that Frank Appleby had accused Wilbur Cosgrove of being a paedophile before killing him in an absolute rage. For their part, they told Jim they now believed that Wilbur Cosgrove was an active member of an international paedophile ring. They thought he was one of those weak sisters lax on security who were systematically being eliminated. Whether in all cases elimination meant murdered, they didn't know. This was one matter they wanted Jim to investigate. Were some ring members simply threatened into better security or were some so lax on security and defiant that they had to be taken out to protect the ring? Liam asked Jim if he still had friends in the FBI, State Police and Interpol he could call on. Jim said he did due to his past career as an FBI agent. Some of his old buddies were still in place with the various agencies. In fairness, he said as time went on he had lost some to retirement but he was still pretty well connected.

Another area they wanted Jim to investigate was how the shotgun could be stolen from the Appleby home without any of the family members noticing. They found this particularly difficult to understand as Mrs. Appleby was at home all the time and didn't have a car at her disposal, hence, she was only away when Frank drove her somewhere. Frank had a pick-up truck and that was the family's only vehicle. They were also interested in Jim searching for witnesses who actually saw the murder. They realized their existence might be remote as Wilbur Cosgrove had been shot at close range inside one of the buildings in his back garden. If an eyewitness existed, they theorized he was the killer or one of the killers, if indeed there was more than one.

Because Patrick and Liam had the ultimate duty to either hire Jim Brogan or not, Patrick addressed this issue. He asked Jim to leave the office so the team could make their decision. After Jim left, Patrick asked, 'are we all in agreement to hire Jim?' There were nods all around. It was really a settled matter after Jim gave them the new information concerning what the two witnesses had heard. Jim certainly knew how to sell a job. Patrick asked Jim if he could start immediately and when he said yes, he hired him for an initial period of two weeks. After Jim departed they were all pleased to have him aboard. The team was convinced Jim would contribute significantly to the defense's case. His fee of two hundred fifty dollars per day was tasty but not outrageous. Roland had urged him to give them his best offer since it was a court appointed defense team with meagre resources. Jim had cut his normal fee of three hundred fifty dollars per day down under the circumstances. They all felt Jim had bought into the team's vision that Frank Appleby was innocent and deserved the best defense possible.

Thursday morning Patrick was a little late getting to work. He had stopped at the general store in Hillsboro for gasoline and had gotten into a discussion with some locals. They were beginning to recognize him and becoming increasingly friendly. When he was a block from the office he noticed heavy black smoke pouring out of the top of the Dean Building. As he drove closer he could see flames leaping from his office. The scene was bizarre. The fire engines were there pumping huge amounts of water on the building. Heather and Kelly were sitting on files and books which they had saved from the fire. Harry Dean was racing up and down the sidewalk as if to direct all operations. A police car was there and two deputy sheriffs were in the street directing traffic. As Patrick ran up Harry Dean yelled to him, 'the building is insured but I hope to hell you have the contents insured.' Patrick yelled back, 'luckily I do' and Harry nodded while in full flight. The strangest sight of all was Kelly had saved Liam O'Brien's hurley and was using it as a pointer to direct the fireman's stream of water from a giant hose connected to the fire hydrant in front of the building. Another surreal sight was two delivery men looking totally bewildered holding a lemon yellow sofa bed.

A photographer from the local paper was out in the street snapping shots. There was not much question that the office fire was going to be the front page story in the next issue. Patrick asked Heather what happened. She said the fire had been started by a pile of cardboard boxes and rags soaked in gasoline which had been placed outside their door. Kelly and she had been working inside when smoke started to seep under the office door from the hallway. They were able to save the files and some books and made a dash for it out the only escape route. Luckily, the fire had been started a little to the left of the office door so they ran through the doorway covering their faces with files, some of which were slightly scorched. They felt lucky to be alive. Kelly butted in with the comment, 'we should both receive battle pay working for you Patrick.'

Then Kelly told Patrick the most chilling fact of the morning. As she and Heather ran from the building they had both seen a black Lincoln heading out route fifteen north at high speed. When the deputy sheriffs arrived about five minutes later, Kelly told them about the suspicious Lincoln and they had a police car dispatched in pursuit. Only one car was available to be dispatched and it went directly out route 15 north through Lucketts headed for Point of Rocks, Maryland. The deputy reported back that he hadn't intercepted the Lincoln and now was backtracking to White's Ferry. White's Ferry had been a ferrying point across the Potomac River between Virginia and Maryland prior to the War Between the States and was mentioned in many history books on that Great War. It featured in Lee's march towards Gettysburg. Had Lee turned right towards the capital the war may have turned out differently? Additionally, there had been troop crossings at White's Ferry and a small skirmish. A small cemetery attested to those who had perished there. After another half hour had passed they learned the black Lincoln had indeed used White's Ferry to make their escape into Maryland. The Maryland police had been notified but no news on their whereabouts had yet been received. Patrick's own guess was they would make a clean getaway. The ferryman however was able to offer good information. There were two men in the car. They were both between twenty-five and thirty-five in age and looked big and very fit. Unfortunately, the windows were tinted so while he could see their overall shape he couldn't describe their facial features in detail as the driver had only opened his window slightly when he paid the crossing fee.

It took another hour for the fire to be totally brought under control. When it was Harry Dean approached Patrick.

'I am sorry Patrick; your offices are totally destroyed as are three additional offices of other tenants.'

'What on earth will I do Harry, I am right in the middle of a major murder case?'

'Yes, I know Patrick.'

'This is terrible; I can't run a murder trial out of Earl's Café.'

'No, I know you can't Patrick. OK, well, here's what I can do. I have a much larger office on East Market Street. It's probably too large a premise for you now but you'll grow. You can use it for six months at one thousand a month but after that I don't want to hear any shit about a graduated lease. It will be three thousand per month, take it or leave it, understand?'

'Ok, Harry, when can I move in?'

'Today, if you want, it's perfect. Suggestion, go to your bank and get a thirty day loan to outfit it until you settle with the insurance company. The bank will check with the insurance company to make sure you have contents insurance and when they find out you do you won't have any trouble.'

'Thanks, Harry, you just saved my life.'

'Save mine sometime will you. My damn dreams just went up in smoke. You know I just renovated that building before you moved in. It cost me five hundred fifty thousand. Now look at what I have, a pile of shit!'

# Fourteen

THE new offices were nothing short of fabulous. Kelly and Heather kept walking around in amazement at the amount of space. There was a reception area, separate offices for three attorneys or paralegals, a conference room, space for office equipment and two bathrooms. One bathroom was off the reception area and the other was part of the largest private office. Heather knew her domain and left all the files in the reception area. Kelly had her eye on a private office next door to Patrick's. Patrick was admiring the largest office, the one with the ensuite bathroom. They couldn't imagine their good luck. They still looked out over Court House Square and hadn't moved two long city blocks.

Patrick followed Harry Dean's instructions exactly. He called his bank, told them he needed ten thousand dollars for thirty days and gave them his insurance carrier and policy number. They couldn't see any problem and he could sign the note and pick-up the cash late Thursday afternoon. Patrick called the office supply house, told them the circumstances of the fire and ordered the exact furniture which he had previously selected. He then indulged in another of his impulsive acts and ordered a conference table and eight leather chairs. Making this selection took about an hour as the salesman described fully the various suites, prices and availability. Patrick finally decided on a suite they had in stock. The conference table was mahogany as were the legs on the chairs which were upholstered in a rich sounding cranberry leather. The most important factor was speedy delivery. The company made an exception due to Patrick's current circumstances and agreed to delivery all the furniture Friday morning. After all, he was becoming one of their best customers as his furniture was burning up almost as quickly as they could deliver it. Patrick remembered a funny story from his home town. There was a local man who had been married seven times. He went to the local florist to announce his impending eighth marriage. The florist inquired as to what kind of flowers he wanted and the response was, 'oh, just give me the usual spread.' If he kept getting burned out Patrick figured he would have to do the same.

Tomorrow was the grand jury hearing. Patrick and Liam were almost one hundred percent sure that based on the evidence and witnesses that they knew about, Frank Appleby would be indicted. Liam had heard on the grapevine that John Brandywell would handle the presentation of the evidence personally. John Brandywell was a decent man and a highly competent prosecutor. Unfortunately, just like old time defense lawyers, he had grown into his role perfectly over time. He had seen a lot of crime and wrong doing in his time and he had hardened. He visualized himself as a guardian of public security and generally had a negative attitude towards anyone who was arrested, innocent or not. Lock-em-up, burn-em, could be cited as his slogans. In fairness, most of those who he prosecuted were indeed guilty. Patrick and Liam felt pretty sure John Brandywell felt Frank Appleby was guilty of a most horrendous murder and it was his duty to see that justice was done. John Brandywell was also notoriously difficult to plea bargain with and the defense bar would rather deal with any of the five assistant commonwealth attorneys, rather than Brandywell.

Patrick and Liam's job was to meet the press after the indictment and put the very best spin on the situation they could. They would have to act confident without being cocky and Patrick would have to sow the seeds that Liam O'Brien and he were defending an innocent man. Patrick telephoned Liam to coordinate their effort. He felt the Washington, D.C. T.V. stations plus CNN and Fox News would all be present and they should probably double team them. In looks, Liam was almost movie star quality and Patrick certainly wanted to get Liam in front of the cameras. When Joan Collins, secretary to Liam, put him through, the first thing Liam asked was, 'have you seen the local paper?' Patrick told him, 'I don't need to see it; I watched my office burn in person.' 'No', Liam said, 'your office fire photo is on page two.' The front page in two inch color print screamed, 'Child Pornography Ring Exposed in County.' The subtitle stated: 'County Loses its Rural Innocence as International Child Porno Ring Moves In, Child Pornography Found in Home of Murder Victim.' Patrick was delighted at the timing of the release the day before the grand jury hearing but was also a little shocked that their press friends had dug out the truth so quickly. This changed the nature of the press conference. They were bound to be asked about the existence of an arm of an international child pornography ring right here in the county. The problem was the more they talked about the horrors of paedophilia and child pornography the more the public would feel Frank Appleby had killed Wilbur Cosgrove in a rage over the rape and molestation of Frankie. Oh, true, public opinion would demonstrate more empathy for Frank Appleby while at the same time copper fastening their view that he was the murderer.

Liam and Patrick decided their best approach concerning the paedophilia and child pornography issue was to raise the spectrum that there may have been other children who where violated, giving rise to other relatives who might also have reason to murder Wilbur Cosgrove. It was now firm in their minds that if this case went to trial they were going to have to demonize Wilbur Cosgrove. Liam said, 'I hate to dishonor the dead but when I get through with that little pervert the world will think he is on trial, not Frank Appleby.'

Late Thursday afternoon Liam and Patrick visited Frank at the jail. After introducing Liam, as his new co-counsel, Patrick carefully briefed Frank that they both thought he would be indicted tomorrow. They then explained the next step, arraignment. They told Frank he would be brought before the Loudoun County Circuit Court to plead to the criminal charge in the indictment. The charge would be read to him and he would be asked to plead guilty or not guilty. He would be given a copy of the indictment for his information before he was called upon to plead. They told Frank they wanted to confirm he would enter a not guilty plea. Frank agreed that was his intention. Liam tried to lift his spirits by telling him these were all necessary legal procedures but it was at trial that they would prove his innocence. Frank seemed relatively calm and resolute and they left him admiring his courage in the face of such accusations.

Friday, the defense team got the body blow they had expected, Frank Appleby stood indicted. The grand jury returned a 'true bill' in his case. There was therefore, in their collective opinion, enough evidence to demand that Frank Appleby stand trial for the murder of Wilbur Cosgrove. Now Frank was going to be bound over to the circuit court for trial and murder. Undoubtedly, John Brandywell would demand the death penalty.

The press conference went well. Liam was the darling of the T.V. stations. He was handsome and extremely articulate. Words rolled off his tongue as smoothly as honey dripped from the comb. When Patrick complimented him later about his performance he simply said, ' a gift from Ireland, the land of Saints and Scholars.' Patrick didn't perform too badly either. Both of them hammered away at Frank Appleby's innocence. They raised the spectrum that other persons unknown may have had a motive to murder Wilbur Cosgrove. They talked about Frank Appleby's great restraint and courage at not lashing out at the man who had violated and degraded his only son. They shifted attention to the victim and his horribly evil act. They described the pain the child had suffered. In the end they were satisfied they had done enough to cast real doubt that Frank Appleby was the killer and that the real evil rested elsewhere. They had tipped their hand a little to the prosecution as to their approach at trial but figured they weren't so naïve not to know what was going to hit them. At any rate, they figured the prosecution had only seen the tip of the iceberg regarding their defense, what was to come would be even more devastating to their case.

There was no further news concerning the two men in the black Lincoln. They had vanished into thin air but Patrick and Liam knew they would return. Liam and Roland figured they somehow found out the team had hired Jim Brogan with a specific remit to investigate the international child pornography ring and its exact connection with Wilbur Cosgrove. They were sending the team a strong message to back off. Both Liam and Roland suggested Patrick have Jim Brogan sweep the new office regularly for bugs. They felt pretty confident that the old office had been bugged. However, any proof of that fact might prove difficult due to the fire. It was fairly obvious to all of them that the closer Jim Brogan came to busting the child pornography ring, the more violent the ring's thugs would become.

# Fifteen

SATURDAY Pritch reached Patrick at the new office. Patrick had managed to arrange with the telephone company that he could keep the same number.

'Sorry Counsellor, I heard about the fire.'

'Yes, Pritch, it was pretty awful, everything destroyed.'

'What's this about an international child pornography ring up there in Loudoun?'

'Yes, well, the murdered man, Wilbur Cosgrove had a lot of child pornography on a secret computer in a lock-up in his basement. The sheriff already had a signed search warrant when Cosgrove was shot. They were going to raid his house and almost certainly arrest him but he was killed hours before they could execute their plan.'

'The Attorney General, Dan Rivers, has picked-up on the story. He's got a copy of your local paper. You know he wants to run for governor next year and there is no way he wants to sit on the sidelines on this one. Busting an international child pornography ring could put him in the governor's chair.'

'The more the merrier, I can use all the help I can get.'

'Now there is a little more that I must tell you and I hope it doesn't upset you.'

'I don't think I can get too much more upset than I have been the last few days. First, two thugs in a black Lincoln follow me for days, then they burn my office and half of Harry Dean's office building to the ground.'

'The Attorney General knows we are law school buddies and has relieved me of my industrial monitoring duties and assigned me to monitor this child pornography case. He asked me to leave for Loudoun County immediately and keep him fully appraised of the situation on a daily basis. So, I am calling to ask if I can work closely with you on the case?'

'That's fantastic, of course you are welcome, you know that.'

'Well, you understand I can't help you with the defense of Frank Appleby. I'll really be riveting on the victim and his links with the international child pornography ring.'

'Pritch, I have no problem at all with that.'

'Good, I'm driving up tonight and thought I would hook-up with Sarah for dinner and a movie, something casual like that.'

'Look, I just had a great idea. Liam O'Brien, a brilliant young criminal lawyer has been appointed by Judge Draper as co-counsel in the Appleby case. He invited Cindy and me to an Irish night. I understand he has also invited Jim Brogan, our private investigator, who is also Irish. Why don't you and Sarah plan to come along with us. I will clear it with Liam and call you at Sarah's tonight to confirm it is ok.'

'That sounds great, I am sure Sarah would enjoy it, particularly if Cindy is there and it will give me an opportunity to meet your colleagues.'

'Exactly my thought, ok, I will contact Liam and arrange it.'

'Ok Counsellor, call me at Sarah's later tonight.'

Patrick immediately telephoned Liam, who was still at his office. He asked him if he could bring his friend Jonathan Pritchard and his girlfriend Sarah Foster to the Irish night. Liam said, 'no problem, that the beer would be flowing and everyone was welcome.'

Patrick telephoned Cindy to tell her the good news that the Fab II would be joining them Sunday at the Irish night. She was absolutely delighted as Sarah and she had really gotten close over the past year and she adored Pritch. She asked what time he would be home as she was lonely. Patrick told her he would leave the office within the next half-hour and should be home by six p.m. Saturday evening was a quiet one by their standards. They stayed home, drank wine and watched t.v. until about eleven p.m. Patrick telephoned Pritch at Sarah's to confirm he had reached Liam and he and Sarah now had a formal invitation. He made arrangements for them to meet him and Cindy at the new law offices on East Market Street at seven p.m. for a short look around prior to leaving for the Irish night festivities. Cindy would also see the offices for the first time. Luckily, the furniture had arrived and the offices looked fairly good, if a little incomplete, due to its overall size. Patrick thought the minimalist look was modern and ok.

Patrick and Cindy arrived at the law offices first. Cindy was amazed at the size and immediately cut to the heart of the matter, questioning how on earth Patrick was going to pay the rent, which she envisioned must be massive. He decided to use an economy of the truth. He told her that due to the fire and his urgent need that Harry Dean had let him have the offices for the same one thousand dollars per month that he had currently been paying. What he didn't tell Cindy was the thousand per month would soon be elevated to three thousand per month. Cindy didn't probe any further and Patrick was happy as he didn't want the evening spoiled. Let her think Harry Dean was their saviour on a white horse. When Pritch and Sarah arrived they were extremely impressed with the new layout, particularly the conference room which looked quite elegant with its cranberry leather chairs and huge conference table in highly polished mahogany. They also liked Patrick's office. The lemon yellow sofa had been re-delivered and looked smashing against the blue grass-cloth walls. He had really lucked out with his office color. After the office tour was over they departed for the local golf club which was the venue for the Irish night.

Ireland was five hours ahead of Eastern Standard Time so the semi-final Ireland GAA football clash had actually been completed earlier in the day. In the bar a large screen t.v. had been set-up where the transmission would be received delayed via satellite. When they arrived the Guinness was already flowing. Liam and his partners, Mick Kelly and

John Jo Sullivan were hobnobbing with the crowd. It was obvious they were the sponsors of the evening and for the partnership it was a real PR exercise. They had little fact sheets printed that memorialised the 1998 Ireland GAA Football Semi-Final between the Lily White's of Co. Kildare and the lads from the Kingdom as Kerry was nicknamed. Kildare wore all white uniforms while Kerry were kitted out in their traditional green and gold.

The real story of the match was played out both on and off the pitch. Mick O'Dwyer the manager of the Kildare team was a Kerry man from Waterville on the famous Ring of Kerry and had been the most successful manager of his home county in history until his departure for Kildare. Now the inevitable had happened, fate had decreed that Kerry would stand in his way of winning the All Ireland championship. Now he was forced to face the county with which he had enjoyed so many glorious days and won all Ireland medals in 1975, 1978 and 1984 over Dublin. The strangeness of the match didn't stop there. Micko's son, Karl, was to play for Kildare while another son, John, was a selector for Kerry and working alongside Paidi O'Se the current Kerry manager. Together they would try and engineer John's father's downfall. In his corner Micko had Pat McCarthy, another former Kerry star like Micko himself. Now Pat McCarthy was a Kildare selector. The two Kerry greats were now entrusted with the demolition of their home county. Patrick copped on pretty quickly that when it came to Gaelic sports, that county allegiance was everything. The match itself was rough and very close. A goal by Denis Dwyer was disallowed for Kerry and Kildare held a slight advantage throughout the tension filled match. At the end Kildare just squeaked by 0-13 to Kerry's 1-9. Evidently, you got three points for a goal so Kerry had twelve points total to Kildare's thirteen points.

Sometime after the match the two managers' released the following statements.

Mick O'Dwyer's statement; Manager of the Millennium

'I was delighted to have won, of course, but emotionally the whole day took a heavy toll on me. I knew there were people who would be happy to say I was a traitor to my native county; that I only came to Kildare for personal gain and so on. It was a strange feeling and I couldn't join in the celebrations as freely as when we had beaten Dublin and Meath, but already I am looking ahead to the final This is no time for negative thinking.'

Paidi O'Se's statement; County Kerry Manager, a Gaelic Football Legend

'I maintain that had any one else been managing Kildare in 1998 we'd have beaten them by seven or eight points. The longer I was in the job the better I felt I was becoming. More confident, but if anything was going to give me the jigs it was the sight of O'Dwyer on the line. I couldn't believe this was unfolding. No point denying it. O'Dwyer looms large in my life. He's been a constant for thirty years. Less than twelve months earlier I'd shared a couple of my happiest hours with him when he told me how well I'd done leading Kerry back to glory, told me to trust my instincts. Now he stood in my way. My heart sunk after the final whistle. I knew O'Dwyer wanted to beat Kerry, big time. Sure he was dishing out loads of 'oh, I'm sorry that it had to be Kerry.' Truth is, O'Dwyer didn't give a fiddler's that it was Kerry.'

Pritch and Patrick were stunned. They had been weaned on baseball, American football and basketball. Now all of a sudden they had been cast into another sporting world. A world of tribal allegiance to one's county. A world where it seemed almost every spectator carried and waved their county flag. A world where sixty-thousand people would turn out to see amateur players play a sport only played in Ireland or elsewhere only by the Irish diaspora. A sport where as a player you gave everything and you played for a small medal and a team cup and you didn't need a multi-million dollar contract to validate your greatness. Pritch and Patrick were enthralled. They decided that day that some September, they didn't know the year; they would travel to Dublin and attend an All Ireland football or hurling final in Croke Park.

Cindy and Sarah were enjoying their day too. They were drinking Bailey's Irish Cream on ice and getting acquainted with many of the other local attorney's wives. The local legal fraternity was well represented. Roland Albert's wife, Terri was with them as was Liam's wife, Fiona and John Jo Sullivan's wife, Eimear. Later there was a demonstration of Irish step dancing, harp playing and a sing-along. They sang; The Banks of My Own Lovely Lee, Carrickfergus, Danny Boy, Galway Bay, The Hills of Kerry, The Holy Ground, In Dublin's Fair City, Mary from Dunloe, The Mountains of Mourne, The Old Triangle, The Rare Ould Times, The Rose of Tralee, She Moved Through the Fair, Spancil Hill and of course what was fast becoming the Irish anthem abroad,

The Field's of Athenry. When they sang the chorus every Irish person seemed to know it.

> 'Low, lie the fields of Athenry, -
> Where once we watched the small free birds fly,
> Our love was on the wing,
> We had dreams and songs to sing,
> It's so lonely round the fields of Athenry.'

Jim Brogan was there with his wife Kathleen. Patrick introduced him to Pritch. Later, Liam, Roland and Patrick huddled with him on the margins. Jim said he wanted to try and visit Frankie in the hospital and asked if Patrick minded if he took Kelly along. Of course he didn't. He felt the boy might prove less jumpy with a woman along after his horrendous experience. Frankie was going to need surgery. The penetration had been so deep and so violent in nature as to be life threatening. The doctor's were going to have to operate to put some of his intestines back in place as they were now badly twisted and Frankie's bodily functions were not working properly. He also had taken to fits of depression where he cried a lot and became very remote from everyone even his mother on her visits. Still, the doctors hoped for a full recovery but it was going to take time. The psychiatrist was now working overtime with Frankie.

The Irish night was a huge success with their contingent. The four of them literally danced out the door. Pritch was singing ' Fields of Athenry' and Cindy was humming 'The Rare Ould Times.' Coffee, tea, sandwiches and cheesecake had been served about eleven p.m. so they were quite sober for the drive home. Patrick told Pritch that he could work out of the conference room and use his telephones. Pritch seemed pleased. Patrick wouldn't let him down any more than Pritch would him. Besides, now that Pritch had seen their new plush offices, he probably couldn't keep him away. Pritch intended to stay at Sarah's penthouse apartment in Reston. It would be a short drive for him to the offices in Leesburg. It was going to be great to have Pritch around just like law school days.

# Sixteen

MONDAY, Judge Draper called a pre-arraignment meeting in his office. John Brandywell, the Commonwealth Attorney was present with his assistants, Eugene Harrison and Bruce Rodgers, Liam O'Brien accompanied Patrick. Judge Draper announced that Frank Appleby would be arraigned at eleven a.m. Wednesday with several other prisoners. He asked Liam and Patrick if they intended to ask for bail and they indicated they did. He wanted to know the approximate number of witnesses the defense intended to call and they indicated about five or six. He then asked John Brandywell if the Commonwealth intended to oppose bail and Brandywell indicated they did. Judge Draper then indicated he would hold the bail hearing after the lunch break on Wednesday at two p.m. Both sides agreed they would be ready. Judge Draper then wanted to know how long it would take the defense to prepare for trial and they indicated fifty days. John Brandywell was upset as he thought thirty days was more than adequate. Liam and Patrick told Judge Draper the case was proving very complex and they felt fifty days was absolutely the shortest time they could be properly prepared. Judge Draper then addressed his remarks to John Brandywell. ' I am going to allow the fifty days and set the trial date accordingly. I don't want this case appealed because the defense contends they were not allowed adequate time to prepare their case.' 'You should want the same John?' 'Alright, your honor, I accept your logic.' With that word from the Commonwealth Attorney the pre-arraignment conference ended and Liam and Patrick returned to Patrick's office to further plan their strategy for the bail hearing. They both doubted seriously that in a murder case, bail would be granted but they were determined to give it their best shot.

Patrick asked Kelly to go out to the Appleby house and get a suit, tie and shirt for Frank. 'Make the shirt white and the tie conservative if you can, Kelly.' 'Ok boss, I'll pick them out myself.'

Liam thought they should ask Frank's preacher the Reverend Donald Weeks of the local Baptist Church to appear as a character witness. Patrick thought Mr. Horace Granger would also be a good choice as he was the one Frank was working for on the day of the murder. Kelly also thought Mr. Ronald Davidson, Frank's landlord would be a logical choice. Liam thought it would be wise to also have a female witness so they agreed on Mrs. Helen Wright of the local hardware store where Frank bought all of his tools and seeds. Finally, Kelly wanted Mr. Jim Abbott of the local garden center. Patrick told the team Liam and he would contact all parties and report to them if they agreed to appear for Frank.

After Liam left Patrick started his telephoning. He was amazed that everyone enthusiastically agreed to appear as a character witness for Frank. Jim Abbott said it would be an honor. Reverend Donald Weeks considered it his pleasant duty. Horace Granger said Frank was the most honest man he had ever met and if he said he was working all day in his back walled in garden, then he was. Helen Wright said she would trust him with her life. Finally, Ronald Davidson said he was eighty-two and had rented out the old family house for thirty-five years ever since he built his new house in 1963 and Frank Appleby was the best tenant he ever had. For the very first time since being appointed to the case Patrick felt cautiously confident they had a chance at trial even though bail was still probably beyond reach even with the testimony of their group of leading Leesburg citizens. Patrick telephoned Liam and gave him the good news. Liam was delighted.

Wednesday morning Patrick was in his office at ten a.m. when Jim Brogan and Kelly returned from the hospital after their visit with Frankie. Jim spoke first.

'Counsellor, I'm going to make your day.'

'How's that Jim?'

'Frankie took the shotgun to Wilbur Cosgrove's house to show it to his new friend since Mr. Cosgrove had shown him all his pets. Frankie said Mr. Cosgrove looked at it but never touched it and Frankie left it in the corner of the largest outbuilding, intending to take it home when he left, but of course after the rape he ran home in terror without it.'

'Jim, you not only made my day you made my year!' Jim could you and Kelly come over at two p.m. to the bail hearing and testify to what you found out?' 'Wow, wait until Liam hears this.'

When Liam heard the news he was as excited as Patrick was but he wasn't sure they should attempt to use this spectacular evidence at the bail hearing. Liam indicated that Jim and Kelly's evidence was hearsay and they both knew Frankie wasn't healthy enough to testify. Plus, Liam felt even if they could get it in it would give the Commonwealth too much time to re-spin their theory of events and diminish the magnitude of the find. He also felt word was sure to get out and the impact on the jury at trial would be lost. Slowly, Patrick came around to Liam's thinking and they decided to go with their character witnesses and a strong summation and hope for the best. Of course Jim and Kelly's statement would be hearsay and would be disallowed. Patrick had forgotten the basics in his rush to serve his client.

When Patrick and Liam arrived at the courtroom it was packed out. There were many friends and relatives of the prisoners to be arraigned. Additionally, many members of the bar had turned out along with the curious. Murder drew people like a magnet. Luckily, the courtroom was arranged so there was one row of seats inside the bar of the court which was reserved for attorneys representing the defendants to be arraigned, otherwise they wouldn't have found a seat. Normally, after being arraigned, indigent prisoners would have attorneys court appointed to represent them. It would be the same in Frank Appleby's case. Liam and Patrick would be formally appointed to represent him even though Judge Draper had in fact given them a head start due to the seriousness of the case. When case 14392 was called out, the Commonwealth v. Frank Lawrence Appleby, the prisoner was brought from the holding area. Frank looked great in his blue suit, white shirt and muted blue tie with small red flecks which Kelly had selected with the help of Mrs. Appleby. Not that there was a lot to select from as Frank only owned one suit, the one he now wore on his back. Mrs. Appleby was not in court as she was at home with the children. She wanted to be there but Frank didn't want her to see him arraigned for any crime, much less, murder. He had gotten her word through a jailer who Frank had gone to high school with and who secretly was in his corner.

Judge Draper addressed Frank.

'Are you Frank Lawrence Appleby?'

'Yes, I am, your honor.'

'Do you have funds to employ an attorney to represent you?'

'No your honor, I don't.'

'Then I am going to appoint Mr. Patrick Hurst and Mr. Liam O'Brien to defend you. They are both competent officers of this court.'

'Thank you your honor.'

'Have you been served with a copy of the indictment?'

'I have your honor.'

'Have you read it?'

'I have your honor.'

'Have you had an opportunity to discuss the indictment with your attorneys?'

'I have your honor.'

'Now, I must read the indictment to you. The Grand Jury of Loudoun County, Commonwealth of Virginia, having been taken from a true list of lawful citizens of the county aforesaid and having been duly empanelled and sworn and charged with the duty to inquire into crimes committed in said county and having been given authority in the name of the Commonwealth of Virginia have upon their oaths presented that Frank Lawrence Appleby of said county and Commonwealth aforesaid, within the jurisdiction of this court, did on Wednesday twenty-eight June 1998 unlawfully, feloniously and intentionally with malice aforethought, murdered one Wilbur Ralph Cosgrove, a human being, in direct violation of the Code of Virginia and against the peace and dignity of the Commonwealth of Virginia, a true bill, signed John H. Buttress, foreman of the Grand Jury.'

'Do you understand the charges against you?'

'Yes, your honor.'

'And do you understand that if found guilty of these charges that you might be imprisoned for life or put to death by the Commonwealth of Virginia?'

'I do, your honor.'

'Then, how do you plead to these charges, guilty or not guilty?'

'Not guilty your honor."

'Alright, I have set your hearing on a Request for Bail for two p.m. today and trial will be set for fifty days from this date or Tuesday 23 September. All pre-trial motions must be filed no later than 1 September and disposed of no later than 10 September. Next case.'

Liam and Patrick left the courtroom immediately and headed for lunch, it was twelve-thirty p.m. and they wanted to return to the courthouse no later than one thirty p.m. to greet their witnesses and brief them as to the order of the proceedings. To avoid the press, they slipped out a back door emptying onto the parking lot behind the building and walked quickly to Liam's car and sped away. They ate that day outside the center of town and their usual haunts. Luckily, no one followed them.

# Seventeen

ALL of Frank's character witnesses were prompt and Liam briefed them regarding the order in which they would be called.

Judge Draper started the bail hearing promptly at two p.m. 'I am going to entertain a short opening statement from each side then I will allow the defense to call their witnesses. Ok, Messrs Hurst and O'Brien, you may go first.'

Patrick answered on behalf of the defense. 'The defense intends to show the court that the release of Frank Appleby on bail will in no way endanger any members of this community and will better facilitate his complex defense. Furthermore, he will not flee the jurisdiction but will return to this court on the date your honor has set for trial and defend himself and clear his name.'

'Mr. Brandywell.'

'Your honor the Commonwealth contends that due to the serious nature of the crime before the court and the very real possibility that the defendant will take flight and leave the jurisdiction of the court and the Commonwealth it would be unwise to release the prisoner on bail. We strenuously oppose release on bail for this prisoner.'

'Your honor, I object to Mr. Brandywell's reference to my client as the prisoner. He is the defendant in this case, who is presumed innocent until proven guilty.'

'Sustained, in future Mr. Brandywell, I am instructing you to refer to Mr. Appleby as the defendant.' Mr. Hurst, you may call your first witness.'

'I call Reverend Donald Weeks.'

'Will the Bailiff swear in Reverend Weeks.'

'Do you swear to tell the truth, the whole truth so help you God?'

'Oh yes, I do.'

Patrick started the examination, 'Reverend Weeks, please state your full name.'

'Donald George Weeks.'

'And what is your current position?'

'I am pastor of the Leesburg Baptist Church.'

'And how long have you served in that capacity?'

'Twelve years.'

'Do you know the defendant, Mr. Frank Appleby?'

'Oh yes, I have known Frank ever since I was posted to Leesburg in 1986.'

'How exactly do you know Frank Appleby?'

'Frank and his family attend our church every Sunday and Frank has served as a greeter and also for the last eight years collecting the offerings.'

'Do you know Frank Appleby outside church?'

'Oh yes, Frank helps me once a year cut firewood for our kitchen stove and I have from time to time sought his advice concerning where to plant trees and shrubs. Also, I see him frequently in town and we often have short chats. Sometimes we go to coffee together.'

'How would you characterize Frank Appleby as a man?'

'God fearing, a believer, honest, loyal, a good family man, friendly, humorous and knowledgeable concerning his work.'

'Do you admire Frank Appleby?'

'Yes, I do, without reservation.'

'Have you ever known anything negative or evil concerning Frank Appleby?'

'Oh no, never, Frank is a model citizen; kind, caring, faithful and dedicated to doing good.'

'How is Frank devoted to doing good?'

'Well probably many ways but as an example, last year Frank was captain of our food drive for the less fortunate. He organized everything and carried many of the food parcels to be delivered in his pick-up truck. He often worked flat out all weekend.'

'If you had to sum up Frank Appleby's life, how would you do it?'

'Oh, that's easy, Frank is a really good person, he cares for everyone, a shining example for our youth.'

'Does Frank have a temper, have you ever seen him mad?'

'No, Frank has a very mild, laidback demeanor. He must be very slow to anger because I never saw him angry, nor was it ever reported to me that he was.'

'Then to the best of your knowledge he never harmed anyone in the past?'

'No, Frank wouldn't harm a flea.'

'Objection, that is conjecture on the part of the witness.'

'Sustained.' Strike that last answer from the record.'

'That is all our questions for Rev. Weeks your honor.'

'Mr. Brandywell.'

'No questions your honor.'

We next called Mr. Horace Granger. Liam handled the direct examination after Mr. Granger was sworn.

'Please state your name for the Court.'

'Horace Matthew Granger.'

'Do you know the defendant Mr. Frank Appleby?'

'Yes, I do.'

'In what capacity or circumstances do you know Mr. Appleby?'

'Frank has worked for me as a gardener for fifteen years.'

'Where does Mr. Appleby perform his gardening services for you?'

'At my home in Leesburg on West Cornwall Street?'

'How has Mr. Appleby performed his gardening services for you?'

'Mr. Appleby is the most honest, trustworthy man I have ever known, his work is impeccable and he is very helpful and accommodating. When I give him money to purchase plants, trees or shrubs he always brings me receipts and accounts for every penny of change.'

'Does Mr. Appleby have a temper or is he violent in any way?'

'Heavens no, you couldn't make Frank angry if you tried. Anger or violence is simply not part of his personality and I can tell you he didn't kill Wilbur Cosgrove, either.'

'Objection, the witness is offering an opinion and conclusion which is total supposition on his part.'

'Sustained, Mr. Granger please only answer the question asked, don't volunteer additional information. Strike that last sentence from the record.'

'Mr. Granger, how would you characterize Mr. Appleby, in other words, what is your overall evaluation of him?'

'As a worker he is excellent. As a person he is honest, reliable, hardworking, fair, honorable, dedicated to his family and his church, really admirable in everyway.'

'Thank you Mr. Granger, no further questions.'

'Mr. Brandywell.'

'No questions, your honor.'

The Defense next calls to the stand Mrs. Helen Wright. After being sworn Liam conducted the direct examination.

'Please state for the court your full name?'

'Mrs. Helen Elizabeth Wright.'

'What is your occupation Mrs. Wright?'

'I am the owner of Wright's Hardware Store in Leesburg.'

'And how long have you owned this store?'

'I owned the store for twenty five years jointly with my husband George Wright until his death ten years ago. Since that time I have been the sole owner.'

'Now Mrs. Wright, in your business, have you had occasion to know the defendant Mr. Frank Appleby?'

'Yes for years, he is one of my regular customers.'

'How many years has Mr. Appleby been your customer?'

'I don't know exactly, we go back a long time together, certainly over twenty-five years.'

'And during those twenty-five years what type of items has Mr. Appleby purchased from you?'

'Mostly tools, string, chalk, bedding plants, flowers and grass seed.'

'And how would you characterize Mr. Appleby as your customer?'

'Honest, fair-dealing, courteous, friendly, reliable. These are the words I would use to describe him.'

'In what ways did you find him reliable?'

'Well, he always paid promptly and he always did exactly what he said he would do. For instance, if I had to order something for him and told him the day the goods would arrive he always returned on that day.'

'So, he was very reliable?'

'Yes, I would trust Frank with my life, that's how highly I think of him.'

'And how was Mr. Appleby's temperament when he came into your shop, did he ever seem agitated or angry?'

'Oh no, you couldn't make Frank mad if you tried. He thinks everything through and has great empathy for people. I sometimes would be nervous or stressed but not Frank. I attribute his serenity to his work each day out with nature.'

'Finally, Mrs. Wright, how would you sum up Mr. Appleby's character?'

'I would say that he is one of the kindest and softest personalities I have ever known.'

'Thank you very much Mrs. Wright, no more questions.'

'Mr. Brandywell, your witness.'

'No questions, your honor.'

It was now obvious that John Brandywell, elected Commonwealth Attorney, was not going to harass any of Leesburg's leading citizens who were probably part of his hardcore voter base. He smiled and nodded slightly at each one as if to say, so glad to see you. I recognize you are telling the truth. Don't worry, John Brandywell, protector of the people is on the job and all will become apparent at trial. Don't worry, justice will be done.

The testimony of Mr. Jim Abbott of the garden center followed and was very similar to the evidence of Helen Wright's. Frank Appleby was honest, dependable, a bankable quantity, a person who was uniformly well liked, a local treasure. Mr. Abbott made one impassioned statement, ' I don't think Frank did it but if anyone messed with my boy I would probably kill him.' This brought a deep frown to the face of Judge Draper and an immediate command to 'strike that statement from the record.' Patrick wondered as he looked at Judge Draper, if Frank Appleby had ever mowed his lawn, cut his hedge or cared for his flower garden. He never said he did or didn't but it wouldn't surprise him if he had at some point. At any rate, the Judge never attempted to disqualify himself. Liam and Patrick were quite pleased the character witnesses had performed admirably and they both sensed they had made a strong impact on Judge Draper.

'Alright Mr. Hurst and Mr. O'Brien, we will hear your summation.' Patrick handled the summation.

'Your honor our summation is a very simple one indeed. Mr. Appleby was born in Leesburg and has spent his entire life here. Almost all the people except the newcomers know him personally. Over time, he has probably worked for more than half of them as a gardener. He is uniformly liked and respected as some of Leesburg's leading citizens confirmed. He is a god fearing believer and doer of good deeds as his Pastor, Rev. Weeks has testified. He needs to work to support his wife and five children and if released will go back to his normal work posing no threat to any member of this community. He will not attempt to flee from the jurisdiction of this court or from the Commonwealth. He has no where to go and no funds to get there. He loves his family dearly and he would never desert them. He will always place their needs above his own as a pure demonstration of his love for them. He is an innocent man and he intends to make his stand on the soil of his birth among those he loves and who clearly love him. I ask the court to grant him bail on his own recognizance.

'Thank you Mr. Hurst.'

'Mr. Brandywell.'

'Your honor the Commonwealth's position is also very simple. Mr. Appleby has been arrested and indicted by a grand jury of his peers and fellow citizens who feel there is enough evidence against him to bind him over to this court for trial. The crime he is accused of is not some petty crime but the most serious crime known to civilized man, namely taking another person's life. Depriving that individual of all his life's relationships with both family and friends. The victim is no longer alive to support his wife, to see his children, everything for him has ended and violently at that. Additionally, we live in a tri-state area. Within a few minutes and a few miles the defendant could flee over the border to Point of Rocks or Brunswick, Maryland. Taking another route of flight he could leave the county and within minutes be in Harper's Ferry, West Virginia. No one denies that Mr. Appleby is a hard worker and well liked in the community. I too like him, however, if he murdered a fellow human being as the evidence indicates then he must be punished to the full extent of the law. Justice demands no less. I, therefore, urge the court not to allow the defendant to be granted bail.'

'I have heard the testimony of the character witnesses and I have listened carefully to both arguments. I have decided that I am going to grant bail to Mr. Appleby on his own recognizance. I believe the likelihood that he will flee the Commonwealth is very remote, indeed. I believe he will keep his court date and his release will facilitate the formulation of his defense, which is in the interest of Justice. In murder trials bail is almost never granted. However, I feel this case is an exception. I don't believe Mr. Appleby possesses a threat to any member of our community. This can not be said in many violent murder cases. While Mr. Appleby needs to work to support his large family I want to make it very clear this was not a major factor in my decision. I must stress my decision is based on two major points. I do not believe Frank Appleby represents a threat to any of our citizens and I believe as the defense stated that he will not leave the jurisdiction of this court and will appear on twenty-three September for his trial. Now Mr. Appleby, as a condition of your release on bail you must report to the sheriff's office once per day and sign on. Additionally, you will be fitted with a new electronic bracelet so the sheriff will know your whereabouts at all times. You may continue your work in the normal manner and meet with your defense co-counsels as necessary. Mr. Appleby, you should return to the jail with the sheriff's deputy where your bail release will be processed in the normal manner. Court is dismissed.'

Patrick looked over at Frank in his nice blue suit and he was beaming. Liam was so happy he could barely contain himself. His law partners had attended the hearing and were congratulating him. Many local people were smiling and giving me their sign of approval. As Frank was being led away the newspaper boys were closing-in on the defense team. This time they had no intent to avoid them. This time they would be happy to give them the interview they so badly wanted. When Liam and Patrick emerged from the courthouse they were ready for them with microphones outstretched and journalist's pads at the ready. Patrick decided to let Liam go first, after all, he was the senior and much more experienced man.

'My co-counsel, Mr. Hurst and I are absolutely delighted at the outcome of the bail hearing and the release on bail of our client, Mr. Appleby. His release will facilitate his defense as Judge Draper stated and his family will welcome him home with open arms.'

'But, Mr. O'Brien isn't his release highly unusual in a murder case?'

'Yes, it is, and it is a great testimony to our client that the court decided that his release was prudent and acceptable.'

'Mr. Hurst, what do you think?'

'I echo the sentiments of my co-counsel. I am absolutely delighted at the outcome of the bail request hearing. We have always contended that Mr. Appleby was innocent and that Mr. Wilbur Cosgrove was murdered by another. The truth will come out at the trial and we look forward to presenting an extremely robust defense.'

'Well, if Frank Appleby didn't kill Wilbur Cosgrove, who did?'

'We are encouraging the sheriff's department to continue looking for the real killer. In the meantime we will go about the business of defending our client to the best of our ability. Thank you gentlemen, we really have nothing else to add.'

This time it was John Brandywell's turn to return to his office and to tell his secretary he had no statement for the press. John Brandywell was not a man who fancied defeat. Liam and Patrick knew he wouldn't embrace defeat at trial without one hell of a fight.

The victory today was sweet but was not the absolute victory they coveted. Judge Draper had been very brave. He had not followed the normal convention that bail was never granted in a murder case. The defense team was prejudiced but they all felt he had acted properly. Even if Frank Appleby had murdered Wilbur Cosgrove for raping his son, which he didn't, there was no way he presented a threat to any other member of society. Logic had prevailed but it took a daring and confident judge to apply it.

# Eighteen

THE yellow sofa bed started to get a real workout. Patrick started to live in his office. He brought from his house an extra suit and some shirts and ties. He shaved and showered in his ensuite bathroom. Cindy was lonely and becoming increasingly angry with him. Their sex life was suffering. On the few nights he did stay at home he was too tired to perform. There was no question his personal life was suffering. Cindy asked him if he minded if in the evenings she helped a political candidate up in the valley who was facing a tough election. Patrick wasn't too keen on the idea but what could he say, he was never home, their sex life was almost a non-starter and even when he was home he couldn't concentrate on anything but preparation for the trial. He finally told her to go ahead, thinking it would occupy her time and make her happy.

Pritch utilized the conference room each day and undoubtedly noticed Patrick's increased stress level and pattern of almost never sleeping at home. Pritch continued to do his job as directed by the Attorney General, Dan Rivers. Everyday he faithfully telephoned Rivers filling him in regarding any information he had been able to glean from various police authorities. Patrick made a pact with Pritch that he would share with him any important information that Jim Brogan unearthed if Pritch in turn would keep them advised concerning police information. Pritch agreed without hesitation, only cautioning that the arrangement must be kept secret. Patrick had no problem with that.

Finances had reached a critical state. Patrick didn't have the one thousand dollars rent money for Harry Dean and the end of the month was fast approaching. Of even more concern, he didn't have enough money to pay Heather or Kelly. Kelly's arrangement was slightly different as they had originally negotiated so he could probably skip paying her for a few weeks but he had never missed paying Heather and this would cause him great embarrassment. Another looming problem was Jim Brogan's fee. He had now completed the first two weeks of employment. Patrick had enough money in his account to pay him for the originally agreed period but no additional funds to keep him working on the case. He couldn't ask Cindy for money as she was already paying the house rent, buying all the groceries and even giving him money to operate his car and buy lunches. The end of his case and maybe even his fledgling law practice was threatened.

How could Patrick let Jim Brogan go. Jim had already helped them immeasurably with his interview of Frankie and the revelation of how the shotgun had been transported by Frankie to Wilbur Cosgrove's outbuildings. This would be a key aspect of their defense. It would prove that Frank Appleby did not grab his gun in a moment of violent anger and make a wild dash for the Cosgrove residence. Now, they could prove the shotgun was already at the premises and could have been used by anyone. True, John Brandywell would contend that it was Frank who rushed to the Cosgrove home, spotted his shotgun in the corner and used it to murder Wilbur Cosgrove. However, the defense could counter that it was also readily available to another perpetrator.

For the first time in his short legal career Patrick was scared; he was facing square into the jaws of defeat. He couldn't believe it was going to end this way but here he was on an irrevocable march towards disaster. Heather announced that Sarah Foster had arrived at the office. Pritch greeted her with a big kiss and Patrick's greeting was only slightly less enthusiastic. After a few moments of their usual banter, Sarah asked if she might see Patrick alone. Patrick thought possibly she wanted to add a codicil to her will but this was not the purpose of her visit.

'Patrick, I have been thinking about poor Frank Appleby and his defense. Pritch says you are confident he is innocent and I want to help.'

'That is very laudable Sarah, what do you propose?'

'I want to give you twenty-five thousand dollars as a defense fund. You may use it anyway you see fit, to keep your office and the investigation going. Pritch says the Commonwealth doesn't pay you a great sum for your representation and I don't want you under undue pressure during this sensitive period. If you need more funds, all you have to do is simply ask.'

'Sarah I couldn't take your money.'

'Patrick, don't act silly, my fortune earns more interest and profits in one day than the amount of my contribution.'

'I don't know Sarah.'

'You don't have to know Patrick. I am not a free spending fool. I am careful with my money but when I decide I want to use my money for good no one can dissuade me. Plus, I don't want to hurt your feelings but this gift is about equivalent to you deciding to give twenty dollars to a worthy cause. Take this check.'

'Well, if you insist.'

'I do insist, besides don't you think my life was worth twenty five thousand dollars. I owe you much, much more.'

'Nonsense Sarah, you would do the same for me.'

'I can only hope, Patrick, that I would have acted as well as you did under crisis circumstances.'

'A thousand thank you's Sarah.'

'I know you are grateful Patrick, and I am sorry for not having been there for you earlier.'

'Sarah, I will have to do all your legal work free for a century.'

'You will do more legal work for me Patrick, I can almost guarantee it, but you will be handsomely paid.'

'I love you Sarah.'

'I know Patrick and I love you too. Say hello to Cindy for me, when will we see you guys?'

'I will ask Liam what the Irish society has up its sleeve.'

'Bye.'

'Bye, Sarah and thanks again.'

'Please, not another word.'

After Sarah left Patrick felt like someone had taken a thousand pound weight off his shoulders. He called Jim Brogan and told him to continue his investigation. Jim told Patrick that he and Kathleen had planned a vacation in Amsterdam. Patrick knew immediately what he was about and told him he would pay for the airline tickets and hotel if he could support Kathleen's shopping. Patrick asked Jim how long his vacation might take and he said he had a few courtesy calls to make to old police friends and would be away one week. 'Be careful Jim, these bastards are brutal. They burnt me out and they wouldn't have given a damn if my secretary and paralegal had burned up too.'

Heather and Kelly got paid and Harry Dean got his rent. Patrick's life was better except at home where his relationship with Cindy continued to deteriorate. They now only passed notes to each other. Personal time together was now almost non-existent. Patrick couldn't understand how such a wonderful relationship had deteriorated so quickly. He was totally and utterly confused.

# Nineteen

JIM and Kathleen Brogan returned safely from their holiday in Amsterdam. Kathleen had bought Christmas gifts in the city while Jim worked. Jim's connections in the Amsterdam police force had borne fruit. They knew about the child pornography ring and had a suspect for 'Mr. Big' but didn't have enough evidence to arrest him. His name was Jan van der Gaar and he was a ruthless criminal who had served two terms in prison on drugs, prostitution and racketeering charges. The Amsterdam police suspected he had shifted his operation into child pornography but couldn't find proof even after executing two search warrants of his warehouse office and home. Numerous young boys and girls had disappeared in recent months. Several were found brutally murdered but most disappeared without a trace. It was suspected that most were kidnapped by being bundled into vans and carried off. They were usually picked-up on quiet streets where nobody noticed their disappearance. A few pictures had surfaced of the most degrading sexual exploitation. Hoods were placed over the children's heads to shield their identity; however, genital areas were shown in full detail. The average ages of the missing children were six to twelve. As a group they were above average in attractiveness and body form. Many were being raped or forced to perform oral sex. It was thought similar images were appearing on the internet but so far the sites had not been identified. Van der Gaar was under constant police surveillance as they waited for him to make a mistake. So far he had proved too elusive for them. His list of close associates was thought to be somewhere between six and eight but information on these men was sketchy at best. Even the usual underworld informants had almost no information on Van der Gaar.

Patrick was sitting at his desk contemplating how evil this fellow Jan Van der Gaar must be when Kelly came storming in the office.

'Boss, boss, great news. I just heard from the lab in Fairfax they have run nine separate tests on Frank Appleby's clothing and all they could find was grass stains, soil stains, particles of sawdust, some oil stains, Frank's DNA and that's it.'

'That is really good news. I must tell Liam immediately.'

'Wait boss, don't telephone Liam yet, there's more. They will confirm all this to you by letter. Additionally, they have formulated their expert opinion as to whether or not any fingerprints would survive on the shotgun if it was in moving water for an eighteen hour period.'

'Go on, I am vitally interested in their opinion.'

'Again boss, they will confirm everything to you in writing but it is their opinion that some finger prints would probably survive. Basically, they say with new sensitive laboratory techniques all of the residue of the oil from the hands that originally made the prints wouldn't be washed away. True, they may be affected to some degree but not totally cleansed.'

'I see, interesting and obviously not in our favor.'

'Well, boss, they go on to say if there are a lot of prints on the gun from the same person the chances are fairly high that some of the prints will survive in a good enough condition to make a positive identification.'

'Thanks Kelly, now I had better wire Liam in.'

'OK boss.'

'Joan, Patrick, is Liam in?'

'Just a minute Patrick, I'll put him right on.'

'Yes Patrick, what's up?'

'Well Liam, I have some good news and some bad news, which do you want first?'

'Oh hell, give me the good news.'

'The independent forensic laboratory in Fairfax has completed nine separate tests on the clothing Frank wore on the day of the murder. They didn't find any blood stains or any DNA from any individual other than Frank Appleby. All they found was grass, soil, sawdust and oil stains; all consistent with Frank's work.'

'That is good news, now what's the bad news?'

'The bad news is that it is their opinion that all fingerprints, particularly if there were quite a few, would not be washed off the shotgun even if it had stayed in a fast running body of water for eighteen hours.'

'In other words, Frank Appleby's prints, will almost certainly survive on the shotgun, thus making a positive identification.'

'Exactly right Liam, our only hope is if someone else's prints survive, of course, leaving out those of the store clerk at Sears and Roebuck who obviously would have handled the gun too.'

'Patrick, the Commonwealth will introduce a forensic scientist to sort all this out for the jury. I suppose we had better hire a forensic scientist of our own to put our spin on the facts.'

'Absolutely Liam, ok, I'll put Kelly on the job of finding us a good but reasonable expert. Probably one from the forensic lab in Fairfax will agree to serve in that capacity.'

'The two may not go together Patrick, good and reasonable, more likely it will be good but expensive.'

'Thanks partner, leave it to you to bring joy into my life.'

'Sorry counsellor, who said criminal law was a rose garden!'

A few days after their return from the so called vacation in Amsterdam, Jim Brogan was hard at work. On his second day back he stopped by the office and told Kelly and Patrick that he was going to personally interview all the residents who lived around Horace Granger's house. It would be similar to the series of interviews he conducted among Wilbur Cosgrove's neighbors. Of course the purpose would be entirely different. When he interviewed Wilbur Cosgrove's neighbors he was seeking information that would rule out any sightings of Frank Appleby near the Cosgrove home on the day of the murder while at the same time attempting to place the real killer(s) at the murder scene. Those interviews corroborated Frank Appleby's statement that he had never been near the Cosgrove home. However, it didn't unearth a sighting of the real killer(s) either. Now Jim would be attempting to locate witnesses that could verify that Frank Appleby and his truck never left the Granger's back garden on the day of the murder. There was a high possibility that no one would be located who had a clear view of Frank at work but Jim felt that basic investigation techniques often paid dividends. He had seen the benefits of this type of basic police-type work during his long employment as an FBI agent. Kelly and Patrick wished him well and thanked him again for everything he was doing to aid in this case. Patrick particularly thought the information he had uncovered in Amsterdam concerning Jan Van der Gaar and his group of criminals was extremely revealing. Jim had wired in Sheriff Dunn concerning all his findings his first day back and had also briefed Liam, Kelly, Pritch and Patrick. Pritch had been in touch immediately with the Attorney General, Dan Rivers. In fact, the Attorney General had asked if Jim could speak to him and clarify a few points which Jim had done. Based on this new information the Attorney General had decided that he should make a personal visit to Loudoun County to meet with Sheriff Dunn and Jim. Pritch was setting up the high profile visit now with all the relevant police authorities.

Jim said he would be back in touch as soon as he had anything of value to share with the team. When he left the office he looked rather rested and had a real spring in his step. Things were beginning to break and Jim now had a target in his sights. Jim hated criminals and had spent his whole adult lifetime chasing them. However, he held a special anger and disgust for those criminals that would harm a child. They topped Jim's list of those who must be apprehended and punished. It was now obvious that after the Amsterdam visit Jim Brogan had a renewed purpose in life; to crush the international child pornography ring and in so doing free Frank Appleby who had been nothing but an innocent pawn in their evil game.

Two days went by and no word from Jim. This was quite unusual as Jim normally telephoned Heather each day, sometimes even twice per day, to determine if Liam, Kelly or Patrick needed him. Patrick decided to telephone Kathleen, Jim's wife, to see if anything was wrong. Kathleen said Jim had called her late Thursday afternoon and said something big was up and he might be very late Thursday evening. Actually, he never returned Thursday evening at all and Kathleen was just about ready to call Sheriff Dunn and report him missing but she was hesitant because Jim was often secretive when he was working on a case and the last thing he would want was the police involved as they might blow his cover. Patrick told Kathleen he would have Kelly call Deputy Sheriff Wayne Broomfield and see if a quiet search for Jim could be initiated. She agreed to this action as she said she was very worried but also didn't want Jim to think she was interfering in his work, after all Jim's work meant that he sometimes was not at home at night. Kelly called Wayne Broomfield as agreed. When Kelly reached Wayne his voice sounded alarmed. 'Kelly, I am on my way right now to the old civil war cemetery at White's Ferry. A van driver got out of his vehicle to relieve himself in the woods before crossing the Potomac on the ferry and as he walked by the cemetery he spotted a man's body lying at the base of the large monument. I'll let you know what I find when I get there. I have already called for an ambulance.' When Kelly told Patrick of Wayne's response he told her we had better get out there immediately. Patrick had a very bad feeling that the injured man might be Jim Brogan. When they arrived two police cruisers were already there with the emergency lights flashing. The ambulance Wayne called had also arrived. The injured man was indeed Jim Brogan. The back of his head had been smashed with a blunt instrument but miraculously he was still alive, although totally unconscious and just barely breathing. There was a massive amount of blood on the ground, on the base of the monument and all over Jim's jacket and shirt. Kelly and Patrick were absolutely gutted. They had learned to love and admire Jim Brogan. Kelly was crying uncontrollably as she had worked very close with Jim and now they were the best of friends. Patrick was totally shattered. Kelly got in the ambulance with Jim and held his hand as they rushed him to the local hospital. Patrick told Kelly he would call Kathleen and then look around for Jim's car. Patrick telephoned Kathleen from his mobile. It was the hardest telephone call he had ever made. Patrick was a softy and he knew it. He hadn't seen much violence in his lifetime. The worst thing that had ever happened to him was he once broke his arm in a sledding accident. Other than that he had never seen anyone seriously injured. His family had protected him, never taking him to funerals. He had only seen two dead people in his whole life and those were when his parents died. Before he was able to call Kathleen he bent over and vomited his lunch. Wayne Broomfield came over and asked if he was ok., Patrick said yes, but he really wasn't. He pounded his fist on a tree trunk and said to himself, 'we are going to get you dirty bastards.'

When Patrick reached Kathleen she sensed from his voice that something was terribly wrong. When he told her what had happened she became very emotional.

'Patrick, I always knew this day would come, I just never knew the hour or the day. Jim's work is so dangerous.'

'I know Kathleen.'

'But you know Jim, he wouldn't be happy without it. Jim gets a good retirement from the FBI but they let them retire too early. They should know a man like Jim would never stop working at 55.'

'No, of course not.'

'I'll leave for the hospital immediately.'

'Kathleen, do you have anyone to drive you?'

'No, I can make it.'

'No, please Kathleen call a taxi, the firm will cover all expenses. I will leave now for the hospital too and I will arrange all your further transport. Please, please you are too upset; don't even think about driving yourself.'

'Thanks Patrick, you are a lovely, kind and thoughtful man just as Jim said you were.'

'Kathleen, we all love Jim.'

'I know Patrick, I know, me too.'

When Kathleen arrived at Loudoun Hospital Jim was already in emergency surgery. Before Patrick left he just wanted to check two things. Jim's car was indeed parked in the White's Ferry parking lot and locked. The parking lot was simply a flat unpaved piece of ground that had been worn-down by previous use.

Patrick felt Jim's car would be safe there for a few hours until he could arrange for its removal. Patrick decided to ask Wayne what he thought about the car. Wayne and another deputy had already cordoned off the crime scene and were awaiting the forensics team. 'No, Patrick, don't attempt to move Jim's car until after forensics check it out. When they are finished we'll make arrangements to bring it back into Leesburg and impound it at the county vehicle compound'. Patrick thanked Wayne and was about ready to leave for the hospital when the ferry from the Maryland side landed. He took an opportunity to talk to the ferryman. He said his name was Oliver Dodd and he had just come to work but he had been on last evening until dark. The ferry service stopped at darkness and on times the river was swollen with rain water.

'Oliver, did a black Lincoln come over last night?'

'Matter of fact one did. Came over about 8 p.m.'

'And did they return or stay in Virginia?'

'Well, that was the funny thing, they didn't stay too long, I remember taking them back on the last Virginia to Maryland crossing at 8:45 p.m.'

'Do you remember who was in the car?'

'Oh yes, they were two big mean looking dudes, talking some foreign language to each other; definitely not locals.'

'You don't know the language they were speaking?'

'No, sorry, I only went to the fifth grade. I ain't much on languages.'

'Ok, Oliver, you've been a big help.'

'Did they kill that feller? I just heard from a passenger what happened up there in the graveyard.'

'I hope not Oliver; I hope he's only injured.'

'Good, I don't want the ferry to get no bad reputation because I love this job.'

'I hope he's alright too, Oliver.'

'Do you know him?'

'Yes, Oliver, I know him well and now I want to go to the hospital and see how he is.'

'If you tell me his name I'll pray for him.'

'His name is Jim, Oliver, Jim.'

# Twenty

WHEN Patrick arrived at the hospital he found Kathleen and Kelly sitting together in a corner. Kathleen was crying softly. Big tears rolling down her cheeks and smudging her face with mascara. Kelly was holding her hand and consoling her. Jim was in emergency surgery and no one had appeared yet with any news. Patrick joined the vigil. He thought it best if he could keep Kathleen occupied so he asked her how she and Jim had met. When she finished that description he asked her about their early years together. Kathleen understood that he was leading her through their entire life together and she was willing to share that information with them. Kelly and Patrick, for the most part, just sat back and listened. Every once in a while one of them would ask a question to make sure they had relationships or family names correct. If necessary, one of them would ask a question obviously intending to keep the story flowing.

They had a very interesting life together. They both graduated from American University in Washington, D.C.

Kathleen had majored in education while Jim had majored in criminology. They had started to date in their senior year. The romance had developed rapidly and two weeks after graduation they married. The year was 1958 and like most young couples of their era they started with little or nothing. Kathleen got a job teaching third grade in Arlington, Virginia and Jim joined the Falls Church police force as an officer. They found an apartment in Clarendon, which wasn't too far for either to travel to work. Their early years were very happy and slowly they were able to furnish their apartment. When they moved in all they had was a bed which was very difficult when they wanted a place to sit comfortably. It wasn't too long however before they were able to purchase some upholstered furniture for the living room and this changed their life immeasurably. Each piece of furniture was carefully selected and Jim always accompanied Kathleen on their shopping adventures. Kathleen was always very proud of the fact Jim would also accompany her on trips to the supermarket. After three years of apartment living Jim and Kathleen bought their first house, a small three bedroom one bath rambler in Falls Church. Kathleen now had a car of her own, a VW beetle and continued to teach in nearby Arlington. After five years of marriage their first child was born, James Brogan, Jr.; two years later the couple had a daughter, Caroline Anne Brogan. Jim's big break came in 1966 when he applied for a job at the FBI. He scored very high on the required tests and at age twenty-nine he became an FBI agent assigned to the main FBI building in Washington. Kathleen had returned to teaching after each child but in 1970 they sold the house in Falls Church and purchased a much larger four bedroom two bath two story house in Fairfax County. The house was on four acres. Kathleen had given up work shortly after the move to the new house as the children really needed full-time attention. They had worked for years planting trees and shrubs. Over the years they had converted the grounds into a shady green oasis. Kathleen felt they had lived the American dream, they weren't rich but they were comfortable.

Kathleen felt that one reason for their success was their thrifty attitude. Sure they went to the many malls and shopping centers that had grown-up around them but they didn't buy just to get that 'feel good feeling' or simply to possess things. They bought what they and the children needed but no more. They tried to pay cash for everything avoiding the pitfalls of credit cards. They had some credit cards but used them very sensibly. They did have one excess, Jim always insisted that appeals for less fortunate or starving people around the world be answered. He said his fore-bearers had been driven out of Ireland during the famine and it was a moral duty to take care of the less fortunate who through no fault of their own were simply born in the wrong place at the wrong time. When they heard Kathleen tell of Jim's real passion for helping others it confirmed their own view that Jim was a true American hero. He had fought crime, stood up for what was right but also he was waging his own personal war against famine, starvation, drought and pestilence. They didn't come more admirable than Jim Brogan. Greed and self-seeking were never going to be features in his life.

Kathleen had just completed that portion of their life where they had sacrificed to put the children through university. James, Jr. was a practicing attorney in Boston. He had graduated from Holy Cross in Worcester and then graduated from Boston College, School of Law. Caroline was a medical doctor. She graduated from Yale and went on to graduate from Tuft's Medical School. She was a general practitioner in a small town near Worcester named Shrewsbury. It was obvious the children were bright and high achievers influenced undoubtedly by their parents who placed a high value on education and an even higher value on service to others.

The white swinging doors opened and a doctor in green operating room garb with his mask dropped down around his neck approached. 'Mrs. Brogan, I'm doctor Ralph Dodson, the operation on your husband has just been completed. The next twenty-four hours will be extremely critical. If he successfully gets by that period his chances of survival will rise. He may remain in a coma for days or even weeks but we feel that if he gets that far his chances of coming out of the coma are fairly good. His chance for a full recovery is now only fifty/fifty but with the successful passing of each day his chances will increase. He is resting comfortably. I will check on him again in about two hours. He will remain in intensive care for a few days. You may see him shortly but I should caution his head is heavily bandaged. After your visit you might as well go home. We will call you in an emergency. Once he is moved to a regular room you will be allowed to be with him as much as you like. I will personally update you concerning his medical progress regularly. He looks a fighter and we are all pulling for him.'

About a half-hour later a nurse told Kathleen she could see Jim. Kelly and Patrick waited. Kathleen's visit was only about ten minutes but when she returned she was badly shaken. 'He doesn't look good, he's so pale and tubes are running out of him everywhere. I don't think I should go home. We live too far from the hospital. If there was an emergency I couldn't get back in time.' Patrick called the inn on his mobile and made a booking for Kathleen. He told her not to worry the law firm would pay the hotel bill, it was the least they could do. The inn was within walking distance of the hospital. If needed Kathleen could be back to the hospital within five minutes. The location was perfect and Kathleen was very pleased with the arrangements. Before they left the hospital Patrick left the number of the inn at the nurses' station. They promised to call Kathleen the minute there was any problem.

Kathleen's attention had now shifted to notifying the children. They would both be shocked. Kathleen was particularly hoping that Caroline could join her in Leesburg for a few days, particularly in the early stages so she could understand the medical ramifications of Jim's treatment. This was obviously the largest single crisis of their long marriage and their hearts went out to Kathleen.

Once they got Kathleen settled Kelly and Patrick drove back to the office. It was now evening so Patrick drove Kelly directly to her car. Before dropping her off he told Kelly to remind him to send flower's to Jim's room once he got out of intensive care and to see that fresh one's were sent every week he was in hospital. He also asked Kelly if she could locate a good forensic scientist who could testify regarding the fingerprints on the shotgun. Kelly suggested that one of the forensic experts from the laboratory in Fairfax might be appropriate or if not they certainly could recommend one. Finally, Patrick asked Kelly to check with Deputy Wayne Broomfield and see if there was any news about who attacked Jim or if the forensics turned up anything.

After Kelly left Patrick tried to reach Cindy but she wasn't at home and her mobile was powered off or she was out of area.

# Twenty One

CINDY Hurst was a bright, energetic girl. There was no doubt that when she married Patrick she felt it was going to be forever. They got along very well from the very beginning. When they were dating at William and Mary they were not only lovers but best friends. Their classmates who knew them well considered them the ideally suited couple. The idea of leaving Patrick had never entered Cindy's mind. When Patrick started the Appleby case Cindy figured out early-on that she was going to be left alone during the trial preparation and trial. She didn't mind, she understood, and only started to work on the campaign of Giles Burnette for congress in the Seventh Congressional District of Virginia to help fill-up her empty hours. The 'lucky seventh' district, as Giles called it, took in twenty-three counties and five small cities. It was an extremely large geographic area which ran from the West Virginia border at Harpers Ferry all the way down the valley of Virginia ending up in Hanover County on the outskirts of the capital, Richmond. It was composed of mostly rural areas and small cities hence had to be geographically large to meet the population equality mandated for every congressional district in the nation.

Giles Burnette was thirty-five years of age and very handsome. He had never been married and was considered a real heartthrob by the ladies. He not only was good looking and very mannerly but he was extremely articulate. He lived for politics. He was also an attorney and had run unsuccessfully for public office on two previous occasions. However, each time he ran he had learned and made additional friends. The public which didn't take to him originally were getting to know him better and feel more comfortable with him. The second outing he had come very close to winning and he was hoping he would be third time lucky. With this in mind he had put together a large group of youthful supporters who were full of energy and enthusiasm. Cindy was just one of many and she found the atmosphere electric. From the very beginning she was physically attracted to Giles and Giles to her but nothing happened. Cindy worked in Giles' campaign headquarters making telephone calls setting up appointments and taking care of many small but important duties. Often she travelled with Giles to party caucuses at night. They would arrive home late and extremely exhausted. One night they had been in Orange County and the meeting had gone on particularly late. On the drive back Giles had broached the idea of staying over night at a motel. Cindy had said she would have to call her husband but when she called home there was no answer. Sensing Patrick was staying at the office she decided not to call him as it was one thirty a.m., she told Giles ok. They checked into separate rooms but Giles invited her to his room for a nightcap, she accepted and matters soon developed in a manner she hadn't anticipated.

They each had one bourbon and water and Cindy said goodnight. When she was leaving Giles went to kiss Cindy on the cheek but she turned her head and took the kiss directly on the lips. Giles acted a little surprised but then responded with a full-blown French kiss and started to rub her bum. Cindy then upped the smouldering passion by reaching down and rubbing Giles. Giles pulled her back into his room and shut and locked the door. They both removed their clothing as fast as they could while kissing and fondling each other as they undressed. The sex was wonderful. Cindy had no idea what Giles' sexual past had been but this was only the fifth man she had ever had full sex with. She had a boyfriend her senior year in high school and they had sex once after the senior prom. It was a nervous affair that wasn't too satisfying but it at least constituted a bridge crossed in the march toward adulthood. In college she had two brief sexual encounters with fellow students. Both were meaningless one night stands that took place after late nights of partying and after quite a bit of drink taken. When she met Patrick things changed. They had sex regularly and when they married it even got better. Now she was the first to break their commitment to each other. When she returned to her room she was scared and wanted to tell Patrick she was sorry but she wanted Giles and she knew if he wanted her she would give herself to him again.

The inner conflict went on for days. Cindy was alone so there was no confrontation or arguing with Patrick like there might have been if their life was normal. Finally, she decided on a course of action. Under no circumstances would she ever tell Patrick what she had done. If matters didn't work out with Giles she would stay with Patrick and try to make it up to him. If she left Patrick she would try to shield him from hurt as a token of the love they had shared. She would leave but he would never have to deal with the pain of knowing his wife betrayed him. Meanwhile sex with Giles was now a regular event.

Kelly Madison had a crush on Patrick from the moment they met. When she learned he was married she was setback. However, during their long association she never showed any affection towards Patrick. He was the boss, she called him the boss and their relationship remained a professional one. Kelly didn't have a lot of time for dating but occasionally she went out with old friends and often in a group. Kelly had met Cindy several times, liked her and also thought she was very pretty. Kelly didn't sense that Cindy was jealous that she had an opportunity to spend so much time with Patrick. She viewed this as good because she never wanted to be seen as the other woman.

While Kelly would never unsettle another person's marriage, one thing was certain; her crush on Patrick had not diminished over time. If he ever became available Kelly would certainly be interested in making him her own. Heather, being an observant woman, occasionally kidded Kelly in a sort of good natured office banter. When she did so Kelly's face would get red and her embarrassment was obvious but she never denied that she was in love with Patrick. Patrick for his part was far too involved in the Appleby case to notice anything that was going on. This sort of innocence was part of his great charm for Kelly. So every day Kelly dreamed of being with Patrick. Patrick dreamed of freeing Frank Appleby and Cindy dreamed of the next hotel night with Giles Burnette.

Word reached the office from several sources that Frank Appleby had returned happily to his gardening chores. Interestingly, not one of his former customers spurned him, in fact, all were clamouring for his services. He was back at the local hardware and garden center making his usual purchases and meeting with Reverend Weeks for the occasional chat or coffee. The citizens of Leesburg were obviously voting in the quiet way most small towns do and the result of the vote was they were happy to have Frank Appleby back among them. Mrs. Appleby and the children were greatly relieved. Sheriff Dunn had ordered a discrete surveillance to make sure Frank would not leave the jurisdiction and was so far satisfied that there was no indication that Frank would run. Judge Draper was being kept fully informed by Sheriff Dunn concerning Frank's activities and was extremely pleased that his risky and unorthodox decision was being supported by the facts on the ground.

Patrick, for his part, was becoming more and more confused about his relationship with Cindy. She was never home when he called and her mobile was always powered off. If she wasn't at home there was no real reason to drive to Neersville and leave the yellow sofa.

Jim Brogan had survived the first critical twenty-four hours and Kathleen's spirits were slightly raised, particularly, since the arrival of her daughter Caroline from Shrewsbury, Massachusetts. Liam, Roland and Patrick were taking turns visiting the hospital, in an effort to support Kathleen. Liam had arranged that the Irish Society send a massive bouquet of flowers and a card of well wishes signed by over one hundred members. The local Catholic priest had learned of the vicious attack on Jim and was making regular visits to comfort Kathleen. Jim had been given the last rites of the church, hopefully, as a precaution. Patrick was satisfied that everything that could be done for Jim and Kathleen was happening. Then an interesting development occurred. A beautiful bouquet of flowers arrived from Cindy. The card read, 'Jim, you are in our prayers, we love you' Patrick and Cindy. This made Patrick extremely happy but also gave him a false sense of security which he would later regret. Cindy in fairness was a considerate and caring person and had wanted to reach out to Jim and Kathleen in their hour of need. She had to put Patrick's name on the card as matters between them were not yet final.

# Twenty Two

IN light of the attack on Jim Brogan, Patrick thought it would be a good idea to call the 'so called' board of directors together to discuss personal security among other subjects. Heather telephoned everyone and set it up for five p.m. on Friday. This was obviously an hour that wouldn't interfere with Liam's or Roland's court appearances. The group was the usual five; Liam, Roland, Kelly, Heather and Patrick but without Jim, who had been added after his employment but was now missing. Everyone was quite nervous and jumpy after the attack on Jim. They all realized they were soft targets and if the ring could reach the most streetwise member of the team it could reach anyone of them. Kelly and Heather were particularly spooked. They had talked it over between themselves and feared they might be kidnapped and forced into prostitution or some other horrible act would befall them. For two very attractive young women this was not a remote possibility. When the meeting started, Heather and Kelly served coffee, tea and sweet rolls as usual. They made sure Roland received two or three on his paper plate which only seemed fitting remembering his size. The meeting took place in the conference room with Heather answering the outside calls from there. No one was therefore in the outer office but it was now beyond normal office hours and no clients were expected. The first order of business had been a review of Jim's medical situation. Each person contributed what bits of information they had picked up from their most recent hospital visits. The consensus was Jim was surviving but just barely. The doctors were not very positive in their pronouncements, they weren't negative so as to alarm Kathleen but they were very guarded. The local papers, the Washington papers and all the TV and radio stations carried the story. CNN, Fox News, NBC, etc. had also picked up on the attack. Ten TV trucks were positioned outside the hospital.

Next on the agenda Patrick briefed the defense team regarding Frank Appleby's reintroduction to the community. With great pleasure Patrick portrayed how Frank had been uniformly greeted back with great warmth by all his old customers. Those who had testified for him at the bail hearing were also delighted. Just as Patrick was concluding with this good news, noise was heard in the reception area. Liam was nearest the door so he got up and went to the outer office. When he got there the scene he met was threatening to say the least. Roland had also got up and his huge frame now completely filled the doorway to the conference room. Liam met two large men wearing balaclavas and wielding handguns. As Liam backed into a corner, a shot rang out and shattered the reception's only window. Liam reached back and grasped his hurley which had been propped up in the corner ever since the move into the new offices. A second shot rang out this time from the gun of the second intruder. This shot hit Roland in the chest; he momentarily stepped back about half a step. As the first assailant was watching this action, Liam clubbed him with the hurley across the side of his head. It was a mighty blow. The assailant crumpled to the floor as if he was a matchstick in a windstorm. Meanwhile, Roland was now moving forward at lightening speed, an NFL linebacker couldn't have moved any faster. As he wrapped his massive arms around the chest of the second would-be assassin, the intruder's right hand which held the gun was forced skyward and he fired two additional shots into the ceiling. Then Roland applied such pressure that we actually heard the intruders ribs crack. By this time Heather, Kelly and Patrick were behind Roland. As they moved forward into the reception area they were able to go past him. The second intruder slipped to the floor in an ungainly heap. Both men were now unconscious. Liam immediately got on the telephone and called the emergency number requesting assistance from both the sheriff's department and an ambulance. Kelly assisted Roland back into the conference room and helped him sit down. His shirt, tie and suit coat were now covered with blood. Heather rushed in with a towel and she and Kelly unbuttoned Roland's shirt and placed the towel over the bullet wound and pushed gently. Roland had lost a lot of blood but was still able to talk. He was directing Heather and Kelly which was at least a good sign. Patrick hadn't played any part in the defense of the team and now felt the necessity to do something constructive so he removed the balaclavas from the faces of both men. The man Liam had hit with the hurley had a large haematoma on the left side of his face. His head in truthfulness had grown twice its normal size and an obvious mark was left by the metal band which was attached to the mallet like top of the hurley. It was a good thing Patrick had removed the balaclava or he might have suffocated. Not that at that moment they had much compassion for these two violent thugs, they didn't. The other thug lay motionless where he had fallen to the floor after Roland had finally released him from his crushing grip.

The response from the emergency services had been swift, they arrived in minutes. Sheriff Dunn had answered the call with three deputies, among them Deputy Wayne Broomfield. Roland was receiving priority treatment but a second ambulance arrived minutes later and their paramedics were attending to the two thugs, both of whom were still out and were being strapped onto stretchers. The office was total bedlam and at that very moment Pritch returned. He had been at the hospital setting-up the visit of the Attorney General, Dan Rivers, to Jim Brogan's bedside and his statement to the TV and press afterwards. Now Rivers would have a lot more to do and talk about. Roland was feeling a little faint but indicated he could walk with assistance to the ambulance which was parked just outside. Looking at the size of Roland compared to the paramedics, they were probably relieved. They had already quickly determined that the bullet that hit Roland hadn't hit any vital organs. Within five minutes what had been a wild scene had subsided and everyone evacuated the office for the hospital except Sheriff Dunn and Patrick.

Sheriff Dunn sat down in the conference room placing his large Stetson hat on the conference room table and began. 'Patrick, we have to talk.' Sheriff Stanley Dunn was a no nonsense man. He had been re-elected by the citizens of Loudoun County by a landslide. He was a rare mixture of excellent politician without ever giving up one iota of police professionalism. He looked like a sheriff should look; he was physically fit yet was greying enough to indicate he was a mature man who possessed enough wisdom to deal with any situation. As Patrick looked at him now he thought that Marlboro cigarettes would have died to get him to do a 'Marlboro man' commercial. Sheriff Dunn started slowly.

'Patrick, you have really been through it.'

'Yes, I have, we all have. The girls are really traumatized.'

'We just found the black Lincoln at the Wal-Mart parking lot; I guess they walked to your office from there.'

'How do you know it's theirs?'

'It's a rented vehicle from Maryland. We called the car rental company and two Dutch nationals rented the car about two months ago. Their description fits our two captives perfectly.'

'That's really good news.'

'Yes, they are undoubtedly the two who started the fire at your office, attacked Jim Brogan and today they returned to finish off your entire defense team.'

'We were getting too close.'

'Yes, and you were damn lucky today, they almost finished their work.'

'If it hadn't been for Liam and Roland they would have gotten us for sure.'

'Liam and Roland are both great men. They are a real credit to the legal profession.' Now, before I leave I wanted to tell you I think your ordeal is over but I can't guarantee that one hundred percent. That is why I have decided until the trial to place a deputy in a car outside your office twenty-four hours a day.'

'Thanks sheriff, I didn't want to ask for any special treatment but I know the girls are very scared.'

'Ok, Patrick consider it done. Now we had both better get up to the hospital. Why don't you come with me?'

'Ok sheriff, I always wanted to ride in one of those shiny popcorn poppers that we tax payers have to pay for.'

'Well, here's your chance, let's go.'

Upon arrival at the hospital the media circus was in full swing. As they walked in the main hospital doorway there were reporters firing questions at the sheriff from both sides of the walkway. Sheriff Dunn fired back. 'Today, the Attorney General of Virginia will answer your questions. Mr. Rivers will be with you shortly.' Patrick found Liam, Kelly and Heather, they were seated on the benches awaiting word about Roland, who was in emergency. Evidently, the bullet hadn't exited Roland's back although x-rays had indicated it was near the surface. They were now going to make an incision in Roland's back and attempt to retrieve the bullet that way. Terri, Roland's wife had been called. She was now rushing to the hospital from Waterford. About two hours later the report arrived that they had removed the bullet successfully and Roland was in intensive care. Terri was with him.

As the remaining members of the team discussed this latest news, Pritch came up and introduced the Attorney General, Dan Rivers. The general, as Pritch called him, at least when Rivers couldn't hear him, was a man about six feet tall and approximately one hundred seventy-five pounds. He was a good dresser and walked very erect like he was ex-military. Rivers was a friendly man but also a man with a purpose. He told the team he was going to visit Jim Brogan and have a quiet word with Kathleen. After that he would visit Roland and have a word with Terri. Unfortunately, the two principals, both Jim and Roland would be unable to communicate with the general now. Jim was still in a coma and Roland would be groggy from the general anaesthesia. The general sent Pritch to find out the status of the two captives. Once all this was accomplished, Rivers would meet with the press. We all decided we would wait and attend the press conference. Heather called her husband, Kelly called her mom and Patrick called Cindy, but as usual her mobile was powered off.

# Twenty-three

AFTER visiting the rooms of Jim Brogan and Roland Alberts, Dan Rivers was ready to go on the attack. Pritch filled him in that both captives would survive although both needed two to three weeks in hospital to recover sufficiently before they could be moved to the county jail. Sheriff Dunn had a deputy sheriff on guard outside their rooms twenty-four hours per day. Between guarding Kelly, Heather and Patrick and guarding the two captives Patrick figured Sheriff Dunn's forces were stretched but in characteristic style he didn't complain.

The press conference started by Dan Rivers outlining the havoc the two Dutch captives had wrought. He described what he called the cowardly from behind attack on Jim Brogan. He went on to describe in detail the attack on our defense team as Pritch had filled him in with all the details. He lauded Liam O'Brien and Roland Alberts as true Americans and great Virginians up for any challenge and he congratulated Kathleen and Terri for their courage in the face of such adversity. Finally, he turned his attention to the foreign-based child pornography ring. He felt they had been dealt a dramatic defeat in Leesburg today. He congratulated all Loudoun people for their steadfast stand against the abhorrent crimes perpetrated against innocent children. He vowed that all the resources of the Commonwealth would be marshalled to crush this evil in their midst. He indicated he had just gotten off the phone with the Governor and he had wished to assure the people of Loudoun that everything that could be done to destroy this evil child pornography ring would be done. He praised Sheriff Dunn for his outstanding leadership and the great police work completed by his department. Finally, he cautioned that while two members of the ring were now in custody this did not constitute the end of the ability of the ring to function. They had suffered a set-back but were not yet broken. For his part, Dan Rivers was on a crusade and personally would not rest until all remnants of the ring were put out of business for good and every member punished to the full extent of the law.

In fairness, it was a masterful performance and the media lapped it up. Rivers was a politician but above all he was a good attorney. It was this perceived separation that gave him great credibility with the people. Everyone went away feeling better. Good was winning out over evil and there was a very personal pride that four of their own, some battered badly in battle, were still winning. Jim, Liam, Roland and Sheriff Dunn had been elevated to hero status. Patrick supposed he felt the same way too but he was an insider and his concerns ran deeper. He knew the situation with Jim Brogan was still touch and go as to whether he would make it. He also worried about Roland.

Sure he would recover and his hospitalisation would pay most of his medical bills but what about his practice. He was a solo-practitioner like Patrick and when they stopped working they stopped eating. It wasn't like working for a big company that could carry him on full pay for quite a few weeks and then pass him over to their insurance carrier who would pay fifty or seventy five percent of his salary for a few more weeks. Attorneys were like tight-rope walkers who worked without a safety net. If they fell they crashed some forty or sixty feet to the tarmac below. Patrick had placed Roland in that predicament and he now felt very guilty. Liam noticed Patrick was looking pretty glum and came over and put his arm around him. Not a word was spoken but they walked out of the hospital together. The team's ranks were thinning but they weren't beaten yet.

John Brandywell, much to his credit, telephoned Patrick and Liam and told them in an extremely sincere manner how sorry he was for all their troubles. Liam told him he was out there doing his best to send him new criminals to prosecute. John immediately saw the irony in the situation and they all had a good laugh together. While Patrick and Liam knew they were probably destined to do battle with John quite a few additional times during and beyond the Appleby case they appreciated that moment. For an instant they were all on the same team and they knew they had one hell of a strong dislike for the two captives who burnt them out, attacked Jim and finally attempted to kill the entire team. They were confident John Brandywell would prosecute the assailants' cases as vigorously as he had ever prosecuted any criminal.

# Twenty-four

THE time for Frank Appleby's trial was edging closer. The defense team was now down from six to four members but they would have to do their best to work on jury selection even with their reduced resources. The first order of business would be to determine a profile of what might constitute the best jury candidates. There would be generalizations made which wouldn't fit everyone on the panel hence, the margin for error. In preparation for this discussion Patrick jotted down his thoughts.

**Not Wanted:**

(1)   Any past or present members of police or security forces including members of their families. The concept was fairly obvious; they would tend to believe the police and the prosecutors. In their work they visualized themselves as fighting crime in all its forms. It would be a big leap for them to see an arrested individual as innocent.

(2)   Older whites, both men and women brought up in a gentler and stricter time when crime was not as widespread,

families were tighter units and morals and good behaviour were the expected norm. Also, had too much acceptance of authority. They wouldn't ask the hard questions regarding the prosecution's theory.

**Wanted:**

(1)     Blacks of all ages and both sexes, black people had often been brutalized, particularly in earlier times. They grew distrustful of authority and often saw themselves in the role of the accused, the underdog, the unwanted, the cast-outs and cast-offs. It was easy for them to project themselves into the role of the accused.

(2)     Young people, both men and women; Patrick's rationale was young people have a more modern outlook and would be more susceptible to a good persuasive argument concerning the facts. They carried little or no baggage from the past and would not stand in awe of authority figures like the police and prosecutors.

(3)     Women generally preferable over men; the rationale was women are for the most part the carers of young children and they would hold anyone who harmed a child in great disdain. Hence, their view of Wilbur Cosgrove would be extremely low and their view of Frank Appleby, even if guilty, somewhat justifiable.

(4)     Fathers, preferable to single men; the rationale is fathers would generally favor direct action to stamp out a threat to their child and would have great sympathy for any father who wouldn't tolerate his child being sexually molested.

(5)     Hispanic men and women; the rationale here was many members of the Hispanic community would be

devout Catholics and very family oriented often coming from or having large families. As a group they would be very protective of young children and would hold great animosity against anyone who would harm a child while at the same time elevating to hero status anyone who righted a serious wrong against a child. Like many new immigrants they might tend to fear authority figures as opposed to feeling comfortable openly supporting them.

Patrick was under no delusion that he was totally correct in his analysis. What he hoped he had accomplished was to provide a starting point for Liam who had more experience in these matters to enhance his own thinking. It was quite obvious that they were going to have to figure out their own best case scenario as there was no money to hire a jury selection consultant to assist them. Patrick was determined not to ask Sarah Foster for more funds, as he believed she had already done enough. Patrick telephoned Liam to tell him what he was working on. Liam listened carefully and agreed this should be the main subject of their next meeting. Liam also strongly suggested that Patrick seek the advice of a well established older member of the community, one who would know many people across the spectrum. One who would know people's political affiliations and social positions, including their conservative or liberal leanings would be perfect.

Patrick racked his brain to figure out who in the community would be the best person to fulfil this role assuming of course, their willingness to support Frank Appleby's defense. Finally, Patrick had it. He would ask Irving Johnson to assist. Irving was now about seventy two years old but was still actively working in the family funeral business started by his father in 1899. Irving knew all the old and young people in Loudoun and more importantly he knew all of the extended families and their political affiliations. Patrick didn't know Irving too well but had been with him on few occasions and was always intrigued by his reference to the original owner of a particular dwelling. Assuming the house was older Irving always skipped over the current owners and reverted to the original family associated with that house, hence, a sample reference might sound like, 'oh yes, he lives in the old Early house.'

When Patrick reached Irving Johnson and laid out the proposal that he help the team behind the scenes with jury selection Irving didn't immediately warm to the idea. He was very sympathetic to Frank Appleby but he wasn't sure his type of information about local people would help. Patrick marked it to modesty and slowed down and explained the role and the value of the exercise in great detail. Finally, Irving grasped what they were after and agreed to assist them. Patrick immediately invited him to their next meeting so he could better understand the process they would be involved in.

Patrick also wanted to recommend to Liam that he and Liam conduct a very well prepared voir dire. Patrick felt the voir dire was not only useful to qualify jurors, which is its major purpose, but also because it allowed the future jurors to see the defense counsel operating in a very structured manner as officers of the court. Patrick viewed it as a wonderful get acquainted period when the future jurors could hear the defense lawyer's voices and see a normal and necessary court process playing out. Those who were not struck off could feel that their fairness and impartiality had been vindicated and they had received the stamp of approval from both the prosecution and the defense. In a way the voir dire would be their first opportunity to shine.

The news from the hospital continued to be good. Jim was still in a coma but there was talk he would be moved today to a private room. Roland was very hungry which was a good sign and the hospital kitchen was on alert that Roland's normal food intake was about three times that of a normal man. Kelly was spending some time daily with both Kathleen and Terri and the word from that quarter was both wives were staying positive. Kathleen was also being supported by her daughter.

Frank was continuing to work in his usual manner and for his regular customers. Frank called the office every few days to see if he was needed. Mostly, he talked to Heather and Kelly who kept him posted on developments and also buoyed up his spirits from time to time as needed. Frank had contacted us immediately after hearing about the capture of the would be assailants. The assailants for their part were also improving in hospital and Wayne Broomfield told Kelly that Sheriff Dunn was going to order their questioning as soon as possible. The FBI had been working with the Sheriff's department almost since the beginning of the case as soon as the child pornography aspect had been revealed. Now they were doubling their efforts since one of their own had been taken down. Jim Brogan might have been retired from their number but as far as they were concerned he would always be FBI. Additionally, the perpetrators of the crime had crossed state lines which had created their jurisdiction.

All the good news was shattered when Cindy called Patrick and asked if they could meet for lunch. Patrick had a premonition that things might not be too good between them. He thought he would get one hell of a scolding concerning all his nights on the yellow sofa but he had no idea how dramatically his life was about to change. At first, things seemed normal. He was glad to see Cindy and she seemed genuinely happy to see him. In fact, she gave him a big kiss in the restaurant parking lot when they arrived at the same time. Rather than the expected scolding Cindy became very sombre and serious once they had placed their orders. She started out in a calm but determined manner; she had taken the opportunity during their forced separation, not formal of course, but real all the same, to think over many aspects of their married life together. She had decided that while she still admired Patrick and might even still love him that she needed time away from him. Patrick protested that was exactly what she already had but Cindy continued in an even more strident manner. No, what she needed was to move out of the house in Neersville and be on her own for a period. Maybe after a period of formal separation and reflection they could get together again, she wasn't sure. Patrick was absolutely stunned and he told Cindy so. He told her how he knew he had neglected her due to the Appleby case but would make it up to her. He told her he loved her and he was sorry he had spent so many nights in the office on the sofa. He told her he expected her to be angry at him with cause but her reaction was too extreme.

Finally, she stopped him and said, 'it's finished, last night, I moved all my clothes out of the house and said goodbye to Ralph and Eleanor.' Patrick was totally crushed. The food arrived and they both only picked at it. Patrick pleaded for more time to make things right. He promised to return home at a reasonable hour each evening. He indicated he would do anything to make Cindy happy. They could go out more, plan some weekends away. He would involve Pritch and Sarah in more social outings and things would soon return to normal, she would see. Un-swayed, Cindy stood her ground. 'No Patrick, for now it is over. I have informed my parents and I have leased a new apartment in Stephen's City.' Patrick was simply dumbfounded. He no longer had anything else to say or offer. He realized he would be cut off at every opportunity. They left the restaurant together and Patrick asked one question. 'Is there anyone else?' The response came. 'No Patrick don't be silly, there is no one.' He walked Cindy to her car and watched as she drove out of his life. He wouldn't see his wife again for months. He got in his car and cried. He didn't start the car for over an hour and then finally, tear-stained and totally distraught he returned to the office. There was simply nowhere else to go. He wouldn't be returning to Neersville either, at least not for a long time as he couldn't bear to look at the empty closets and his destroyed life.

When he arrived at the office Heather gave him a look that said, I know something horrible has happened. Patrick went to his office and collapsed in his chair. Heather went to Kelly and told her Patrick looked as if he was deeply upset. They waited for about five minutes, finally, Heather told

Kelly she had better go in it might be about Jim or Roland. When Kelly opened the door and looked at Patrick she was shocked, she had never seen him look so bad. Patrick was still crying and Kelly handed him some tissues. 'Patrick, is it Jim or Roland?' 'No, Cindy has left me.' Kelly picked up the phone and buzzed Heather. 'Don't let anyone in Heather and no telephone calls either until I tell you.' She then helped Patrick up and walked him to the sofa. The next hour or two passed with Kelly cradling Patrick's head in her lap and wiping his tears and soothing his face with her hand. Time passed, after a long time Kelly heard Heather pack-up and leave for home locking the office door on the way out. They stayed together until dark. Finally, Kelly asked Patrick to stand up and she opened the sofa bed, took off Patrick's coat shirt and tie and made him lie down. Then she took off his shoes and pulled off his suit pants, covering him with a blanket. Kelly hung up his suit and kissed him goodnight on the cheek and left the office. Patrick thought, this is the treatment drunks get but he didn't care; he was paralyzed and right now he didn't care if he lived or died. Tomorrow would surely come but he didn't know if he wanted to be part of it. In fact, he was pretty sure he didn't.

# Twenty-Five

KELLY Madison knew her moment of decision had arrived. She loved Patrick very much but she was also a considerate person who would never intentionally hurt another individual and certainly not attempt to break-up a marriage. She decided the best thing to do was to discuss the matter with her mother with whom she was very close. Kelly's mother was a high school geography teacher. She dealt with young people all day, every day and was an extremely sensitive and reasonable person. Her mother wore glasses and had put on a little weight over the years. Still, she was not obese and she wore her clothing well, giving her an air of confidence and authority. She was not overpowering but could and would apply discipline when needed. Her students seemed to respond favorably to her fairness and no-nonsense reasonableness.

'Mama, I suppose you have already guessed that I am in love with Patrick.'

'Kelly, Patrick is a married man.'

'Maybe not for long. Cindy has left him. He is in a terrible state.'

'When did this happen?'

'They had lunch together yesterday and she told him she was leaving him. He evidently pleaded with her to stay but she was determined. She had already moved out of their house in Neersville and taken all her belongings. When Patrick arrived back at the office he was shattered. We had to cancel all our afternoon appointments and block all incoming calls for him.'

'Oh, I am very sorry to hear that, I don't know Patrick personally but from what you have told me he is a very compassionate and lovely person.'

'Yes, mama, he is and I love him. How do I handle matters now? He needs me mama, he is in real pain.'

'Well, Kelly, I will offer my advice but you might not like it.'

'No, mama, I wouldn't have asked for your advice if I didn't want it.'

'Well, you are going to have to walk a fine line, which might not suit you.'

'What do you mean mama?'

'Of course you must support Patrick in his hour of need, particularly since you are in his employ. This is the only Christian way to respond but you also must be very careful not to exploit your position and get between Patrick and Cindy. Maybe they will reconcile and if there is a chance of this happening you must not pull Patrick in another direction.'

'I know mama but she threw him away, she discarded him like so much trash.'

'Does Cindy have another man?'

'She says no mama.'

'And what about Patrick, does he have another woman or did he act badly to cause the separation?'

'Heavens no mama, Patrick would never be disloyal, it's not in his make-up, that's why I love him so.'

'Well Kelly, I think your role is clear. Support Patrick but don't attempt to charm him. Give him time to sort out his problem. Maybe if there is no reconciliation in six months you could start to show your real feelings.'

'I know you're right mama but do you know how hard it's going to be for me. I really am crazy about him but I will try to walk that line.'

'Good Kelly, remember, if he is the one for you it will happen and if he isn't, well.'

Kelly purposely arrived at work early. The law office and all the surrounding offices were dark and very quiet. She opened the door to the outer office and let herself in. She went to her office and left her purse in the usual spot behind her desk on the floor. She then went to Patrick's office. She found him curled up in the foetal position on the yellow sofa-bed. What she really wanted to do was to lock his door, take off all her clothes and lie down next to him but she knew that was the wrong thing to do just yet. So she walked over to the sofa-bed, kissed Patrick on the cheek and said, 'time to get up sleepy head.' Patrick looked up at her with glazed eyes and asked if it was really a bad dream. When Kelly said no in a soft and sympathetic voice, he covered his eyes with one arm. Kelly sat on the bed next to him and explained to him exactly what he had to do and why.

'You have some clients to see today. Heather cancelled all your appointments and blocked all your calls yesterday afternoon. We can't do that again today. Now get up and take a shower. By the time you dress I will be back with hot coffee and those lovely jelly doughnuts you love. When Patrick didn't stir, Kelly took the arm covering his eyes and pulled him up to a sitting position. She then took his other arm and with all her strength, pulled him up to a standing position. She then led him like a blind man to the shower. Patrick dropped his boxer shorts to get into the shower. Kelly looked at his bare butt for the first time. She thought it looked great; strong and athletic and she whispered to herself, that butt's going to be mine.

When Kelly returned with the coffee and doughnuts, Patrick was dressed and looked sad but at least businesslike. Slowly, he started to function and address the work on his desk. Kelly went to her office, shut the door, and telephoned Liam. When Joan put her through she briefly told Liam what had happened, swore him to secrecy and then asked Liam to take Patrick to the hospital to see Jim and Roland and then to take him to lunch. Liam immediately agreed and was very supportive of his co-counsel. Pritch arrived to take up his usual place in the conference room. Kelly briefed Pritch regarding the break-up. Pritch was stunned. He immediately telephoned Sarah and they discussed if there was some way Sarah could try and reach Cindy and talk some sense into her.

There was little chance of that as Cindy and Giles had spent another night at a motel, this time in Fredericksburg and at that very moment Giles was gently rubbing Cindy's bare back. Had Kelly been able to see this scene there would have been little chance she would be walking that fine line any longer. However, because the true situation would not be uncovered for many months she would behave herself although she really wanted Patrick.

# Twenty-Six

LIAM and Pritch were great; they kept Patrick busy day and night between them. They organized lunches with all of Patrick's usual legal buddies and in the evenings concocted reasons they needed to go out for a few beers together. When Liam became exhausted with the pace, Mick Kelly or John Jo Sullivan, Liam's partners, took over. When Pritch couldn't figure out what to do next Sarah would invite Patrick and Kelly out to dinner or for drinks and dancing. Slowly, a small transition was taking place; people were accepting that Patrick and Kelly were sort of a couple. Patrick never objected to this and of course Kelly was thrilled. Patrick seemed to be somewhat better. Of course he received all kinds of advice. Some male friends told him to immediately go out and get laid. There was even some talk of organizing a hot girl to come to his office one evening and give him a good screwing. Kelly was horrified by these suggestions but luckily Patrick didn't encourage these types of false solutions, so over time, happily for Kelly, they stopped.

At the office work on the Appleby case and a few other cases continued. Kelly was pulling her weight and handling all the real estate conveyancing. There was a lot of paperwork involved with these transactions and many of the mortgage companies were very exacting as to the forms and further assurances they wanted. Heather and Kelly worked very hard to keep them satisfied as they knew the practice could extract their fees at settlement and this up-front money was paying the major bills including their salaries. Patrick had made friends with numerous real estate agents and some of them were pushing work his way. Kelly felt they were taking financial pressure off Patrick this way and was happy to make this end of the practice succeed. The practice was up to about twenty-five settlements per month which kept everyone very busy.

One day Kelly was in the outer office with Heather when Deputy Wayne Broomfield walked in. Wayne was single and an old friend of Kelly's as well as the office's best police informant. He invited Kelly to go to a dance at the Lovettsville Community Center. Patrick just happened to walk into the outer office as Wayne was making his date offer. Kelly gently turned Wayne down; indicating that Patrick and her had to be in Fairfax Saturday evening at a legal meeting. Patrick knew this was a lie the moment Kelly said it and quickly retreated to his office. After Wayne left, a little disappointed, Kelly went in to see Patrick. Patrick asked why she had turned Wayne down as he seemed to be a really nice guy. Kelly told Patrick she would much rather go out with him. She was shocked when he said ok. He took out the yellow pages and made a reservation for dinner at a Fairfax restaurant. When he got off the telephone he said they could take in a movie after dinner if she liked but it would have to be in Fairfax or at least out of Loudoun so Kelly wouldn't be caught in a lie with Wayne. After all he had helped them tremendously in the Appleby case, they owed him. Kelly almost danced out of Patrick's office and when she told Heather what had happened, Heather smiled a most beautiful smile and said, ' well, well, little miss has her first date.' Kelly was on a rocky mountain high all day.

When Saturday came Kelly encouraged Patrick to pick her up at her house in Hamilton so he could meet her mother and father. He seemed quite willing to do so. Maybe he was a little curious about her family life. She introduced him first to her mother, Rachel and then they went together into the living room where her father, Ronald, was reading the newspaper. Her father was a very pleasant and approachable man. He was still youthful looking at fifty. He also dressed in a modern way which made him look five years younger. Her father was a medical doctor, a GP. He had a good practice and was widely appreciated and loved. He wasn't greedy for money, although they never wanted for anything. He was one of the few doctors left in upper Loudoun County who would make a house call if someone was seriously ill. His philosophy was that it was not appropriate for loved ones to rush patients to the hospital who could recover just as well; if not better at home. They often would receive better care at home and with the right medicine would recover just fine in their own surroundings. He also believed some common viruses and diseases could cause extremely painful symptoms and hospitalisation only spread these diseases faster through the community. Finally, he thought medical insurance was too expensive partially driven by unnecessary use of hospital facilities. He was still a rather young doctor but with old-fashioned ideas concerning the type of service he wanted to deliver. Of course, to do so, he had to pay a personal price Almost every night he responded to at least two or three home calls. Luckily, his patients didn't abuse him and only called after eleven p.m. if it was something terribly urgent.

Ron and Patrick got on fine and after their short conversation Ron invited Patrick to play golf with him at the local country club in Purcellville. Patrick seemed to like this idea and agreed that they would arrange a day and time during the next week for a weekend round. When they got to the car Patrick indicated to Kelly he thought she had really nice parents. She was confident from their body language that Patrick too had made a good impression on them. Once Kelly freshened up they were off to Fairfax for their first date.

Dinner was lovely in a small intimate dining room which was highly atmospheric with a rustic beamed ceiling, subdued lighting and candles, not only on each table but on a large antique sideboard which the waiters used to serve from. The red oriental carpets over wide plank flooring suggested one should linger awhile, no one was in a rush to push you out. The food matched the surroundings and was absolutely superb. The romance seemed on too as at one point Patrick took Kelly's hand in his and held it for a good few minutes before the dessert arrived. After dinner they went to the cinema and selected a legal thriller based on a Jonathan Haar book, the movie starred John Travolta. They both liked it and found it quite legally correct. They concluded Harr had done his research well.

Patrick drove Kelly back to Hamilton. When they arrived Patrick gave her a full kiss on the lips. She craved more and pushed her body close to his and kissed him with an open mouth, their tongues touched and their first French kiss was a huge success. Kelly felt like ripping her clothes off and saying, take me, but Patrick thanked her for a lovely evening and told her he would see her Monday morning at the office.

On Monday, Judge Draper's office called to remind counsel that he would hear all motions on the Appleby case on Friday at eleven o'clock. The defense had filed several motions. The main thrust of these motions was to obtain information from the prosecution concerning the existing evidence against Frank Appleby. At the hearing all the defense motions were approved and the prosecution seemed to lean over backwards to convince the court they were sharing all information and fully cooperating.

It was clear that the main evidence against Frank Appleby was his potential motive to retaliate against his son's abuser, his perceived opportunity because he was working nearby and finally that his shotgun was found in the creek behind the victim's home within hours after the crime. As suspected by the defense the prosecution would attempt to prove through expert testimony that some of Frank Appleby's fingerprints on the gun had survived its time in the water.

The huge weakness in the Commonwealth's case was they had no eye witness to the shooting nor could they produce a witness who could place Frank Appleby at the crime scene on the date and time of the shooting or for that matter, at any other time either. On the other hand the defense had no witness to show that Frank Appleby was where he said he was at the time of the murder.

Judge Draper set the trial date for about two weeks after the Motions hearing. He asked the Commonwealth and defense if this would allow enough time and both sides agreed it would. Frank Appleby's trial was thus set for Tuesday twenty-three September. Judge Draper indicated in the first instance there would be sixty potential jurors empanelled and each side would have alternating strikes (meaning they could eliminate potential jurors without offering a cause). Judge Draper would himself question the panel and dispense with the usual array of pleas of illness or inability to serve due to work commitments and an array of personal problems. Finally, the Commonwealth and defense would be allowed to conduct their voir dire and commence their strikes until the final twelve jurors and three alternates were decided. If more potential jurors were needed he would order them empanelled.

# Twenty Seven

TWO weeks seemed a long time but the time available for further trial preparation flew by. Finally, on a crisp but beautiful sunny September morning, Patrick J. Hurst and Liam O'Brien, counsellors at law, laden down with records, files and notes, crossed the street at the corner of Market and King Streets and passed through the iron gates surrounding the old courthouse. They walked through the leaves that had fallen overnight and passed the Civil War monument of a soldier in confederate uniform with rifle in hand and up the stairs of the white columned red brick building that housed the oldest existing courtroom in Loudoun County. Huge paintings of distinguished Virginians and a large clock graced the walls. The courtroom didn't have a second floor balcony but otherwise the entire setting was reminiscent of the courtroom in the movie, 'To Kill a Mockingbird'.

The defense took the counsel table on the right and the Commonwealth, the counsel table on the left both facing the bench. The sixty empanelled potential jurors were too numerous to sit in the jury box so they sat on the left side of the courtroom in reserved places.

Promptly at nine a.m. the bailiff announced: 'All rise, the Circuit Court of Loudoun County, thirty-third Circuit of Virginia is now in session. The Honorable Judge Philip Draper presiding.' Judge Draper strode in and took his place on the bench. Judge Draper said, 'please be seated' and then started by addressing the empanelled potential jurors. 'Ladies and gentlemen of the citizen's panel, I wish to start by asking you a few questions. I would like you to take your time in reflecting on those questions. If you feel you should respond please don't be shy and do so. I will assist you to determine if your answers are important to our proceedings. If at any point you have a question or need clarification please ask me and I will do my best to answer. Most importantly please relax. I know for many of you this is the first time you have been in a court of law and you are somewhat intimidated by the surroundings. I can assure you that you needn't be fearful or embarrassed. Rather, you will simply be asked a series of questions which are critical to the conduct of justice and I ask you to respond promptly and truthfully. Now I would like to ask you these questions.'

'Is there anyone on the panel who is over seventy years of age?' Two hands went up. 'You are excused from jury duty. You may leave the courtroom now.'

Both individuals, one a man and the other a woman, shuffled away.

'Is there anyone on the panel who is too ill to serve, bearing in mind this trial may take several weeks to complete?' Four hands shot up.

'Now, I don't want to pry into your medical case history, but could you in a very few words explain your condition?'

The first to respond was a man with a heart ailment. Next came a woman who was scheduled for major surgery in two weeks. She was followed by a man with severe Parkinson's disease who couldn't eat unassisted; finally, another woman had rheumatoid arthritis and couldn't sit in one position for long periods of time. Judge Draper dismissed them all and wished them well, particularly with their health conditions. They, like the old age pensioners over seventy, left happily and quickly.

'Is there anyone who is related to the defendant, a member of the defense team or a member of the prosecutor's office?' 'No, that's fine.'

'Is there anyone who feels that due to pre-trial publicity or for any other reason they could not render a fair judgement in this case?' 'No, that's good.'

'Is there anyone who feels they cannot serve on this case for personal reasons?'

'Your honor, my name is Jason Richardson and my wife and I booked a trip to California early next month to be with our daughter who is expecting our first grandchild. We made our reservation before we knew I would be called for jury duty.'

'Mr. Richardson, I am going to excuse you from jury service. I understand fully your dilemma and I wish you and your family the very best during this important family time. You may leave now.'

'Thank you your honor.'

'Are there any other personal reasons why anyone feels they can't serve?'

'Your honor my name is Carlton Jackson and I am a local pharmacist. I operate a small drugstore in the Leesburg Shopping Center. I often can find a substitute pharmacist when I want to take a day or two off but I feel it would be very difficult, maybe impossible for me to find a substitute for a protracted period.'

'Mr. Jackson you render a much needed, often emergency service, to the community. Normally, I don't like to excuse a member of the panel simply due to work commitments. However, in your case I will make an exception to my general rule. You are excused, you may leave.'

'Thank you, your honor.'

'Alright, anyone else like to be heard?'

'Your honor my name is Lavel White. My husband and I have four pre-school children at home. My husband is a trash collector and he doesn't make enough money for me to hire anyone to take care of the children. If I hire a babysitter I will have to cut back on the food I buy for the children.'

'Mrs. White, I understand your problem and I agree it is a serious one. I will excuse you from the panel.'

'Thank you your honor.'

'Anyone else wish to be heard? No, then we will proceed. I am going to ask the defense counsel to commence their voir dire, which is simply a Latin phrase that means their relevant examination. The defense is represented by Mr. Patrick J. Hurst and Mr. Liam O'Brien. Gentlemen, who would like to begin?'

'I will your honor.'

'Alright the court recognizes Mr. Liam O'Brien for purposes of the voir dire.'

As Liam was being introduced by Judge Draper, Mr. Irving Johnson, the local undertaker slipped into a place at the back of the courtroom. He held a small note pad.

'I am part of the defense team and an officer of this court; I would like to ask you a few questions today that will assist us in the jury selection. First, are any of you or members of your families a police officer, a deputy sheriff, a member of the FBI, Secret Service, CIA, ATFA, a security guard, a prison guard, military police or any other form of police associate?'

'Mr. O'Brien, my husband is a security guard at Wal-Mart.'

'Thank you, might I ask your name?'

'Yes, I am Mrs. Jerome Black?'

'Thank you Mrs. Black. Anyone else fit this category?'

'Mr. O'Brien, I am Florence Graybone, my daughter-in-law works in Washington for the FBI as a file clerk, does that count?'

'Thank you Mrs. Graybone, yes, we very much appreciate you offering that information.'

'Does anyone else fit in any of these categories? No, well if not I will continue.'

'Is there any member of the panel who feels that if a person is arrested by the police they must be guilty as charged? Yes sir, do you have a comment?'

'Well, I am not sure if I should comment but I do feel that most of the time the police get it right only very rarely do they get the wrong man.'

'Thank you very much for that truthful comment. Might I ask your name?'

'I am Alvin Baker.'

'Is there anyone else on the panel who would agree with Mr. Baker?'

'I suppose I would, I think he has it about right.'

'And your name maam?'

'Rosemary Jenkins.'

'Thanks, Ms. Jenkins, anyone else feel the way Mr. Baker and Ms. Jenkins do?' No, alright, I will move on.'

Is there anyone on the panel who feels that a blue collar worker (a person who works with their hands and does physical labor) is more likely to commit a violent crime than a white collar worker (one who works in an office setting)?'

When no one answered after a reasonable pause, Liam continued. In the back of the courtroom Irving Johnson was watching every facial twitch of the prospective jurors and furiously making notes on his small pad.'

'Is there anyone on the panel who disagrees with the legal principle that an individual is innocent until proven guilty and that in a criminal case the burden of proof is on the Commonwealth and that burden of proof is beyond a reasonable doubt?' No one answered.

'Is there anyone on the panel who believes that the Commonwealth Attorney and his assistants by virtue of their positions should be more believed than other officers of the court, namely; defense co-counsels?' Again, no answer.

'Is there any member of the panel who believes that ownership of a gun, a guaranteed right under the U.S. Constitution, automatically causes the owner to be guilty of a criminal act if that gun is used in the commission of a crime?' Again, no answer.

'Finally, is there any member of the panel who knows any reason why they cannot give the defendant in this case, Mr. Frank Appleby, a fair and impartial trial?" No one answered. The voir dire continued for a long time, finally;

Liam concluded;

'I want to thank each of you for your honesty and candor in answering our questions. No further questions your honor.'

Judge Draper then turned to John Brandywell. 'Do you have any questions Mr. Brandywell of the panel on behalf of the Commonwealth?'

'Only one your honor. Ladies and gentlemen of the panel, would any of you have any difficulty in finding the defendant guilty if the evidence as presented convinced you beyond a reasonable doubt that the defendant was indeed guilty even if finding him guilty meant he might be imprisoned for life or receive the death penalty?' No one answered. 'That's all of our questions your honor.'

'We will now commence with the peremptory strikes. Are counsels ready? We will rotate the peremptory strikes between the Commonwealth and Defense. We will start with fifty one individuals remaining on the panel. After each side has made six peremptory challenges we will adjourn until tomorrow at nine a.m. to finish our work. Those persons who Counsels' strike are free to leave the courtroom with my most sincere thanks for their assistance in this trial. Mr. Brandywell you may make the first strike.'

The Commonwealth strikes Mr. Tyrone Jackson
The Defense strikes Mrs. Jerome Black
The Commonwealth strikes Mr. Clarence Warner
The Defense strikes Mrs. Florence Graybone
The Commonwealth strikes Mrs. Lucy White
The Defense strikes Mr. Alvin Baker
The Commonwealth strikes Mr. Landon Green
The Defense strikes Mrs. Rosemary Jenkins
The Commonwealth strikes Mr. Albert Lapino
The Defense strikes Mrs. Annabel Cross
The Commonwealth strikes Mrs. Jose Jesus Rodriquez
The Defense strikes Mrs. Augustus Rodgers

The peremptory challenge is the right to strike a potential juror without assigning a reason for the challenge. After using up their peremptory challenges, both sides would be required to furnish a reason for all subsequent challenges that met the agreement of the court.

'Thank you gentlemen, the panel is now reduced to thirty-nine individuals. This means that tomorrow each side may make additional strikes assuming proper cause is demonstrated to the court. Once we reach fifteen unchallenged names, I will designate the first twelve as jurors and the last three as alternates, we will start promptly at nine a.m. Court is adjourned.'

The bailiff snappily said 'all rise' and Judge Draper darted from the courtroom to his private chamber. The large crowd started to disburse. When Patrick and Liam got back to the office Irving Johnson was already in the conference room chatting with Pritch. When Pritch saw them coming he quickly vacated the conference room. Heather and Kelly hurriedly got everyone coffee and Patrick asked them both to join the deliberations. Liam turned to Irving and asked, 'what do you think about the Commonwealth's first six peremptory strikes?' Irving answered in a slow southern drawl.

'Well, they struck; three black men, one black woman, one Italian newcomer and one Latino. That tells me they want to keep as many old boys as possible and dispense with as many blacks and newcomers as possible.'

'Why do you think they want to keep the old boys?' Liam asked.

'Well, in many ways it makes sense, the older residents would know the prosecutors, particularly John Brandywell, quite well. I suppose they feel they could influence them better.'

Kelly asked, 'but Mr. Johnson wouldn't many of those older residents also know Frank Appleby well and like him?'

'That would be true Kelly; but John Brandywell would have a much higher profile in the community than Frank

Appleby. Frank is a nice guy but John is someone of power and prestige. People like to side with power.'

'Oh my God,' Heather said, 'is this trial going to be about local politics and power strokes when a man's life is at stake?'

'I'm afraid this comes into it.' Irving replied.

'Ok, Irving, give us your analysis of our first six peremptory strikes?' Patrick asked.

'Well Patrick, you took out four individuals who you determined were clearly inappropriate as identified by Liam's questioning. Your final two strikes were old residents of the county; one man and one woman. I suppose in a way both you and the Commonwealth are moving in different directions toward the same result.'

Liam continued, 'you're right Irving, we had targeted young people, blacks, Latinos and more liberal newcomers as people we wanted. We wanted to stay away from the more conservative establishment figures and older residents generally.'

The defense team worked all afternoon to determine their preferred strikes. It was decided the best approach would be to formulate a strike list in descending array. The first name therefore was the individual they most wanted to strike and conversely the last name the one they least wanted to strike. As a strike by either side occurred they would draw a line through that name. Four lists would be created and Patrick, Liam, Irving and Kelly would continually update them as the strikes continued. Liam would be responsible for conducting the voir dire for the defense. The team decided they would attempt to retain as many as possible of the following groups. First, young people, both men and women; second, blacks, both men and women; third, Latino's, both men and women and finally, anyone from a minority foreign ethnic group who might not have been in the area for long. They would attempt to strike those of conservative persuasion and as many old time county residents as possible. However, they now had to do this with an eye to satisfying the court there was a valid reason a potential juror should not serve.

Irving provided background information on almost everyone. His funeral service also catered to black families so he was very friendly to and knew almost all of them. Admittedly, he felt a little guilty working to eliminate from the jury old timers, many of whom were his pals but he understood the logic of the strategy.

Both the Commonwealth and the defense wanted the voir dire beyond the peremptory challenges to be on an individual not group basis. Judge Draper readily agreed to this arrangement. Now the voir dire of each potential juror would shift to their ability to apply the law and reach a fair sentence. If a juror for any reason could not vote for the death penalty, that the Commonwealth intended to ask for, this was ample reason the Commonwealth would challenge and the court would agree. Alternatively, this would definitely be a juror the defense team would some how attempt to retain. The defense for their part would attempt to find a reason why anyone viewed as too hard nosed toward crime and particularly punishment could be eliminated. The process would be slow with each side attempting to keep the potential jurors who fit their predetermined profiles.

# Twenty Eight

WHEN September twenty-four came, again Patrick and Liam took their same route to the courthouse. Just as on the previous day, the t.v. cameras picked them up as they left Liam's office and tracked them all the way to the courthouse door. As they got close there were many requests for interviews. Patrick told Liam, their t.v. star, to go ahead and give them a word or two and he would meet him inside. They wanted to know how things were going and what the team's reactions were. Liam wasn't going to get caught in that trap. He indicated they were in the jury selection process and that they looked forward to a fair and sympathetic jury who would recognize the truth when they heard it and he fully expected Frank Appleby to be acquitted if the trial went to the jury. The possible idea that the case against their client might collapse and be dismissed before ever reaching the jury intrigued the journalists and they craved more information but Liam cut them off and left them in their frenzied state, having taken them halfway down that unexpected road, he then left them there.

Court proceedings commenced exactly on time and it became obvious that Judge Draper was going to run a tight ship. He addressed the panel again and thanked them for their time and patience during the jury selection process. He told them he knew many were making sacrifices being away from their jobs and lauded them for doing their civic duty. Actually, they were there because they had been summoned and had little or no alternative. Still, his words went down well basically because he was sincere and everyone likes to be thanked for doing even those things which they must do.

After several hours of penetrating questioning Judge Draper had his jury in record time. When they were completed, Judge Draper invited the jurors and alternates to take their place in the jury box. He then gave them some specific instructions asking them to stay alert and listen carefully to every word said throughout the trial. He indicated they were the triers of fact and as such had to affix the proper weight to the testimony of all witnesses including expert witnesses. Testimony that rang false should be discounted while testimony that rang true should be elevated. Finally, Judge Draper dismissed them for lunch and set two p.m. that afternoon for the opening statements.

In the final analysis the jury was certainly acceptable to the defense. It was composed of; two black women, two black men, one Latino man, one Latino woman, and one newcomer whose nationality was Mexican. For the other side there were three white men and two white women. Four of the five were long time Loudoun residents. Two of the five Irving thought to be quite conservative. Since everything was now decided it was time to forge ahead. We thanked Irving for his input but told him we might need him again at critical stages of the trial.

They had agreed that Patrick would make the opening statement so he practiced his presentation all evening on Tuesday. By eleven p.m. Tuesday evening he was at least halfway confident that he could pull it off. When Wednesday afternoon arrived he was not at all sure. Everyone had returned to the office for lunch. Heather and Kelly had gone to Pizza Hut and bought more than enough personal pan pizzas for everyone. At one point about one-thirty p.m. Patrick felt sick to his stomach. He went to the bathroom and looked in the mirror, sweat was rolling down his face. He splashed cold water on his face and towelled off. Kelly entered the bathroom and wedged her way between him and the washbasin. She looked him straight in the eye and told him he would do just fine to stop worrying. He was looking over her shoulder into the mirror. Her ass was sticking out over the basin. The rim of the basin had cupped under her ass and pushed her skirt inward to allow it to show off its most perfect form. He had the strongest desire to grab her ass in his two hands and draw her to him. He gave in and did what he wanted to do. He forced his body hard against hers. She kissed him with full lips with her mouth slightly open. She accepted his advances without hesitation. Finally, he said he would have to cool down, he couldn't go to court like that. She slipped from between him and the washbasin closing the door behind her as she left. Patrick composed himself. He felt great, like a man again. All his fear had disappeared. He felt he could whip the world if necessary. He laughed to himself, if just a little embracing and kissing could do that to him imagine what full sex would do.

When Liam, Patrick, Kelly and Irving arrived at the courthouse, the crowd was even larger than the day before. The t.v. and print journalists were even more numerous too. Once inside they met Frank, who looked wonderful in his best and only suit. Frank had been fairly passive throughout the jury selection process. Now, his spirits seemed to lift as he sensed the real fight for truth was about to begin.

Again, exactly at nine a.m. Judge Draper entered the courtroom. There seemed to be a real urgency in his demeanor. He asked the bailiff if all the jurors and alternates were in place. When he was assured they were, he addressed them. 'Ladies and gentlemen of the jury, the trial is about to begin. I wish you the best as you struggle with the facts you are about to hear. Under no circumstances are you to talk to anyone regarding this case and that means to each other. Do not talk to the press and certainly don't give any interviews to anyone. When you are at home do not discuss this case with your families or let them tell you what other people are saying about it. Do not read newspapers or watch television or listen to radio news programs that are sure to report on the progress of this trial. If you violate the strict rules which I have laid down I may have to dismiss you from the jury, dismiss the entire jury or sequester the entire jury. Please don't place me in that situation. Listen to the arguments presented to you by the Commonwealth and Defense counsels. Listen carefully to all witness testimony. Weigh carefully the truthfulness of what you hear.'

'Is the Commonwealth ready?'

'Yes, your honor.'

'Is the defense ready?'

'Yes, your honor.'

'Then the Commonwealth will commence with their opening argument.'

'Your honor, ladies and gentlemen of the jury. My name is John Brandywell and I am the Commonwealth Attorney for Loudoun County. It is my obligation and the duty of my assistants to prosecute all criminal acts perpetrated within our jurisdiction. It is that function that brings me before you today. However, today is different than almost every other day because this trial is not about; assault, breaking and entering, shoplifting, armed robbery, etc., all serious crimes. No, this trial is about murder, about the wrongful taking of life in a most violent and abhorrent manner. We are a peaceful county, luckily over the years we have been spared such violent acts as murder. Only a few times in the modern history of our county has a jury been forced to hear a murder trial. I, therefore, stand before you as a very sad prosecutor forced to prosecute a fellow member of our community for killing, in cold blood, with prior intent, another member of our community. The fact that it was a premeditated act carried out with full prior intent saddens me even more.'

'Let's look at the facts of what happened on the day that Mr. Wilbur Ralph Cosgrove was so brutally gunned down on his own property. It was Wednesday, twenty-eight June on a beautiful sunny summer day that the defendant, Mr. Frank Appleby, sometime between two and two-twenty p.m. went to the Cosgrove home, found Mr. Cosgrove in a storage building in the back lawn of his house, argued with him and killed him in cold blood by firing a single shotgun blast into Mr. Cosgrove's chest at close range. The Commonwealth will prove that Mr. Frank Appleby is the killer of Mr Cosgrove. We will prove further that on the day of the murder he travelled from a home on West Cornwall Street in Leesburg, where he was working as a gardener in his truck to his rental home on Route fifteen north (the old Davidson house). At his home Mr. Appleby (the defendant) took a shotgun he owned from its storage place beneath his bed, left his house this time on foot and ran from his yard across open fields in a westerly direction toward the Old Waterford Road, the place of the residence of Wilbur Cosgrove. As he approached the Cosgrove backyard where the storage buildings are, he had to cross a small creek and then move along unnoticed in the heavy summer foliage of this wild un-kept area which had grown up outside Mr. Cosgrove's backyard. The defendant entered the back lawn and found Mr. Cosgrove alone in one of the storage buildings. They argued, he fired one shot at close range into the chest of Mr Cosgrove. The blast killed Mr.Cosgrove who may have survived for a short time but was pronounced dead upon arrival at the Loudoun Memorial Hospital at approximately two-fifty-four p.m'.

'Mr. Appleby went home for lunch sometime around one-thirty to two p.m. When he arrived home he found his son, Frank, Jr. in a state that might suggest he had been raped or otherwise molested. There was blood and semen dripping from his rectum. Frank Appleby Sr. became so enraged that he took matters into his own hands instead of reporting the matter to the police, which is what he should have done. Rather, he ran to the Cosgrove home and killed Mr. Cosgrove in cold blood. In rushing away from the Cosgrove home after the murder, the defendant discarded the murder weapon in the creek previously described behind the Cosgrove home. It was recovered there by police.'

'It therefore is clear for all to see that the defendant had both the motive and opportunity to kill Mr. Cosgrove. He also possessed a lethal weapon with which he carried out this violent murder. We can sympathize with a father whose only son is molested but we can't forgive him for murdering another human being. Mr. Cosgrove did not receive a fair trial; he was killed in a vigilante revenge act. This type of behaviour is totally repugnant to our way of life and the rule of law. Sympathy can only stretch so far, it is not a justification for murder. The defendant is an intelligent man. He knew at all times what he should have done, namely; report his son's abuse to the sheriff's department. He didn't do that. He took the law into his own hands and with malice aforethought he murdered Wilbur Cosgrove. He had time to reflect, to stop, to turn back, to abandon his plan as he ran towards the Cosgrove home. He did not, he forged on, determined to kill Wilbur Cosgrove, which he did.'

'The Commonwealth will prove that the defendant killed Mr. Cosgrove (the actual criminal act). We will also prove that he had (prior intent/malice aforethought) to carry out this act. We will prove that he pulled the trigger of the gun that killed Mr. Cosgrove and we will ask, if you find the defendant guilty, that he be sentenced to death.'

'Many people are confused about the concept of intent, they say, how do I know what is going on in another person's mind? I know a way to help you. I am fairly confident that many of you own dogs or a member of your family does. If so, you know how sometimes they can get under your feet. Most of you can probably recall accidentally stepping on your pet and hearing him or her howl in pain. However, that dog always knew whether you stomped on him intentionally or conversely stepped on him accidentally. By the way, the pain is the same for the animal either way, what isn't the same is his perception of intent. If a dog can judge intent perfectly every time, I have full confidence that you will have no difficulty determining the intent of the defendant when he murdered Wilbur Cosgrove in cold blood with malice aforethought'.

'Ladies and gentlemen of the jury, I want to thank you for your courteous attention.'

When John Brandywell finished Judge Draper turned to the defense table and asked; who will make the opening statement for the defense.' Patrick answered.

'I will your honor.'

'Fine, Mr. Hurst, please proceed.'

'Your honor, ladies and gentlemen of the jury. My name is Patrick J. Hurst and I am co-counsel for the defense. As you can observe, I am a young lawyer. I have only practiced law for one plus years and this is my first murder trial. I am therefore not the most experienced lawyer in Loudoun

County, far from it. I am not the best lawyer in Loudoun County, far from it. I am not even the best criminal lawyer in Loudoun County, far from it. So how do I conceive in my wildest dreams that I can prove that my client is innocent? Because ladies and gentlemen I have a magic ingredient on my side. Can you guess what it is? Yes, that's right, it is the truth. The truth is that Frank Appleby didn't kill Wilbur Cosgrove. The truth is that Frank Appleby never physically hurt another human being in his entire lifetime. How do I know, because my client told me? No, because the truth told me. You see the truth is so powerful it speaks for itself if we are but ready to listen. Unlike my experience and skills as a lawyer there is no second or third class truth, there is no inexperienced truth. There is no best or worst truth; there is only the truth, nothing more, nothing less.

The truth in this case is that Frank Appleby's son was raped and molested by Wilbur Cosgrove. We know this for sure because the DNA from the semen oozing out of Frank Jr's. rectum was DNA tested and then compared by the laboratory with blood samples taken from the body of Mr. Wilbur Cosgrove. Recall please that they were taken to the same hospital on the same day at approximately the same time. This is part of the truth and we will prove this through expert medical testimony and DNA testing.

The truth is that Frank Appleby Sr. never went home from work on the day of the murder. He received an emergency telephone call from his wife to the home of Mr. and Mrs. Horace Granger where Mr. Appleby was working as a gardener in their back garden. Mrs. Granger called Mr. Appleby to the telephone at approximately three-thirty p.m. on the day of the murder and his wife told him their son had been badly hurt and to come immediately to the Loudoun Memorial Hospital. This is exactly what he did. This is the truth and we will prove it through the testimony of Mr. Horace Granger.

It will be interesting to see if the Commonwealth can produce one witness to the murder, one witness that places Mr. Appleby at the crime scene, one witness who can even testify they know for certain that Mr. Appleby and Mr. Cosgrove ever met. Our investigation could not produce one witness to the murder, one witness that places Mr. Appleby at the crime scene and not one witness who can testify that the two men ever met. This is the truth. You see how loud it is speaking to us.

You will undoubtedly hear testimony that the weapon that fired the shot that killed Wilbur Cosgrove was found in a small creek which runs directly behind the Cosgrove property. You will learn that this weapon was the same shotgun which was purchased some months earlier by Frank Appleby from Sears and Roebuck. We don't dispute these facts because they are the truth, however, Frank Appleby did not transport that shotgun to the creek behind the Cosgrove property and Frank Appleby did not throw his shotgun in that creek. We will prove another person took Frank's gun to Wilbur Cosgrove's, that is the truth.

Some of you may own a shotgun, a handgun, a rifle. This is your right under the Constitution of the United States. Some of you may be hunters; some may like target or skeet shooting. However, this ownership and usage does not make you murderers and this is the truth.

Ladies and gentlemen of the jury, can I ask you to assist me? I would ask you to close your eyes and think of yourself when you were a child, you select the age; 6, 7, 9, 13, 15, you choose. Can you see yourself? Oh, someone is accusing you of something. Is that your father or your mother or a teacher, I can't tell. They want to punish you but you are protesting. You are telling them you didn't do it. You are trying to tell them the truth but they are not listening. They are mad at you, they say you did do it, can you see them? Now you are begging for them to believe you, you are pleading, but they are not persuaded. Maybe, they perceive you did do it. Maybe, they are too busy to listen. Maybe, circumstances point to you and this is enough for them. Oh, they are spanking you, you are crying, you are very upset. The truth was there, speaking loudly, but they didn't want to hear the truth so they blotted it out.

Please open your eyes, don't cry anymore. That time in your childhood, the truth wasn't heard but today it will be heard. You know it must be heard, you will ensure it will be heard. You are the guarantors of the truth. I humbly salute you.'

'Thank you your honor. That concludes our opening statement.'

'Thank you Mr. Hurst.'

'Mr. Brandywell rebuttal?'

'Ladies and gentlemen of the jury, you may find it strange but we agree wholeheartedly with Mr. Hurst. We too want to have the truth speak to us. Justice demands that truth prevail. That is why we have prepared our case against the defendant so carefully. We will put on the stand both expert witnesses and lay witnesses who will scrupulously tell you the truth. Listen to them carefully. Don't be deflected by emotional appeals, listen for the facts. Remember the defense has no monopoly on truth. As Mr. Hurst said himself the truth stands on its own legs. Look for it in the testimony of our witnesses and you will find it. Thank you.'

'Mr. Brandywell are you prepared to call your first witness?'

'I am your honor. I call to the stand the Sheriff of Loudoun County, Mr. Stanley Dunn.'

After the sheriff was sworn, Mr. Brandywell commenced his questioning.

'Mr. Dunn, could you tell the court your position?'

'I am the Sheriff of Loudoun County.'

'How long have you held that position?'

'For nine years.'

Were you working on Wednesday twenty-eight June, the day Mr. Wilbur Cosgrove was murdered?'

'I was.'

'Did you go to the murder scene?'

'I did.'

'What was the situation when you arrived?'

'Our office picked up the emergency call from the police scanner. Our dispatcher immediately sent an ambulance to Mr. Wilbur Cosgrove's home.'

'Did you arrive before or after the ambulance?'

'My deputy, Mr. Wayne Broomfield and I arrived just before the ambulance.'

'Was Mr. Cosgrove alive when you arrived?'

'I am not sure, he may have been; I don't have any medical knowledge. He was very still and not making any sound but after the medics arrived they were working on him frantically.'

'Do you recall the time you arrived at the Cosgrove home?'

'Yes, it was approximately two thirty-five p.m.'

'Was anyone other than the medics and yourself and Deputy Broomfield at the scene?'

'Yes, Mrs. Cosgrove was there.'

'What was her state?'

'She was quite hysterical, extremely upset.'

'Did you interview Mrs. Cosgrove?'

'Yes, I did.'

'What did she tell you?'

'She said she was working in the kitchen and she heard a loud bang like a gunshot. The sound came from the backyard. She rushed to the outbuilding and found Mr. Cosgrove on the floor with a gunshot wound to the chest. She ran back to the house, called the emergency number and then ran back to her husband.'

'And then what did she do?'

'She tried to help her husband. She cradled his head and kept telling him to hold on not to leave her.'

'And what was the murder weapon?'

'From my experience the type of wound to Mr. Cosgrove's chest was consistent with a shotgun blast.'

'And did you ever find the murder weapon?'

'Yes, in a search of the area we found a shotgun submerged in a small creek which runs behind the Cosgrove's premises.'

'And how do you know this was the murder weapon?'

'We had the shotgun and one spent cartridge tested at the State Police Ballistics Laboratory in Richmond and they ascertained that the shotgun found in the creek fired the one cartridge which we had located.'

'And where did you locate this one cartridge?'

'In the outbuilding in the backyard of the Cosgrove property on the floor about six feet from the body.'

'And did the gun automatically eject the spent cartridge?'

'Yes and no. The shotgun was a pump action type and the cartridge was not automatically ejected after the shot was fired but would have been ejected automatically when the pump portion of the shotgun was pulled back towards the shooter.'

'So the shooter would have had to open the breach so to speak?'

'Yes, that's correct.'

'Was there any evidence the shooter loaded another cartridge into the shotgun?'

'No, but the shotgun was loaded with two further cartridges which could have been fired but were not.'

'And were these cartridges still in the shotgun when it was found?'

'They were.'

'I show you four exhibits, a shotgun, one spent cartridge and two unspent cartridges, do you recognize them?'

'I do.'

'Is this the murder weapon and its cartridges?'

'Yes sir.'

'I would like to submit this shotgun and spent and unspent cartridges to the court as prosecution exhibits number one through number four and note your honor that the defense has been previously given an opportunity to have their ballistics expert examine the shotgun and the spent and unspent cartridges.'

'Very well Mr. Brandywell, please continue.'

'And Sheriff Dunn, I now show you the report of the State Police Ballistics Laboratory concerning the shotgun in question, do you recognize this as authentic?'

'I do.'

'Your honor the prosecution would like to submit this report to the court as prosecution exhibit number five and note that the defense has previously been given a copy of this report.'

'Thank you Mr. Brandywell, please continue.'

'Sheriff Dunn, did you have occasion to talk to the defendant, Mr. Frank Appleby, concerning Mr Cosgrove's murder?'

'I did, I went to Mr. Appleby's house late Wednesday evening, the same day as the murder to discuss the events of that day with him. I enquired about the condition of his son Frankie and asked him if he knew anything about the murder of Wilbur Cosgrove.'

'And what did you find out?'

'Mr. Appleby said Frankie was in critical condition and acted very shocked to learn of Mr. Cosgrove's murder.'

'Was Mrs. Appleby present during this conversation?'

'She was.'

'Did she say anything?'

'No, not a word. She didn't seem too shocked at the murder and acted very passive throughout the conversation.'

'I told the Appleby's that Mr. Cosgrove had been killed by a single shotgun blast and I asked Mr. Appleby if he owned a shotgun?'

'And what was his answer?'

'He said he did and took me to his bedroom where he stored the shotgun and ammunition under his bed.'

'And was Mr. Appleby's shotgun under his bed when you looked together?'

'No sir, it was not.'

'What did you do next? I asked Mr. Appleby if I could take a sample of the ammunition and a book on the shotgun and its operation. He readily agreed.'

'Did you arrest Mr. Appleby Wednesday evening?'

'No, sir.'

'When did you arrest Mr. Appleby?'

'The next day, on Thursday twenty-nine June.'

'On what basis did you arrest Mr. Appleby for the murder of Wilbur Cosgrove?'

'I arrested him on the basis that he had the opportunity, the motive and that his shotgun matched the description of the murder weapon found near the murder scene.'

'Thank you Sheriff Dunn, no further questions now, although I may have additional questions on redirect.'

'Mr. Hurst and Mr. O'Brien, who will conduct the cross examination?'

'I will your honor.'

'Alright Mr. O'Brien, please proceed.'

'Sheriff Dunn, when you arrested Mr. Appleby on Thursday, twenty-nine June, did you read Mr. Appleby his full Miranda warning?'

'I did.'

'And when you went to the Appleby home, did you have a search warrant?'

'No, I did not but I never searched the Appleby home.'

'But you did take certain items away from the Appleby home, did you not?'

'Yes, I did but only with the full agreement of Mr. Appleby.'

'I see, and when you went with Mr. Appleby to look under his bed for his shotgun did he act surprised when it was no longer there?'

'Yes, he did act surprised.'

'And what did he do when he couldn't find the gun?'

'He and his wife searched everywhere in their bedroom and throughout the house for it.'

'And how would you describe this search?'

'Mr. Appleby seemed quite frantic and very upset when he couldn't find his gun.'

'And his wife helped him search?'

'She did.'

'And how would you characterize her emotions?'

'She was calmer, far less excited.'

'And when you arrested Mr. Appleby the next day, how did Mr. Appleby act?'

'Well, he didn't resist arrest or anything like that.'

'But how would you characterize his emotions?'

'Objection your honor, the Sheriff is not a psychiatrist or psychologist. He is not medically trained to judge emotions.'

'Overruled, Sheriff Dunn is an intelligent and perceptive man and I believe he is competent to judge when individuals are upset or distressed.'

'Upset, very upset and disbelieving.'

'Sheriff Dunn, did Mr. Appleby ever state he killed Mr. Cosgrove or alternatively ever state that he did not kill Mr. Cosgrove?'

'Well, he never said he killed Mr. Cosgrove but he did say many times that he did not kill Mr. Cosgrove.'

'And when you interrogated Mr. Appleby after his arrest, did he continue to claim his innocence?'

'He did.'

'And did he at any time confess to the murder of Mr. Cosgrove?'

'No, he did not.'

'In fact, he always stated his innocence?'

'That's correct.'

'No further questions your honor.'

Mr. Brandywell, any questions on redirect?'

'No, your honor.'

'Then please call your next witness.'

'The Commonwealth calls Dr. Albert Panski.'

'Dr. Panski, would you state your full name.'

'Albert Stephen Panski.'

'And what is your occupation?'

'I am a forensic scientist.'

'And where are you employed?'

'I am self employed but do a great deal of work for the Commonwealth of Virginia Forensic Laboratory in Richmond on a freelance basis.'

'And you are a doctor in what discipline?'

'I am a doctor of criminology and forensic science.'

'And where, Doctor Panski, did you receive your higher education?'

'I received a Bachelor of Science degree in Criminology from the American University in Washington, D.C., a Master of Criminology and Forensic Science from the University of Maryland and a Doctor of Criminology and Forensic Science from the University of Virginia.'

'And do you have any publications concerning criminology and forensic science to your credit?'

'Yes, I have written three books on the subject of criminology and forensic science and have written eighteen articles on various aspects of criminology and forensic science published in learned journals.'

'And do you belong to any professional associations or societies?'

'Your honor, the defense will stipulate to the court the acceptance of Dr. Panski as an expert witness in his field.'

'Thank you Mr. O'Brien.'

'Fine, Mr. Brandywell, please continue.'

'Thank you your honor.'

'Dr. Panski, in your capacity as a freelance forensic expert were you asked by the Commonwealth Forensic Laboratory in Richmond to examine a shotgun in the Wilbur Cosgrove murder case?'

'I was.'

'And were you able to find any fingerprints on the shotgun in question?'

'I was, it was somewhat difficult because the shotgun was in fast moving water for a period of approximately eighteen hours. The shotgun was lying on the bottom of the creek bed and the prints on the side that faced upward towards the fast running water were substantially undermined. However, the side that was lying on the sandy bottom was much less effected by the moving water.'

'And whose prints did you find on the murder weapon?'

'I found several clear prints that matched those of Mr. Frank Appleby and also one clear thumbprint of Mr. Ralph Hightower, the salesman at Sears and Roebuck who sold Mr. Appleby the shotgun. I also found the outline of some small prints consistent with those of a child or a small adult but these were not clear enough to positively identify.'

'And how do you know that the prints found match those of Mr. Appleby and Mr. Hightower?'

'I matched Mr. Appleby's prints with those taken at the time of his arrest and I requested a set of finger prints from Mr. Hightower once it was established by the sheriff's department that he was the clerk at Sears and Roebuck who sold Mr. Appleby the shotgun in question.'

'And were the prints on the shotgun of Mr. Appleby clear and convincing from your experience?'

'Oh yes, I would call your attention to the fingerprint charts on the two easels which show blow-ups of the right thumb print of Mr. Appleby's taken from the shotgun and compared with the right thumbprint taken from the police finger print records, again, on the left index finger print of Mr. Appleby taken from the shotgun compared with the left index finger print of Mr. Appleby taken from sheriff department records.'

'And in your expert opinion are they clearly the fingerprints of the same man?'

'Absolutely, the prints lifted from the shotgun are extremely clear and compare exactly with the fingerprints of Mr. Appleby taken at the time of his arrest. I would call attention to the numbered key similarity points shown on the charts.'

'And Dr. Panski, in your expert opinion, what is the chance for error in regard to these prints?'

'Oh, it is hard to say exactly, a fair estimate might be ten million to one.'

'Thank you Dr. Panski, that will be all the questions for now.'

'Mr. O'Brien your witness.'

'Thank you your honor. Dr. Panski, did you look elsewhere for any DNA evidence?'

'Yes I did, the clothing worn by Mr. Appleby on the day of the murder was offered to us for examination by the defense after they had sent the garments out to a laboratory in Fairfax for analysis.'

'And did you thereafter have occasion to analyze the clothing Mr. Appleby wore on the day of the murder?'

'I did.'

'And what were your findings?'

'I found stains of soil and grease consistent with his work as a gardener but no blood stains or DNA from Mr.

Wilbur Cosgrove or any other individual other than Mr. Appleby himself.'

'And were the work clothes of Mr. Appleby accompanied by a sworn and signed statement showing the chain of custody from the moment they were turned over by Mrs. Appleby to the moment they were turned over to you for examination?'

'Yes, such a statement accompanied the clothing and I signed, dated and placed the time on the form when it was tendered to me.'

'Now, Dr. Panski, did you have an opportunity to examine the body of Mr. Cosgrove after the murder?'

'No, I did not.'

'But you did read the coroner's report concerning Mr. Cosgrove and also the police reports?'

'I did, they were made available to me along with photographs of the dead man.'

'And Dr. Panski, did those reports indicate an estimate as to how far away the murderer was from Mr. Cosgrove when he or she fired the shot?'

'Yes, they did.'

'And what was that estimated distance?'

'Three to four feet.'

'In other words, Dr. Panski, at point blank range?

'Yes, that's correct.'

'And Dr. Panski, in your professional opinion could an individual fire a shotgun blast into another human being; namely, an adult male at point blank range without having blood and tissue propelled back towards the shooter's clothing?'

'Yes, that could be the result if the shooter fired from behind a large shield, door, wall, etc.'

'And was there any evidence at the murder scene to indicate that such a blood spray was left on a shield, door, wall, etc?'

'No, not to my knowledge. Another possible way the shooter could have avoided the blood spray was to place the gun in a form or rack and use a cord to pull the trigger from a distance.'

'And was any such form, tripod or rack found at the murder scene?'

'No, not to my knowledge at least there wasn't any mention of such a device in the police reports I read.'

'Now, Dr. Panski, if a shooter was standing directly in front of the victim wouldn't their body stop the blood spray leaving their silhouette on the floor or objects behind the shooter?'

'Yes, that is correct.'

'And did your study find such a silhouette?'

'Yes, I did.'

'And would you describe that silhouette for us?'

'Yes, well it was consistent with a small individual of about 5'4" or 5'6" in height.'

'And are you aware that Mr. Appleby is at least six feet in height? Please stand for a moment if you will Mr. Appleby, thank you.'

'Yes, I note the defendant is taller, however, the blood spray may have been of such force that it actually wrapped around the shooter, somewhat, particularly if he was standing a little sideways.'

'Now, Dr. Panski, you didn't mention the possibility the shooter could have been a woman?'

'That of course is a possibility.'

'So, you really can't be sure if the murderer is a man or a woman or a teenager?'

'No, not from the forensic evidence presented to me.'

'No further questions your honor.'

'Thank you Mr. O'Brien. Mr. Brandywell, any questions on redirect?'

'Yes, your honor, only a few questions.'

'Dr. Panski in your professional opinion did the blood spray hit the murderer?'

'Yes, if there was nothing to impede it such as we have discussed.'

'Then how do you explain the fact that Mr. Appleby's work clothing had no blood or tissue on them?'

'Well, those clothes were clean but other work clothes, possibly now destroyed, may have had the blood spray on them.'

'Objection your honor, attached to the chain of custody form was a signed affidavit from Mrs. Appleby that those were the work clothes Mr. Appleby wore on the date of the murder and that she had not washed or otherwise altered them in any way. The court has that exhibit before it.'

'Objection sustained.'

'Any further questions Mr. Brandywell?'

'Yes, your honor, only one. Dr. Panski you stated you saw photographs of the victim?'

'Yes, I did.'

'Are these the photographs of the dead man you viewed?'

'They are.'

'The prosecution submits these photographs to the court marked as exhibit number six.'

'Then the court will adjourn for today and commence at nine a.m. tomorrow.'

Patrick and Liam were not too unhappy with the second day of the trial. True, the prosecution had scored heavily in the early going but Liam had clawed back some lost advantage in the late afternoon, particularly in his cross examination of Dr. Panski.

When Patrick arrived back at the office, Heather presented him with some bad news, Cindy had filed for divorce. Evidently, Cindy's attorney had filed the day she left. A process server had pinned the filing to the front door of the house in Neersville. Ralph Harrington had finally spotted it sometime later and brought it to Patrick's office. Under Virginia law, the fact that they had no children would allow for a rather quick no fault divorce. There was little or no property to split as they had always lived in rented, fully furnished accommodation. Cindy had a good company car so she didn't need the one car they owned together. There was something very sad that the old car that Patrick drove looked like it was going to outlast the marriage. They had purchased it just after their wedding and it was still going strong even though the marriage was ending. Patrick hadn't seen his wife since the separation or better stated, desertion. Patrick never entertained the idea of charging Cindy with desertion, what was the use. He had been expecting Cindy would want a divorce but now that it was clear she did, he was very upset. Patrick felt it was as if his best friend had died, even though he knew she was alive and well. The fact that Cindy had filed for divorce the day she left further upset Patrick.

Kelly had been in court all day watching the trial. She had sat in the front row with Irving Johnson. As a paralegal, she could perform many legal acts under Patrick's supervision but one thing she couldn't do was try a case in a court of law. She could if Patrick agreed, sit at the counsel table and even pass notes to either co-counsel and she thought one day she might do just that. However, today she had been content to sit with Irving and simply observe. She thought Patrick's opening statement was brilliant although she knew she was totally bias in its evaluation. She also thought Liam's cross examination of Dr. Panski was excellent as he had cut to the heart of the matter with an economy of words. When Patrick went to his office, Heather told Kelly that Cindy had filed for divorce. Kelly thought this would make her very happy, which it did, but she had to balance her happiness with her sadness at the hurt and pain Patrick must be feeling. She waited a discrete amount of time and then knocked on Patrick's door and entered. Patrick was seated at his desk with his fingers steepled with a far-away glazed look in his eyes. Kelly guessed Patrick was thinking over the memories of his time with Cindy, both before and after their marriage and of course she was right. She started the conversation slowly and deliberately.

'Heather told me, I am sorry Patrick.'

'I am sorry too Kelly, I just can't figure out what I did wrong.'

'Maybe you didn't do anything wrong, maybe it was just some cruel twist of fate.'

'Maybe you're right. I have been thinking a lot about what happened and while I can't really make any sense of it I have finally decided it is not in my interest to twist and turn what happened over and over in my mind. It's punishing me unnecessarily and I know I must stop.'

'Well Patrick, if you have come that far you are definitely on the road to recovery.'

'If I am Kelly, and yes I think I am, it is all down to you and your support. You are marvellous.'

'I don't know about marvellous but I do care for you.'

'Yes, I know you do and I am very grateful. In fact, I have been thinking a great deal about us over the last few days.'

'Patrick, that's the first time you ever referred to us; like us together, like we instead of just you and I, just boss and Kelly. Mind you, you're still the boss.'

'Look Kelly, when this trial is over we will discuss our future.'

'Really Patrick, wow, ok.'

'Patrick, there is a little secret I must tell you. I promised my mother I wouldn't get between you and Cindy and your marriage, I am not a home wrecker. But now that Cindy filed for divorce sometime ago I don't feel compelled to follow that tact any further. I just wanted to put you on notice.'

With that Kelly left the office for a moment and told Heather to hold all calls. When she returned she locked Patrick's office door and walked over behind his chair and started to massage his neck and shoulders. The desired results were achieved. Patrick reached back and started to rub her right calf with his right hand. Slowly he worked his way up her thigh to the bottom of her ass. This was as high as his arm could reach. After a few more moments Kelly took the initiative again. She hiked her skirt up and slid her panty hose off, stepping out of her high heel to complete the operation. She then slid her thong panties off and stepped back into her high heels. Patrick watched intently and was almost instantly aroused. It had been months since he had sex and he was extremely horny. Kelly pulled her skirt up over her ass and bent over Patrick's desk. Patrick unzipped his pants and let them drop to the floor; he did the same with his boxer shorts. Cindy was well endowed but Kelly had an even better body and a mind to match. Kelly was gently groaning as she came, she climaxed just a second after he had and he kept his deep thrusts going to make sure she achieved maximum pleasure. Patrick patted her beautiful ass as a signal to disengage. Their first sexual encounter had been a great success.

As the trial continued there would be many more opportunities for sex with Kelly. In fact, as the pressure in the trial built to its natural climax there were plenty more climaxes in Patrick's office. If Heather ever caught on she was polite enough never to say so but she wouldn't have to guess too much because after the first encounter, a rumpled Kelly with hair somewhat messed up, pumped the air with one closed fist and said 'yes' as she left Patrick's office.

# Twenty Nine

AGAIN Judge Draper started exactly on time.

'Mr. Brandywell is the prosecution prepared to call your next witness?'

'We are your honor.'

'The prosecution calls to stand the coroner of Loudoun County, Dr. Roger Case.'

After Dr. Case was sworn questioning by Mr. Brandywell commenced.

'Dr. Case please explain to the court your position?'

'I am the coroner for Loudoun County; this means I am a medical doctor and examiner specializing in pathology.'

'How long have you served in that position?'

'Fifteen years.'

'And in the conduct of your function did you have occasion to examine the body of Mr. Wilbur Cosgrove?'

'I did.'

'And did you formulate an opinion as to the cause of death?'

'Yes, Mr. Cosgrove succumbed to one shotgun blast fired at close range into his chest.'

'And was this single shotgun blast the cause of Mr. Cosgrove's death?'

'Yes, Mr. Cosgrove died from massive loss of blood and massive trauma to several vital organs located in the chest area. His lungs were collapsed, pellets were lodged in his heart and two pellets almost completely severed the aorta, the main artery delivering blood from the heart. It was this severing of the aorta that actually caused his death.'

'Was there further damage?'

'Yes, some pellets entered and severely damaged Mr. Cosgrove's stomach and intestines.'

'Any additional damage?'

'Yes, a few pellets entered Mr. Cosgrove's legs and genitals. However, these were not life threatening, assuming prompt medical attention of course.'

'Did Mr. Cosgrove die instantly?'

'No, he may have survived for a few minutes, possibly five minutes maximum.'

'Was Mr. Cosgrove in pain after he was shot?'

'No, not really, his body would have been in massive shock, he would have been unconscious.'

'Thank you Dr. Case, no further questions.'

'Mr. O'Brien, your witness.'

'Thank you your honor, we have no questions for Dr. Case.'

'Mr. Brandywell, please call your next witness.'

'The prosecution calls to the stand Mrs. Sally Ross.'

After Mrs. Ross was sworn the questioning began.

'Mrs. Ross, would you state your full name?'

'Sally Elizabeth Ross.'

'And where do you live Mrs. Ross?'

'On the Old Waterford Road, just outside the Leesburg town limits.'

'And do you live close to the Cosgrove family?'

'Yes, I am their immediate next door neighbor on the Leesburg side, meaning you come to my house while leaving Leesburg just before the Cosgrove's property.'

'And going toward Waterford from Leesburg are you on the right or left side of the road?'

'We are on the right.'

'That would mean the Cosgrove's too are on the right?'

'Yes, that is true.'

'And how close is your house to the Cosgrove's home?'

'Well, not too close as the houses on the Old Waterford Road are country type properties and not too close together.'

'Would you say fifty, one hundred, two hundred yards away?'

'Oh, I would guess about one hundred fifty yards away.'

'And on Wednesday twenty-eight June, the day of Mr. Cosgrove's murder did you hear any strange noises coming from the Cosgrove's home?'

'Yes, I was out hanging up my clothes in the backyard about two p.m. on that day and I heard some loud voices coming from the Cosgrove's property and a few minutes later what sounded like a gunshot.'

'How many gunshots were there?'

'Only one.'

'Could you hear what the voices were saying?'

'Not too clearly, but they sounded like they were arguing.'

'Could you tell what they were arguing about?'

'Not fully.'

'Could you identify any of the words being spoken?'

'I heard the word pervert at one point and child porn at another.'

'Could you identify who the parties arguing were?

'Well, one sounded like the voice of Mr. Cosgrove and the other was a much lighter voice that I didn't recognize.'

'Explain what you mean by lighter?'

'Well, not as deep, higher pitched.'

'Were you able to see the people arguing?'

'No, it was summertime and all the trees were out, shielding off our property from the Cosgrove's property.'

'Did you see or hear any cars going up or down the Old Waterford Road about that time?'

'No, during the time I was outside no cars passed on the road.'

'How long were you outside?'

'Oh, maybe twenty minutes.'

'Did you hear any noise after the gunshot?'

'None until about fifteen minutes later when the police and emergency vehicles started to arrive.'

'And what did you do when you heard and saw the emergency vehicles arrive?'

'I ran up to the Cosgrove's but when I got there a deputy sheriff held me and another neighbor back.'

'Who was this other neighbor?'

'Mr. George Rankin.'

'And where does Mr. Rankin live?'

'He lives across the street from us. He is a retired gentleman.'

'Did you see the ambulance take Mr. Cosgrove away?'

'Yes, I saw them place Mr. Cosgrove in the ambulance and drive off, sirens blaring.'

'And when did you learn that Mr. Cosgrove had died?'

'My husband told me when he arrived home about six p.m. He had heard in town that Mr. Cosgrove had died from a gunshot wound. He didn't know any other details.'

'No further questions for this witness your honor but we may have additional questions on redirect.'

'Mr. O'Brien, are you going to continue today with the cross examination?'

'Yes your honor.'

'Alright, please proceed.'

'Mrs. Ross, you stated you heard two people arguing, one you identified as Mr. Cosgrove and the other voice you said you could not identify, is that correct?'

'Yes.'

'And you stated the second voice was higher pitched, not so deep?'

'That's correct.'

'Was the second voice more consistent with a man or a woman's voice?'

'I am just not sure.'

'Could it have been the voice of a woman or a teenager?'

'Yes, possibly.'

'Now Mrs. Ross, when you heard the gunshot were you surprised?'

'Oh no, we hear gunshots here all the time, more during hunting season in the Autumn but many people out in this area have guns and do target shooting all year round.'

'Do you know the defendant, Mr. Frank Appleby?'

'Yes I do, he does gardening for my friend Sara Butler. I sometime see Mr. Appleby when I play bridge on Thursday afternoons at Sara's house.'

'Did you ever see Mr. Appleby working out in your area on the Old Waterford Road?'

'No, I never did. I don't think anyone out this way ever used him.'

'And how about on social visits, did you ever see Mr. Appleby in your neighborhood?'

'No, never.'

'Do you know what kind of vehicle Mr. Appleby drives?'

'Yes I do, an old pick-up truck. It's always parked at Sara's when he works there.'

'And did you ever see that pick-up truck go up or down the Old Waterford Road?'

'No, I never did.'

'Do you know if Mr. Cosgrove knew Mr. Appleby?'

'No, I really don't know if they knew each other.'

'Mrs. Ross, do you know if Mr. Cosgrove ever had children visit his home?'

'Yes, he had a lot of pet animals so quite a few children stopped by to play with the animals.'

'And did they come alone or with their parents?'

'Both, some with their parents mostly on weekends and some alone.'

'How many children per month would you say visited Mr. Cosgrove and his animals?'

'Well it would vary with the weather and the time of year but I would say it might average twelve different children per month, mostly they came on weekends.'

'And were the children boys or girls?'

'Both, probably in equal numbers.'

'Mrs. Ross, do you know if any of the visits by children ended with problems or parental complaints?'

'If there were any problems I was not aware of any.'

'Mrs. Ross, what was your impression of Mr. Cosgrove?'

'He was very hard working at his business and of course at tax time he had to work very long hours. Other than that he seemed a nice person and was a good neighbor.'

'Mrs. Ross, did you find his relationship with so many children odd?'

'Well, different in the sense that he was the only person in my acquaintance that invited so many children onto his property. As to his relationship with the children, I really don't know anything about that.'

'Thank you Mrs. Ross, no further questions.'

'Thank you Mr. O'Brien. Mr. Brandywell any questions on redirect?'

'Only one your honor, Mrs. Ross, from your personal experience, how did Mr. Cosgrove interact with the children who visited him and his animals?'

'Well, I have two children under ten years old and they visited Mr. Cosgrove and his pets on several occasions, some of the time I was with them. He always seemed polite and very patient. He loved his pets and would let the children help feed them. The children loved their visits.'

'I have no further questions for this witness your honor.'

'Fine Mrs. Ross, you may step down.'

'Mr. Brandywell please call your next witness.'

'Your honor, the prosecution calls to the stand Mr. George Rankin (after the swearing in of Mr. Rankin). Your honor the questioning of Mr. Rankin will be conducted by Mr. Eugene Harrison, Assistant Commonwealth Attorney.'

'Very well, Mr. Harrison please proceed.'

'Mr. Rankin please tell the court your full name?'

'George Hobart Rankin.'

'Where do you reside?'

'On the Old Waterford Road just outside the Leesburg town limits.'

'What is your occupation?'

'Well, I am retired for the last four years from the Potomac Electric Power Company (PEPCO).'

'Did you know the deceased, Wilbur Cosgrove?'

'Yes, quite well, he was my neighbor for many years.'

'Where is your house in relation to the Cosgrove's home?'

'I am about one hundred fifty to one hundred seventy-five yards away on the opposite side of the road.'

'Were you home on Wednesday twenty-eight June last between one p.m. and three p.m.?'

'Yes, I was working in my front yard cultivating around some flower beds.'

'Did you hear or see anything strange around the Cosgrove's home between one p.m. and three p.m. on twenty-eight June?'

'I did, around two p.m. or a little after I heard some loud voices arguing.'

'Could you make out who the people were who were arguing and what they were saying?'

'Well one voice was definitely that of Wilbur Cosgrove, the other voice I didn't recognize. Mr. Cosgrove was being accused of something because he kept saying I didn't do it.'

'Did you pick-up on what he was being accused of doing?'

'No, not exactly but I heard the other person call him a filthy faggot and a pervert; then about two fifteen or twenty p.m. I heard a shotgun blast.'

'How do you know it was a shotgun blast as opposed to a rifle or pistol gunshot?'

'Well, I own both a shotgun and a rifle so I pretty much know the different sound they make when fired.'

'Can you describe the voice of the person arguing with Mr. Cosgrove?'

'Well, I can tell you first off it was a very angry voice and a very high pitched shrill voice.'

'And would you say this was a man or woman's voice?'

'I couldn't be absolutely sure as shrill and high pitched as it was it could have been either because the person was very agitated or the voice was screaming.'

'And after the shotgun blast what did you hear?'

'Well, nothing for quite a few minutes then I heard Mrs. Cosgrove screaming; help, help, Wilbur's been shot.'

'And what did you do then?'

'I ran over to the Cosgrove's property. As I left my driveway my neighbor across the street, Mrs. Ross, was coming around the side of her house to the front gate. I waited for her and we ran together to Cosgrove's.'

'Then what happened?'

'Just as we arrived Sheriff Dunn and Deputy Broomfield arrived in a police cruiser. Deputy Broomfield held us back and Sheriff Dunn ran down to one of the storage buildings in the back garden.'

'Then what happened?'

'The ambulance arrived and Deputy Broomfield waved them down the Cosgrove driveway. We stayed at the mouth of the driveway talking to Deputy Broomfield.'

'Did Deputy Broomfield tell you anything about what was happening?'

'Yes, he was very polite and said Sheriff Dunn had told him not to let anyone down the driveway except the ambulance, that they might have a crime scene on their hands.'

'Then what happened?'

'Well they brought out Mr. Cosgrove on a stretcher and put him in the ambulance. They drove up the driveway and I looked in as they slowed to turn out on the road. Mr. Cosgrove looked dead to me.'

'Anything else happen of significance?'

'Not really, Deputy Broomfield was called by Sheriff Dunn and was evidently told to start roping off the area which he did quickly with some bright yellow tape that said crime scene on it.'

'What did you do then?'

'Nothing really, my wife Kitty had come-up by that time and Mrs. Ross; my wife and I talked for a few minutes about the shocking and sad event. We didn't see Mrs. Cosgrove. I think she was talking to Sheriff Dunn, so we couldn't comfort her. After awhile we just went home; word must have spread fast because when we got home people started to ring us to find out what happened.'

'Do you know Mr. Frank Appleby?'

'Yes, I have known him for years.'

'Did you see him on the day of the murder around the Cosgrove's home?'

'No, I never did see Frank up this way. I guess he doesn't have any customers out here.'

'Did Frank Appleby ever work for Mr. Cosgrove?'

'No, I don't think so, the Cosgrove's were both keen gardeners they did all their own garden work.'

'Did you see anyone else around the Cosgrove's property on the day of the murder?'

'No, not a soul.'

'How about children?'

'No, never saw any children either.'

'I have no further questions your honor.'

'Fine, Mr. O'Brien, your witness.'

'Mr. Rankin, how well do you know Mr. Appleby?'

'Fairly well, we go to the same church. Oh, I'd say I've known him since we were in elementary school together.'

'And you testified that Frank never comes out your way and certainly was not there on the day of the murder?'

'That's correct, I was working outside almost all day and I never saw him.'

'Now I want to ask you about the second voice, you heard the one that was shrill, high pitched and very agitated. Could that have been the voice of Frank Appleby?'

'Well, I suppose anything is possible but no it didn't sound like Frank's voice at all. Plus, I never saw or heard Frank Appleby angry in his life.'

'Thank you Mr. Rankin, no further questions.'

'Mr. Harrison, any redirect?'

'Yes your honor.'

'Please proceed.'

'Mr. Rankin, under the circumstances that Frank's only son Frankie was molested, could that have made him agitated and angry?'

'Well, I suppose it could, it would have made me angry.'

'No further questions your honor.'

'Fine, court will adjourn for today. We will resume this trial as usual promptly at nine a.m. tomorrow.'

Patrick and Liam were fairly pleased with the third day of the trial. The prosecution had been able to produce two witnesses to the argument between the murdered man and his probable assailant and to the gunshot but neither witness could place Frank Appleby at the crime scene. This testimony had been consistent with Jim Brogan's investigation. Thus far there had been no surprises.

Liam and Patrick agreed to meet at Liam's office at eight p.m. to review their strategy for tomorrow. Kelly, who had sat again with Irving Johnson throughout the third day walked with Patrick back to the office. When they arrived both Kelly and Patrick wanted to go to his office, lock the door and make love. Patrick guessed Heather knew what was going on but he also knew she was very discreet. However, he wasn't quite ready to announce his intentions toward Kelly to Pritch. He was therefore delighted to learn the General, Dan Rivers, had called Pritch to Richmond for consultations. Pritch had left shortly after arriving at nine a.m. He had loaded up his briefcase with police reports and information on the international child pornography ring and told Heather not to expect him back until late tomorrow evening.

Patrick told Heather to hold all calls and book appointments for any clients as Kelly and he would be reviewing trial strategy for tomorrow. After Patrick locked his office door, both he and Kelly acted as happy as two children mysteriously locked in a chocolate factory for the night. This time Kelly wanted more than a bend over job. She slowly and provocatively undressed in front of Patrick. Patrick watched intently so much so that he was slow to undress himself. Kelly pulled out the yellow sofa bed as Patrick watched her bend and stretch in awe. When she was done she lay down and beckoned him to join her. Patrick gladly obeyed.

After their sexual tryst was over they collapsed in each others arms and held each other for a full ten minutes before Kelly got up and went to the bathroom. When she returned she dressed quickly. When Patrick got up to go to the bathroom Kelly folded up the lemon yellow sofa bed. Finally, when they got themselves together, Kelly asked Patrick, 'do you think I earned the right to move my toothbrush in?' Patrick replied, 'you can move anything you want in as long as your beautiful ass comes in the bargain.' They laughed, hugged but no kisses as Kelly had just refreshed her lipstick. Patrick unlocked the door and Kelly left. The office was hot and sticky and smelled like sex. Patrick opened the window and praised the fact that it let light in but faced the brick wall of the building next door. He had cursed that feature when he moved in, now he loved the privacy.

# Thirty

JUDGE Draper seemed somewhat irritated when he entered the courtroom at 9:20 a.m. on the forth day of trial. He had been informed one of the jurors had telephoned that he was caught in traffic and would be a little late. Judge Draper addressed the jury; 'today we are starting a little late because one of the jurors was caught in traffic. I understand these types of occurrences do happen and sometimes they are beyond our control, however, I would ask each of you to do everything possible to avoid these types of occurrences in the future. If this means leaving your homes earlier, please do so to guard against such eventualities'. Norris Green, the late juror sunk down in the jury box and hung his head. His failure to arrive on time had been noted and duly admonished even if the warning had been a general one addressed to all jurors.

Having laid down the law on tardiness, Judge Draper seemed to cheer up slightly.

'Mr. Brandywell, will the prosecution call your next witness?'

'Yes your honor, the prosecution calls to the stand Mr. Ralph Hightower.'

After being sworn the direct questioning of Mr. Hightower began. Again, Mr. Harrison conducted the examination.

'Please state for the court your full name.'

'Ralph Edward Hightower.'

'And where do you reside Mr. Hightower?'

'2324 Cherry Orchard Lane, Ashburn, Virginia.'

'And where are you employed?'

'In the gun department of Sears Roebuck in the Hunting Chase Mall in Chantilly, Virginia.'

'And do you recall selling a shotgun to Mr. Frank Appleby about one year ago this month?'

'Yes, I do.'

'You must meet many customers in a day's time, how is it you recall Mr. Appleby from one year ago?'

'Well, I don't remember everyone, sadly, even though I try to but Mr. Appleby was different.'

'How was he different?'

'Well, he was what I would call a cautious and thoughtful purchaser. He took a long time to make a decision and he asked me to show him many shotguns and he asked a lot of questions before he decided. I wasn't busy at the time and I was able to spend a lot of time with him.'

'What type of questions did he ask?'

'Mostly technical questions about the operation of the various guns. I think the price of a good shotgun kind of shocked him and I think all the questions were an attempt on his part to justify the price, so I showed him where the quality was built into the better guns.'

'And in the end what price and type of gun did Mr. Appleby purchase?'

'Well, he didn't buy the most expensive or least expensive gun. He paid three hundred eighty-nine dollars for a good serviceable Remington pump action shotgun which fell somewhere in the middle.'

'Give the court a sense of the price range of shotguns which you carry.'

'We have one very special shotgun; a real collector's item which retails for fifteen hundred ninety-nine dollars. However, the great bulk of our shotguns start at about one hundred seventy-nine and go up to six hundred ninety-nine.'

'And did you ask Mr. Appleby what he wanted to use the shotgun for?'

'Yes, the subject came up when Mr. Appleby purchased ammunition. I asked Mr. Appleby if he wanted birdshot for shooting; ducks, pheasant, partridge, etc. He answered no; he only wanted the gun for protection, particularly for protecting his wife and children.'

'Did you find this unusual?'

'No, not really, although pistols are normally the largest sellers for protection because they are easier to carry.'

'But shotguns would be even more menacing, would they not?'

'Well, all guns can kill, it's just that shotguns at close range really can't miss as there are so many pellets in one shell, whereas you have to aim a pistol more carefully or you could miss.'

'Would you call a shotgun an extremely dangerous weapon?'

'All guns can be dangerous in the wrong hangs but certainly not too many people are going to argue with a man with a shotgun at close quarters.'

'So a shotgun is a pretty potent weapon?'

'At close range, very potent.'

'Let's get back to what Mr. Appleby told you about protecting his family.'

'He said if anybody attacked his wife or children he would have no trouble using the shotgun on them. He left me in no doubt that he would use the shotgun if the necessity ever arose.'

'Did Mr. Appleby mention anyone in particular he might use the gun on?'

'Oh no, no one was mentioned specifically, only if a real threat to his family arose.'

'And Mr. Hightower, do you recognize prosecution exhibit number seven, the sales records on the shotgun?'

"Yes sir, I do.'

'And what was the serial number of the shotgun you sold Mr. Appleby?'

'The serial number is; FAK 197329463.'

'Your honor, we submit this record as court exhibit number seven.'

'No further questions for Mr. Hightower at this time your honor.'

'Mr. O'Brien, your witness.'

'Mr. Hightower, did Mr. Appleby tell you where he intended to store the shotgun?'

'Yes, he said he thought he would keep it near to where he slept in case of a break-in at night.'

'Was a break-in at night what Mr. Appleby feared?'

'Yes, that's the gist of what I understood?'

'Was Mr. Appleby unique in his fear of a break-in during night-time?'

'Oh no, this is probably why we sell fifty percent of our guns.'

'And would both men and women have this fear of night-time break-ins?'

'Oh yes, women living alone are very afraid of night-time break-ins but just as many men are too.'

'Did Mr. Appleby ever mention to you that he intended to protect his family outside his home with the shotgun?'

'No, he didn't.'

'And you stated earlier a pistol could be easily transported and hence better protection outside the home?'

'Yes, that's right, far better for more varied use.'

'Now, Mr. Hightower, did Mr. Appleby ever state to you that he would use the shotgun outside his home?'

'No, he didn't say anything about where he would or wouldn't use it.'

'And he never indicated anyone he wanted to hurt?'

'Certainly not, if he had I wouldn't have sold him the gun and would have called the police.'

'And you wouldn't have sold him the gun if you thought him a risk to any member of the public?'

'Certainly not.'

'No further questions your honor.'

'Mr. Brandywell, any questions on redirect?'

'Only one your honor?'

'Was Mr. Appleby checked by the police prior to buying the shotgun?'

'No, he wasn't. If he had purchased a handgun he would have but not for a shotgun.'

'Thank you Mr. Hightower, no further questions your honor.'

'Alright Mr. Brandywell, please call your next witness.'

'The prosecution calls to the stand Mr. Stanley Ward.'

After being duly sworn the questioning commenced this time by Assistant Commonwealth Attorney, Mr. Bruce Rodgers.

'Mr. Ward, what is your full name?'

'Stanley John Ward.'

'And where do you reside?'

'At 1593 South King Street, Leesburg, Virginia.'

'And do you know the accused, Mr. Frank Appleby?'

'Yes, I do.'

'How do you know Mr. Appleby, are you a friend?'

'Well, I suppose I am a friend although we don't visit at each others houses or anything like that. I really know Frank because we play cards together every Monday evening.'

'During these Monday evening card games, what subjects do you discuss?'

'Well, everything really; current affairs, politics, sports, local news.'

'And how many persons are in your card game?'

'Well, there are four regulars; Frank, myself, Harry Bennett, and Roy Harris. Then we have two substitutes who fill-in if there is an illness or someone is on vacation, etc.'

'And do you play year around?'

'Yes, fifty-two weeks per year without fail.'

'Do you gamble at these card games?'

'No not really, it's only penny anty stuff; we bet ten cents each per hand. The total pot seldom goes over four or five dollars. It's not serious gambling, just enough to say we played for something.'

'And did you ever discuss crime and possible self-defense?'

'Oh yes, on quite a few occasions, particularly if there was a rash of house break-ins. Then we all got a little spooked.'

'And did Frank Appleby have any views on the subject?'

'Yes, he told us he had purchased a shotgun for protection and said he would use it straight away if anyone broke into his house at night or harmed his wife or children.'

'And did you believe him when he made that statement?'

'Sure, Frank never lies, if he said that's what he would do, then that's what he would do.'

'And did Frank Appleby indicate he would use the gun to defend his family outside the family home?'

'No, Frank never got specific about where he would use the gun but he left us in no doubt he would defend his family if they were threatened.'

'Your honor, I have no further questions for this witness on direct but would like to reserve the witness for redirect.'

'Thank you Mr. Rodgers, your witness Mr. O'Brien.'

'Thank you your honor. Mr. Ward, you testified that after a rash of break-ins in the area Frank Appleby indicated he would use his shotgun as a defense to protect his family if someone broke into his home in the night-time?'

'Yes sir, that's true.'

'Mr. Ward, that sounds a reasonable statement that many men would make, isn't it?'

'Oh yes sir.'

'Mr. Ward, do you own a gun?'

'Yes I do.'

'What type of firearm do you own?'

'A pistol. Had it for years.'

'And where do you keep your pistol Mr. Ward?'

'I keep it right in the top drawer of my bedside table"

'Do you have a license for your pistol?'

'Well, not a license, but I was cleared by the police before I could purchase it. I guess I checked out ok because a few days later the gun shop telephoned me and told me I could come in and collect my handgun.'

'During your card game, did you make any statements about protecting your family if there was a night-time break-in at your home?'

'Objection your honor, what Mr. Ward said is irrelevant to this case.'

'Overruled, I am going to instruct Mr. Ward to answer that question as it is relevant to the nature of the conversation that took place.'

'I said the exact same thing that Frank said, in fact, we all did. We all felt the same.'

'And Mr. Ward, please explain more fully to the court how you felt.'

'Well, if anyone broke into my house at night, I would figure they were very dangerous and would use my pistol to stop them.'

'Now, Mr. Ward, was it only in the context of night-time break-ins that all these statements regarding the potential use of firearms were made?'

'Yes, that's true.'

'Mr. Ward, was there any mention of the use of firearms for self or family defense outside the specific context of night-time break-ins?'

'No, that's true, our conversation centered around night-time break-ins only.'

'I have no further questions your honor. Your witness Mr. Rodgers.'

'Mr. Ward, you previously testified that Mr. Appleby was a man who didn't lie and who said if his wife or children were threatened he would use his shotgun to protect them, did you not?'

'Yes sir, that's true.'

'So do you think Mr. Ward that Mr. Appleby would have used his shotgun to defend his family outside the family home?'

'Objection you honor. Mr. Rodgers is asking the witnesses to comment on pure conjecture outside the original conversation?'

'Sustained. I instruct you Mr. Ward not to answer that question.'

'No further questions your honor.'

'Alright then Mr. Rodgers, call your next prosecution witness.'

'Your honor, the prosecution calls to the stand Mr. Roy Harris.'

After being duly sworn Mr. Harris was questioned again by Mr. Bruce Rodgers.

'Mr. Harris, would you state your full name for the court?'

During the questioning of Roy Harris, Patrick was sitting at the defense table doing what he had done basically throughout the trial, monitoring the proceedings, making copious notes and attempting to assist Liam by making suggestions where he thought appropriate. He was quite happy to let Liam handle the cross examinations and further learn his profession from a more experienced trial lawyer. They had agreed that Patrick would concentrate on the opening and closing statements, the emotional appeals, while Liam would handle the bulk of the cross and later direct questioning. So far Liam had done extremely well ameliorating to a great extent much of the impact of the evidence the prosecution had attempted to place before the court. As Bruce Rodgers continued the direct questioning of Roy Harris it was obvious Liam was going to have a difficult time cross examining Harris. Roy Harris was a sour man who was aggressive and belligerent. He had testified in no uncertain terms that Frank Appleby had stated he would kill anyone who touched his children. In so doing Harris had gone much further with his damning testimony than Stanley Ward. Patrick anticipated that Liam would have a much more difficult job getting Harris to soften his testimony than he had with Ward. Frank Appleby's card playing friends were of course under oath but it was fairly obvious that they were not as kindly disposed toward Frank as the team had expected they would be. Patrick had been watching Frank during the testimony of Ward and Harris and he looked distraught. It was patently clear he felt betrayed by their evidence.

The prosecution was winding up their case and the defense team had felt they hadn't presented much of a case. The problem was the defense had even less. They intended to use the character witnesses again that they had successfully utilized at the bail hearing. Deputy Sheriff Wayne Broomfield had agreed to testify that neither Frank nor his truck had been seen around the crime scene on the day of the murder. This was already in evidence and Wayne's testimony would only serve to solidify that fact in the minds of the jurors, particularly as Wayne would be in uniform and it was already in testimony that he had responded to Mrs. Cosgrove's emergency call with the sheriff. Sheriff Dunn had no problem with Wayne testifying for the defense which indicated to the defense team that the police were not convinced Frank Appleby had killed Wilbur Cosgrove. The most convincing witness the defense had was an employee of the forensic laboratory that examined

Frank's work clothes who would testify there was no blood spray found on the garments. Finally, they had their own forensic scientist, Dr. Rey, who would also testify about the shotgun, fingerprints and blood sprays, etc. The team felt their total defense would only take from two to two and one half days. Collectively, they were hoping they had enough to tip the scales but there was no doubt in any of the team members' minds that Patrick would have to make the closing statement of his life if they were to win.

Patrick had noted Kelly had been sitting in the courtroom with Irving Johnson and today Fiona O'Brien, Liam's wife, had joined them. About twenty minutes ago, Kelly had received a telephone call and rushed out of the courtroom. Patrick had noted her departure out of the corner of his left eye and had wondered what that was all about. About fifteen minutes later Kelly returned and rushed directly to the defense counsel's table, whispering in Patrick's ear that Jim Brogan had come out of the coma and was calling for Patrick. Patrick scribbled a note to Liam, 'Jim out of comma and calling for me. Must go with Kelly to hospital immediately.' He quickly packed his gear and followed Kelly out of the courtroom noting Judge Draper's interest had been peaked by his quick departure and was staring at him as he moved away.

On the short walk to the hospital, Kelly filled him in that she had received a call on the mobile from Heather. Kathleen, Jim's wife, had telephone in an excited condition and said that Jim had come out of the coma and was pleading with her to get Patrick. Additionally, Pritch had received word that the Attorney General, Dan Rivers, was to hold a major news conference in Leesburg tomorrow at twelve noon. As Patrick took all this in they rushed on toward the Loudoun Memorial Hospital.

When they arrived in Jim's room, Kathleen and her daughter were both smiling but also crying tears of happiness. Kathleen hugged Patrick and said, 'he's back, Jim's back, it's a miracle. Patrick sat on the bed next to Jim and Jim reached out a feeble but very alive hand. The muscles in his once strong arms had atrophied but the physiotherapist had been doing her best to keep Jim halfway flexible. Now that he could answer her and push against her force, Jim would recover his muscular strength faster.

'Good to see you back partner, what happened?'

'Oh, I made a big mistake Patrick. They suckered me out to the cemetery at White's Ferry on the pretense they would give me information about who killed Wilbur Cosgrove.'

'And they hit you from behind?'

'Yes, I entered the small graveyard and saw the figure of a man at the back of the cemetery up near the tree line. He was smoking and I saw his face in the dim light. As I approached him his partner must have clubbed me from behind. I don't remember anything after that.'

'They got them Jim, they're in the county jail here in Leesburg but they deny they killed Wilbur Cosgrove. The police interviewed them for days but were unable to break them. They are sticking to their story that Wilbur Cosgrove was alive when they left him. I am convinced the FBI and police believe their story.'

'I'm glad they caught them but that's not what I wanted to tell you.'

'No, I gather you have big news?'

'Yes, earlier in the day before I went to the cemetery I found an eye witness that can confirm that on the day of Wilbur Cosgrove's murder, Frank Appleby never left the Granger's back garden.'

'If that's true Jim, that's going to free Frank.'

'I certainly hope so Patrick. I found this elderly man Mr. Ralph Johnson. He lives in his daughter and son-in law's house in an upstairs apartment they created for him. On the day of Wilbur Cosgrove's murder, he was sitting looking out his bedroom window which overlooks the Granger's back garden. He said he watched Frank work all day and he never left Granger's, even eating his lunch there just as Frank said.'

'But all day, how can he testify he looked out all day, is that reasonable?'

'In this case, yes, Mr. Johnson is eighty-nine and fairly immobile. He can walk but doesn't move around much. But the ringer is his wife died on the twenty-eighth day of June five years previously and he stated he sat there and mourned her passing from sun-up to sun-down, never leaving his chair.'

'Wow, this is the break we had prayed for. How on earth did you find him?'

'Strangely enough, it was just plain old police work. I had called at the house and interviewed both the husband and wife, Mr. and Mrs. Russell. Luckily, the husband was off work that day. I was just about to leave when I remembered to ask if anyone else lived in the house. Mrs. Russell said her father lived in the apartment upstairs. She took me up.

He was in his bedroom in his favorite chair looking out the window. When I approached Mr. Johnson I could see the Granger's back garden clearly through his window and knew I was on to something.'

'Jim, unless I miss my guess, your routine police work is going to save Frank's life.'

'I hope so Patrick. Kathleen, I am starving, do you know when they will bring my lunch?'

'Darling, I don't know but I will get them to hurry, after all they have been feeding you through tubes for so long they owe you a lot of meals!'

Everybody laughed and Patrick and Kelly left to return to court. When they arrived court had been adjourned and Liam was packing-up.

'How did it go with Roy Harris?'

'Not as good as I had hoped for. I tried to break him down into a softer posture but he wouldn't budge much. Some friend to Frank.'

'Was Frank upset?'

'Yes, of course. How's Jim?'

'Well, let me make your day. Jim is fully out of the coma and roaring for food, but more important, before he was assaulted he found an eyewitness who will swear that he watched Frank work and eat lunch in Granger's back garden.'

'Who is our angel?'

'He's an old man who lives in an apartment on the second floor of his daughter and son-in-law's house. His name is Ralph Johnson.'

'Any relation to Irving?'

'I don't know, forgot to ask in my excitement, we will ask Irving.'

'How old is Mr. Johnson?'

'Jim says eighty-nine but he has all his faculties, just doesn't walk very fast.'

'We can live with slow walking and right talking.'

'Another bit of news. Pritch says the general will hold a big news conference tomorrow at twelve noon.'

'You had better handle that while I continue to deal with the prosecution. I think they may have another witness although nobody else is on their list of witnesses they gave us.'

'Maybe you should talk to Judge Draper and Mr. Brandywell , tell them we have a new witness too and see what arrangements can be made since both sides have a new witness not previously announced.'

'Ok, consider that done, but I am extremely worried about their mystery witness.'

'I am too, I will see if Kelly can dig up anything with the help of Wayne Broomfield.'

'Ok, see if the general reveals anything that will help us?'

'Right, I will be with you in the morning and will leave court around eleven-forty-five a.m. and return as soon as the press conference finishes. Keep the faith we're going to win.'

'Right, see you in the morning.'

Patrick decided there wouldn't be any activity on the yellow sofa-bed tonight. It was time Kelly was introduced to the house in Neersville. He had continued to pay the rent each month to Ralph and Eleanor Harrington even though he hadn't set foot on the premises since Cindy left. He hadn't even gone back for clothes as he had enough at the office to survive. As they drove out towards Hillsboro he was turning in his mind how he would handle the situation with the Harrington's. They obviously knew that Cindy had left him and filed for divorce. He decided honesty was the best policy. So when they arrived at the Harrington's he took Kelly immediately to the main house to meet Ralph and Eleanor. The Harrington's were as warm and friendly as ever. Ralph asked how the trial was going while Eleanor showed Kelly through their house. Patrick had intended to tell the Harrington's about his and Kelly's relationship but under the circumstances they made matters easy and no explanation seemed necessary. When they left Ralph and Eleanor wished Patrick well with the trial and told Kelly they hoped to see her often. It was evident the Harrington's were people who understood life and human relationships and were very tolerant of others feelings. Good for them Patrick thought and they shot-up even further in his estimation. As they parted Eleanor gave Kelly some milk, bread, eggs and butter, which was a much appreciated gesture.

Patrick then took Kelly to the cottage. Kelly loved the house and she started to feel comfortable and at home almost immediately. They had a bottle of wine and opened a tinned can of spaghetti and heated it up. It wasn't haute cuisine but they were happy to be together. They watched t.v. and went to bed early. They talked long about the day's spectacular events and fell asleep in each others embrace. Sex was not a feature; it could wait for another night.

# Thirty One

PATRICK arose early as was his habit. He shaved, showered and dressed quickly and set about making some coffee, toast and eggs for Kelly and himself. She was impressed as she stumbled into the living room with only her bra and thong panties on. However, with the promise of food she dressed quickly and joined Patrick at the table. All and all her introduction to the house in Neersville and their landlords, the Harrington's, had been a great success. Kelly was happy, Patrick was pleased and they quickly agreed they would set-up house together in Neersville and abandon the yellow sofa-bed unless the practice called for a long night of work where they were too tired to drive. Cindy's name was never mentioned and any hold she had on the Neersville house seemed long ago dissipated.

When the trial promptly progressed at nine a.m. as usual John Brandywell called to the stand a Mr. John Bentley. Mr. Bentley appeared in leisure clothes but with no tip off as to who he was. Liam asked if he could approach the bench. When Judge Draper indicated his approval, Liam told the judge that Mr. Bentley was not on the list of witnesses supplied to the defense. Mr. Brandywell apologized to the court but indicated that Mr. Bentley was a witness that possessed very relevant information concerning the murder and his existence and the nature of his knowledge had just come to light to the prosecution. Liam asked if the judge would meet with opposing counsels in his chamber for a few moments as the defense had a similar situation where a key witness had just been identified and maybe both matters could be handled at the same time. Judge Draper agreed and recessed the court for thirty minutes. Once in his chamber, Judge Draper threw off his gown and asked his secretary to serve coffee all around. Bruce Rodgers joined John Brandywell in the conference and both Liam and Patrick were present.

'Alright gentlemen, who are these new witnesses; John, maybe you would like to start us off and tell us about Mr. John Bentley?'

'Certainly your honor, Mr. Bentley is a plumber by trade who was recently in the county jail for a few days during the time Mr. Appleby was confined.'

'And very generally what will he testify to?'

'He will tell the court of certain conversations he had with Mr. Appleby during the recreation periods.'

'And are these conversations relevant to this case?'

'Oh yes your honor, very relevant.'

'Mr. O'Brien, what new witness for the defense do you have?'

'We have a gentleman, Mr. Johnson, who will be able to shed some light on the whereabouts of Mr. Frank Appleby on the day of the murder. His existence just came to light when our private investigator, Mr. Jim Brogan, came out of his coma today and informed us of the knowledge of this witness.'

'And will Mr. Johnson's testimony be relevant to this trial?'

'Absolutely your honor.'

'Then does anyone have any objections to the introduction of these witnesses?'

Both John Brandywell and Liam O'Brien had objections but both remained silent for fear their objections, if voiced, might jeopardize the introduction of their witness.

'Alright gentlemen, if there are no objections I will allow both these new witnesses to testify but I will hold you to your pledges that in both cases their testimony will be relevant. By the way, I am delighted to hear Mr. Brogan is out of his coma. Will you see to it Mr. O'Brien that you send him my best regards for a speedy recovery from this point onward?'

'Thank you your honor, we will. We know your good wishes will mean a lot to Jim.'

'Fine, Mr. Brandywell will you be handling the direct of Mr. Bentley?'

'I will your honor.'

'Fine, Mr. Brandywell, let's go back and get started.'

It was obvious that both sides were apprehensive even though they were putting on brave faces. The idea of last minute mystery witnesses was always unsettling. The defense was probably the most fearful simply because they had to face the testimony first. John Brandywell obviously had something up his sleeve, but what? Both Liam and Patrick knew John Brandywell would want to end the prosecution's case with a real flourish.

After Mr. Bentley was sworn John Brandywell started the questioning.

'State for the court Mr. Bentley your full name.'

'John Robert Bentley.'

'And where do you reside?'

'Strawberry Hills Drive, Hamilton, Virginia.'

'And what is your occupation?'

'Plumbing contractor.'

'And how long have you resided in Loudoun County?'

'All my life, I was born here.'

'And do you know the accused, Mr. Frank Appleby?'

'Sure, I know Frank.'

'And did you have occasion to talk to Frank Appleby recently?'

'Yes, I did a few weeks ago.'

'Explain to the court the circumstances surrounding that conversation.'

'Well, I was spending a few days in jail for driving while intoxicated and I talked to Frank during the recreation period. The young guys were playing basketball and Frank and I were walking around the yard together.'

'And what exactly was said between you?'

'Well, I asked Frank point blank if he killed Wilbur Cosgrove?'

'And what was Mr. Appleby's reply?'

'He didn't answer for a long time, then he said, John, that man was a bad man you know he raped my little Frankie. He was a real bad man, he needed killing before he hurt other little children and destroyed their lives.'

'And was he serious when he made that statement?'

'Oh, dead serious.'

'And what did you reply?'

'I told Frank he was right, that kind of man we didn't need or want in our community.'

'Was anything else said between you?'

'Not much, it wasn't too long after that they took us back to our cells.'

'And do you know the date of this conversation?'

'Well, I would have to look at a calendar to tell you the exact date but I was only in for a Saturday, Sunday and Monday and the conversation took place on a Monday about the first week in July.'

'Thank you Mr. Bentley, no further questions at this time.'

'Mr. O'Brien, your witness.'

'Thank you your honor. Mr. Bentley you testified that when you asked Frank Appleby point blank if he killed Wilbur Cosgrove there was a long pause?'

'Yes sir, that's right.'

'How long would you estimate that pause was?'

'Well, you know I don't really know but it seemed a real long-time, maybe fifteen seconds or so. I know we were able to walk quite a distance on in silence.'

'Mr. Appleby never answered your question Mr. Bentley, did he?'

'Well, only in a fashion.'

'Mr. Appleby never said he killed Mr. Cosgrove, did he?'

'No, he didn't.'

'He just said he was a bad man who had to be stopped before he hurt other children, isn't that right?'

'Objection your honor, counsel is leading the witness.'

'Sustained, please rephrase your question Mr. O'Brien and try not to lead the witness.'

'Yes your honor, Mr. Bentley let me rephrase my question; was it your testimony that Mr. Appleby said Mr. Cosgrove had raped his son Frankie and was a bad man who had to be stopped before he hurt other children?'

'Yes sir, that's correct.'

'And did you generally agree with that statement?'

'Yes sir, absolutely.'

'And you didn't kill anyone or say you were going to kill anyone, did you?'

'Oh, no sir.'

'And Mr. Appleby didn't say he killed anyone, did he?'

'No sir, he only said Wilbur Cosgrove needed killing, he didn't say he had killed him.'

'You recognize the difference between an admission of guilt for killing someone and a general statement that someone is so bad they needed killing, don't you?'

'Oh, yes sir, I do recognize the difference.'

'Thank you, no further questions.'

'Your honor, a couple of questions on redirect.'

'Mr. Bentley, did Mr. Appleby tell you the name of another person who he thought killed Wilbur Cosgrove?'

'No sir, he didn't.'

'Mr. Bentley, do you think it is normal to go around saying people need to be killed?'

'Oh no sir.'

'Mr. Bentley, do you ever recall any other person telling you someone needed to be killed?'

'No, not really. Well, maybe my daddy said that about Hitler when he was a soldier in the Second World War, but no, I never heard it since.'

'Is it proper language to talk about someone needing killing?'

'No sir, I don't think so.'

'Thank you Mr. Bentley, no further questions.'

'Alright Mr. Brandywell, call your next witness.'

'The prosecution rests your honor.'

'Alright, since that completes the Commonwealth's case, I am going to adjourn court for today and ask the defense to be prepared to start their case in the morning at nine a.m. as usual.'

Patrick and Liam were delighted as this would allow Liam to join the others at the general's press conference. They packed-up quickly and proceeded next door to the Juvenile and Domestic Relations Court which had been made available for the press conference as the presiding judge, Judge Ryan Gossett was away at a two day judicial conference in Richmond. Pritch had made sure all the necessary dignitaries had been invited . All the mayors of Loudoun towns were there including of course the mayor of Leesburg. Jeremy Ricketts, Loudoun's Delegate to the House of Delegates was present and had been asked to chair the press conference. Sheriff Dunn was there as were representatives of the; FBI, Virginia State Police and police departments of all of Loudoun's incorporated towns. Hillsboro, Virginia's smallest town had no police but the mayor had brought along three members of the town council plus the water commissioner to make sure Hillsboro would not be forgotten. Even the mayor of the city of Winchester, atop the Shenandoah Valley, was present as was Winchester's police chief. With all the police brass there in uniform, it added to the color and seriousness of the occasion. Of course the press was there in astounding numbers. The print media and radio stations were well represented but it was the T.V. journalists with their camera crews and large lights that really made an impact. The entire defense team save Jim Brogan and Roland Alberts were present, although they had to fight the scrum to enter the rather small, intimate courtroom. The district and circuit courtrooms were larger but not available. Judge Draper's courtroom was now empty although that fact was not known in time. Sinclair Munro, the Clerk of the Circuit Court suggested to Delegate Ricketts to move into the larger old circuit courtroom that Judge Draper had just vacated. The general was agreeable so the entire entourage was moved. The T.V. crews were put out as they had the most equipment to carry. The defense team ended up back in the same courtroom they had just left. Sinclair Munro looked greatly relieved as the chief of the Loudoun County fire department had obviously raised total hell about the overcrowding. After about fifteen minutes the move was accomplished.

Delegate Ricketts commenced by first apologizing to everyone for the inconvenience of the move and thanking everyone for their cooperation, particularly the T.V. crews who had so much equipment to move. This statement seemed to pacify the T.V. people and almost certainly, after the Attorney General himself, insured Delegate Ricketts would get honorable mention on the six p.m. and nine p.m. news. Delegate Ricketts then welcomed every local politician and police chief by name before welcoming the Attorney General of the Commonwealth back to Loudoun County. He reviewed briefly the important announcement that the Attorney General had been able to make on his last visit to the county and how Loudoun County and its people appreciated his return to brief them and indeed the state and nation concerning the biggest paedophile ring bust in international history. Ricketts had done his job well and Dan Rivers seemed duly pleased as he strode to the microphone. Camera bulbs flashed and T.V. footage rolled.

Rivers looked more like a movie star than an attorney. He had a shock of snow white hair immaculately combed into place. He always carried a heavy layer of tan which contrasted perfectly with his white hair. Today, he was wearing a handsome grey striped three piece suit with a beautiful grey silk tie and matching handkerchief stylishly cascading out of his breast pocket. His black shoes were shined to perfection in military fashion, a habit Rivers had never lost from his years of military service. All in all he was by any reasonable judgement a class act and possessed presentation skills to match his impeccable appearance.

After the cameras had stopped flashing he started his presentation in a slow deliberate manner. 'I want to thank Delegate Ricketts for his kind introduction and to acknowledge the presence today of many mayors and police chiefs and police force members from Loudoun County and surrounding areas. I particularly want to thank the FBI, the Virginia State Police and Sheriff Dunn's Loudoun County Sheriff Department who have worked so assiduously to crack this international child pornography ring and bring the ringleaders to justice. Today, I am pleased to report to you that through the combined efforts of our local, state and national police forces working in close cooperation with Interpol and the Dutch police, the international child pornography ring has been crushed. Thousand of pictures and images exploiting young children, both boys and girls, have been confiscated. These young children, some as young as six years old, were forced to commit acts of oral sex or were raped or sodomized. Many of these children I am sad to report were forced by their own parents or guardians to submit to these violent and illegal acts. In other cases, young children were kidnapped for these specific deplorable purposes. Evidently, the child pornography ring had set-up an elaborate system of intricate passwords to access the child pornography on the Internet. Nevertheless, the Dutch police have captured thousands of credit card billing records where suspected paedophiles paid money for the opportunity to view and download child pornographic images from the Internet. I am very saddened to report to you that over thirty thousand of these paying customers are from the United States and there are over three hundred thousand worldwide. Two Hundred and seventy two suspects are from the Commonwealth of Virginia. Early this morning in a coordinated state-wide police effort over two hundred Virginia suspects were arrested in pre-dawn raids under, 'Operation Freechild'.'

'It is shocking that many of those arrested in Virginia today were people form nice homes, in attractive neighborhoods, who had responsible jobs. They represented many of the professions we have grown to respect. They are; doctors, lawyers, judges, government employees, businessmen, teachers, tradesmen, salespersons, clergy, social workers, etc. Each paid twenty-nine dollars to access these illegal images on the Internet. Sadly, behind each of these images on the Internet is an abused child whose life undoubtedly will be seriously scarred by this horrible exploitation. Right now we are going through hundreds of confiscated computers, computer discs, pieces of photographic equipment, books, video tapes, letters, invoices, etc. I can assure you those people who are guilty will be prosecuted to the full extent of the law. They run the gambit all the way from teenagers to those in their eighties. In many cases their spouses and family members had no idea what they were up to and I sympathize with those who did no wrong but will be shamed by the actions of their loved ones. I can tell you the sinister kidnapping and exploitation of children is far worse than even hardened vice-squad police officers had ever expected.'

'Medical and applied psychologists have indicated to my office that the intent of those viewing and downloading these images from the internet is to feed their sexual fantasies for the express purpose of facilitating masturbation. Research tells us that one out of every five individuals who downloads child pornography from the Internet actually also abuses one or more children. Normally, the more pictures downloaded the more dangerous the individual. I bring this statistic up to show that there is no such thing as a mild form of child pornography. It also should be mentioned that it was once thought paedophilia was a rare perversion. This evidently is not correct and this activity is much more serious and widespread than previously thought. Additionally, I should point out these paedophiles are highly manipulative people who are often very well resourced.'

In addition to viewing and downloading child pornography from the Internet many paedophiles are utilizing young peoples' chat rooms to groom children for future sexual exploitation. This is an evil activity that we must stop. My office is currently working on new draft legislation that will soon be introduced in the state legislature. Already many of our leading delegates and senators, including I might mention Delegate Ricketts, have agreed in advance to co-sponsor this legislation. I appreciate greatly the assistance my office is receiving in this regard.'

'Now I would like to open the news conference for questions.'

'Mr. Attorney General, you talked about the abuse of young peoples' chat rooms on the Internet, can you explain how that works?'

'First, I would like to state that I am not an expert in this area but the experts who have researched this abuse advise me of the following. The vast majority of young people who use these chat room services enjoy the opportunity to talk to new people their age and make new friends. To this extent the chat rooms serve a valid purpose. Where the abuse occurs is where an adult posing as a young person enters the chat room for the specific purpose of attempting to sexually exploit their target at a later date. Normally, the paedophile first attempts to hone in on a vulnerable target and isolate them by attempting to get them to leave the chat room and go one on one. Usually they say, 'we can talk more privately this way'. Once the target is isolated the first thing the paedophile will attempt is to find out is if there is any adult monitoring the exchange. If not the paedophile will feel more comfortable continuing. If the child is being closely monitored the paedophile will almost certainly end the exchange and look for a new more vulnerable target. At some point the victim will be asked their age. The paedophile will then usually confide falsely that they are a year or two older. Once a real rapport is set-up with the child the paedophile will often confide that they are more than one or two years older but will plead that if the child loves him not to break off the relationship. Obviously, to get to this stage takes many conversations, not just one. Finally, the paedophile will attempt to set-up a personal and secret meeting with the child. If this works successfully further grooming will go on leading the child into sexual exploitation. Of course we don't know every scenario used but what I have told you would seem to be typical. Does that answer your question adequately?'

'Yes, thank you.'

'Yes sir.'

'Attorney General, what can be done to fight this exploitation of our children?'

'Well, I think the first step is to tighten up our legislation, both to identify new illegal acts as crimes and to provide for very stiff sentences. As I stated earlier, we are working on this at the very moment and I believe we will succeed. Beyond that the International Congress Against Commercial Sexual Exploitation of Children urged that a child pornography observatory staffed by highly trained professionals from relevant disciplines be set-up to monitor, educate and address the problem. However, I should point out the problem worldwide is massive. It is estimated that fifty thousand illegal images of children are generated each month and the trend is increasing upward. Additionally, we must work much closer with the Internet service providers and credit card companies to flush out more quickly these perpetrators. If they don't assist us and self-regulate the industry then we must legislate at federal and state level to make them comply. We also need to fund more research in this area at our leading universities. Virginia universities could take a leading role in this area. I hope my answer helped.'

'Yes sir, thank you.'

'Attorney General, were all the children in the downloaded images being abused?'

'No. they were not, some were shown naked in erotic poses. However, we have no idea if the children were later abused by their controllers. Our assumption is, many were.'

'Thank you.'

'Mr. Rivers, is there any indication organized crime is involved in child pornography?'

'Yes, there is hard proof that organized crime is involved in trafficking in human organs of children and trafficking in children for erotic posing and child sexual abuse.'

'Thank you.'

'Mr. Rivers, how many other countries are involved in this operation?'

'Well, as you know the hub of the illegal activity was in Amsterdam in this case. The operators of this illegal operation were clearing almost three million dollars per month. Credit card subscriptions were being received from every country in Europe and as far away as Russia and many of its former republics that are now separate countries. Authorities in almost all those countries have been given lists of credit card subscribers and as we speak these people are being closed in on around the world.'

'Many thanks.'

'Attorney General, have many of the abused children been identified?'

'Yes, some but compared to the number of abused children the number is very, very small indeed. You can appreciate it is difficult to give you an exact number due to the number of police authorities involved.'

'Thank you.'

'Mr. Rivers, are there underlying reasons in society why these prurient activities are on the rise. And if so, what can be done to abate them?'

'Well, my own opinion is we must all work together and that includes; parents, clothing manufacturers of children's clothing, key retailers, Internet service providers, credit card companies, law enforcement authorities, legislators, etc. We must focus on the hard facts that these paedophiles are playing off their fantasies. Anything that needlessly fuels those fantasies should be avoided where possible. Children who are provocatively dressed beyond their years may say to the paedophile, the child wants sexual relations and would be a willing partner. Some mothers wrongly think their little girls look stunning in flashy clothes and padded bras designed for older girls. This acts as a magnet for paedophiles. I will give you an example of dress codes gone wild. Recently, Kidprotect, a Canadian charity for the protection of children campaigned against high-street stores selling thong panties for pre-teen girls decorated with a pussycat and the words, 'stroke my fur'. I think this is an example of where a more mature view and a better focus must be adopted if we are to succeed.'

Delegate Ricketts called for one last question.

'Mr. Rivers, could innocent people stumble on child pornography sites on the Internet?'

'That is a very good question. Yes, it is possible that an Internet user could hit on an Internet site somewhat innocently. However, I should point out that these child pornography sites do not offer these images for free. They must be paid for; therefore, it is almost inconceivable that an individual would order access to child pornography images by giving credit card information without knowing what they are doing. No, these people know exactly what they want, they are not innocents. Thank you very much; I hope I have assisted you to understand this growing legal problem and how we must attack it to protect young children in our society.'

The Attorney General was given a standing ovation led by the strong contingent of police officers. Patrick caught Pritch's eye and gave him the thumbs-up. There was no doubt that the general had done his homework as well as being a smooth performer at the podium. His greatest attribute of all was his sincerity and the soft spoken and polite way he delivered his message. If the general ran for governor he had just won Patrick's vote.

When the team was filing out of the courtroom Patrick found Irving Johnson on his right side. He asked Irving if he could have a word with him outside. As the crowd dispersed Patrick and Irving moved out on to the grass, away from the sidewalks. Patrick asked Irving if he was related to Ralph Johnson?

'You mean Dr. Ralph Johnson who lives with his daughter up on West Cornwall Street?'

'I didn't know he was Dr., what kind of doctor is he?'

'He was a medical doctor and before he retired a damn good one.'

'Jim Brogan interviewed him before he was attacked but I doubt he knew he was a medical doctor.'

'Now, back to your original question, are we related? Yes, slightly, around these parts we would refer to our relationship as dog-kin. Maybe we are third cousins or something.'

'I doubt Liam had time to mention it to you but Dr. Johnson has agreed to testify for the defense.'

'That's wonderful Patrick. You just hit the jackpot; Dr. Johnson is just about Leesburg's most distinguished and best loved citizen.'

'How is that?'

'Well, during the Second Word War Dr. Johnson was a young GP. He had worked his way through university and medical school and had married shortly after qualifying. He was born in Leesburg so he returned home to practice. When he started out he didn't have anything. He and his new bride rented a small flat over one of the shops on King Street. The living room was turned into his office. When America entered the war Dr. Johnson made a decision, he was four-F himself due to an old and serious back injury, so he decided that for the duration of America's involvement in the war he would never charge a family member of a U.S. serviceman or woman for his medical services. Black or white, yellow or brown, it made no difference to him. Well, you can imagine with all the young men and women away at war almost every family had a serviceman or woman in one branch or another. Dr. Johnson was poor and got even poorer but he soldiered on never once complaining to anyone. His dear wife Elaine supported him one hundred percent. They did without and probably if the truth was known didn't even have enough food to eat. I remember my daddy taking them up vegetables from the garden regularly. I suppose they lived on what food friends and relatives gave them. I recall when I went off to war; Dr. Ralph and Elaine looked of normal weight. When I returned in 1945 they both looked tired and emaciated. All I have to say is, may he live one hundred years. There is no way Leesburg will ever forget Dr. Ralph Johnson. He is Leesburg's heart.'

'Wow, what a story, what a man!'

'True for you Patrick, true for you.'

It was about two p.m. when Patrick left Irving Johnson on the courthouse lawn. Kelly had mentioned that tonight she was going home to pack her clothes for the move to Neersville. Patrick didn't want to start their life together with the distrust and hatred of Kelly's mother and father, so he decided that today was the day they would become engaged. He crossed King Street and went immediately to the local jewellery store. Once inside he lost his courage a little. Sarah Reed, one of the shops salesclerks asked him politely if she could help. At first he feigned that he was just looking. When the owner of the store, Tobias Ridge came over to shake hands with him, Sarah gave way. After the usual small talk Patrick confided that he was looking for an engagement ring. Toby was very discreet, he didn't ask any questions about who the girl was or where she was from, he just promptly produced a tray of engagement rings with various size diamonds.

'Do you know if she would prefer a yellow gold, white gold or platinum setting?'

'Gee Toby, I really don't know.'

'Can you recall the color of the jewellery she currently wears?'

'Yes, well it's all yellow gold come to think of it.'

'Well, then I think a yellow gold setting is probably our best bet. However, if it isn't right rest assured I will change it for you at no extra cost. Now about the size of the diamond?'

'Can you give me an idea of price and quality Toby; I am a real novice in this area?'

'Well, I suppose the first thing you need to know is that I don't deal with low end diamonds. That means you will get a smaller stone but a higher quality diamond for your money. Operating in a small town I feel it would be ill advised to sell diamonds that later some other jeweller can point out all the flaws and discoloration in. So you will get a high quality stone, remembering diamonds are natural substances, hence, very few are absolutely perfect. With that one caveat let me give you an idea about prices. Most of my selection is about four thousand dollars per carat; hence a one-half carat diamond is about two thousand dollars while a two carat diamond is about eight thousand dollars. Do you have any idea what price range you might want?'

'Well Toby, if I gave you all the money in my pocket at the moment it might be one fourth of a carat.'

'Don't worry Patrick, very few young men slap down the total amount. Give what you can and I will carry you on my books without interest for a year or two.'

'Well, that's great Toby, then let's shoot for about a one carat and I will give you one thousand dollars today.'

'Here's a lovely one carat ring I can offer to you for four thousand three hundred dollars. Here, I think you should view this stone carefully with my loop.'

'It looks brilliant and pure crystal color.'

'Yes, it looks very good Patrick, no carbon deposits, no obvious flaws and it's not cloudy or discolored. I would rate this stone very highly.'

'Fine, Toby, that's the one for me then.'

'Now, luckily this stone is already set in yellow gold and is size six and a half. Does your fiancée to be have very thin, normal or large hands?'

'I think normal but could I use your telephone a minute and telephone Heather?'

'Sure Patrick, use this one right here.'

'Heather, is Kelly in the office?'

'Yes, she's right here. Do you want to talk to her?'

'No, just answer yes or no and don't let on what you are talking about.'

'OK'

'Do you think Kelly has thin, normal or large hands?'

'Normal.'

'Do you think her ring finger might be about six and a half?'

'Yes, that sounds right.'

'Wonderful, see you in a few minutes.'

'Toby, Heather thinks a size six and a half sounds about right.'

'Great, then you take this ring and if it needs to be resized, bring the young lady in and I will take care of it in a few hours.'

'Ok, well here's the one thousand dollars down.'

'Would you like me to gift wrap the box?'

'No, just in the box is fine.'

'Ok Patrick, good luck.'

'Thanks Toby, see you soon.'

Patrick returned to the office and put in an hour or so of good work. Every ten minutes or so he flipped open the top of the jewellery box and stared at the ring. He was very excited, the diamond seemed more beautiful each time he looked. Finally, five o'clock came and Heather packed up to leave. Pritch had never returned to the office as he was with the general and would be until the instant he was airborne for Richmond from Leesburg Airport. Kelly came into his office to indicate she would go home and quickly pack her cloths for their new life together in Neersville.

'Will you wait in the office for me Patrick, I will only be about one hour?'

'I have decided I will drive home with you. We can take my car and you can leave your car here.'

'That would be great Patrick.'

'There is one important matter we must discuss before we go.'

'What's that?'

'Your parents are very proper people, they won't like the fact we are going to live together without being married. Word will get out quickly and they will be very embarrassed.'

'Well.'

'I think this might help a little and I give it to you with all my love.'

'Kelly opened the box and gazed in amazement at the beautiful diamond ring. Then she started to cry, real tears of joy and happiness. Patrick took out the ring and slipped it on her finger. It slid over her knuckle without a great deal of pushing and yet it was not loose. It was a perfect fit and Patrick was delighted. Kelly hugged him and actually jumped up and down several times. He didn't jump but he did the next best thing. He lifted Kelly off her feet and spun her around several times all the while kissing her. It was indeed a magic moment, they were like big kids together. Later that night each would confide in the other that it was the happiest day of their life.

When they arrived at Kelly's house both her father and mother were home. Patrick and Kelly carefully outlined their future plans including of course the short-term plans of living together in Neersville. Both parents had known for a long time of Kelly's love, loyalty and total devotion to Patrick. Now with Patrick indicating he had the same strong feelings for Kelly and of course the fact that they were engaged, which did make a huge difference, they accepted with only slight hesitation their plan to live together.

Kelly packed some but far from all her clothing. This was done purposely as Kelly thought if Patrick saw all the clothes she had he would certainly call the engagement off. Later, he could learn of her passion for clothing, shoes and handbags. She hoped by the time it dawned on him that she was a high maintenance dolly-bird he would be hers. They had dinner with Kelly's parents before heading out for Neersville.

When they got to Neersville, Kelly literally ran in to see Ralph and Eleanor Harrington and showed them her ring. They were very pleased for both Kelly and Patrick and Ralph broke out a bottle of champagne that he had placed on ice for just such a special occasion, although at the time he put it on ice he had no idea just what the next good news might be. When they got back to the cottage, a little giddy, Kelly put all her clothes away thus making the living together arrangements formal. Mindful that tomorrow would mark the start of the defense's evidence they made glorious love together and fell asleep in each others arms.

# Thirty-Two

JUDGE Draper did not look happy when he took his seat on the bench promptly at nine a.m. One of the bailiffs had overheard two jurors discussing the trial in their room before they entered the courtroom and reported what he had heard to the judge. The judge commenced:

'Word has reached me that there has been some discussion of the trial between certain jurors while in the jury room this morning. I had cautioned you previously that this was not permissible. You may in fairness think it odd that you are forbidden to discuss the trial among yourselves since in the final analysis you will decide the outcome of the case. You may understand perfectly why you shouldn't discuss the trial with outside sources and yet not see the wisdom of why you can't discuss the trial among yourselves. I thought today, I would take a moment to explain to you why this behavior is prohibited. First, when the jury discusses the case it should only take place after all testimony has been placed in evidence and all jurors should be privy to the comments and discussion points put before it by all other members. Second, jurors too sometimes wrongfully attempt to influence or win over other fellow jurors to see the case their way. This they often attempt to do by isolating a juror they want to wrongfully influence. I am not saying this is what happened this morning but I am reminding you that you must refrain from such activity in the future for the two basic and compelling reasons I have outlined. If there is a repeat of today's activity by any juror or jurors I will be compelled to dismiss the juror or jurors involved and supplant them with one of our alternates. The jurors collectively hung their heads as if all had been wrong doers. They hadn't of course but they had known what had gone on and none had spoken up to stop the conversation and to that degree they all acknowledged their guilt.

Judge Draper, having felt he had temporarily, at least, quashed any contamination of the jury system was ready to move on.

'Mr. O'Brien, are you ready to call your first witness?'

'I am your honor. The defense calls to the stand Dr. Edward Fiske.'

After being duly sworn the direct examination commenced.

'Dr. Fiske, could you state for the court your full name?'

'Edward Christian Fiske.'

'And where do you reside Dr. Fiske?'

'At 2937 Catoctin Avenue in Chantilly, Virginia.'

'And what is your occupation?'

'I am a forensic scientist.'

'And where do you work?'

'I am director of the Fairfax Forensic Laboratory?'

'And is your laboratory an independent business or affiliated with any governmental organization or agency?'

'We are an independent business which has been in operation for thirty-five years. We are not affiliated with any governmental bodies or agencies although many governmental agencies and police forces have historically used our services.'

'In other words, governmental agencies and police forces are some of your regular customers?'

'That is correct.'

'And could you trace for us your personal education?'

'Yes, I have a Bachelor of Science degree from Duke University, a Master's degree in Forensic Science and Medical Criminology from Harvard University and a Doctorate in Forensic Science and Medical Criminology from Johns Hopkins University.'

'And how long have you practiced in this field?'

'Approximately twenty-one years.'

'And how long have you been with the Fairfax Forensic Laboratory?'

'I have been there sixteen years and I have been the director for the last twelve years.'

'And where did you spend the first six years of your career?'

'In the FBI Forensic Laboratory in Washington, D.C.'

At this point John Brandywell had heard enough, not wanting the juror's to hear any further testimony concerning Dr. Fiske's forensic accomplishments.

'Your honor, the prosecution will be glad to stipulate that Dr. Fiske is an expert witness.'

'Fine, Mr. O'Brien, please continue.'

'Dr. Fiske, in your capacity as Director of the Fairfax Forensic Laboratory, did your staff have occasion to examine certain clothing worn by the defendant, Mr. Frank Appleby on Wednesday, June twenty-eight of this year?'

'Yes, we did, we were given one pair of bib overalls and a work shirt for examination and we conducted nine separate chemical and forensic tests on the garments.'

'And what were you primarily looking for?'

'We were attempting to establish if there was any blood or DNA samples of any kind on the garments that would belong to any individual but particularly to the deceased, Mr. Wilbur Cosgrove.'

'And did you find any blood or other DNA samples on the subject overalls?'

'Yes sir, we found perspiration stains and some saliva that were from the defendant, Frank Appleby.'

'Then what else did you find?'

'We found grass stains, grease stains and some metal filings.'

'And these metal filings, could they have come from a gun, particularly a shotgun?'

'No sir, they could not. They were consistent with filings from either a manually operated or electric hedge trimmer.'

'How do you know this to be the case?'

'Because in all cases they were interspersed or sometimes contained in the sap or minute clippings from plants or shrubs.'

'In other words these filings were consistent with the work of a gardener or other individual trimming shrubs and hedges?'

'Exactly.'

'Now, Dr. Fiske, when you received these overalls, how did you know they were the work clothes of Mr. Frank Appleby?'

'There was a sworn affidavit attached, signed by Mrs. Evelyn Appleby, stating that these were the work clothes of Mr. Frank Appleby worn by him on Wednesday 28 June. Additionally, there was the signature of the individual who picked-up the work clothes from Mr. Appleby and delivered them to our laboratory. Once in our control these overalls were maintained at all times in our secure lock-up area and when examined by one of our forensic scientists were signed out and back-in to this secured facility.'

'So would it be safe to say that in your opinion the chain of custody over these particular items of clothing was properly maintained at all times?'

'Absolutely.'

'And in her affidavit did Mrs. Evelyn Appleby state that the overalls had not been washed or in anyway altered by herself or any member of her family?'

'She did indeed state that fact.'

'In her sworn statement?'

'Yes, that's correct.'

'Now, Dr. Fiske, are you totally convinced in your professional opinion that there was no blood or DNA samples from the deceased man, Mr. Wilbur Cosgrove?'

'Absolutely, one hundred percent sure.'

'Now Dr. Fiske, were DNA samples of Mr. Frank Appleby and Mr. Wilbur Cosgrove made available to you?'

'Yes, the DNA profile of both individuals you mentioned was provided to us by the State Police Laboratory in Richmond, Virginia.'

'No further questions your honor.'

'Alright, Mr. Brandywell, your witness.'

'Dr. Fiske, you stated that the metal filings found on the work clothing of Mr. Frank Appleby which your laboratory examined were consistent with filings from either a manual or electric hedge clipper and not a shotgun?'

'Yes, that's correct.'

'And how sure are you of this fact?'

'Very sure, because they were often found surrounded by or alternatively encased in the sap from bushes or shrubs.'

'Were you ever able to determine which shrubs these sap samples came from?'

'Yes, we found they came from a variety of shrubs, including; American and English Boxwood, golden privets and pine trees of several types including blue spruce and white pine.'

'And is it not possible that these filings came from the barrel of a shotgun?'

'No, not really possible, because had that been the case gun powder residue would have been found with the filings and none was detected.'

'None at all?'

'No, none at all.'

'Now, Dr. Fiske, how confident are you that the article of clothing your laboratory tested wasn't altered or substituted before it reached you?'

'Well, I can confirm it wasn't washed for a long period prior to being tested because the amount of detergent residue found was minimal.'

'But detergent residue did exist?'

'Yes, that's correct, in low amounts.'

'Could the item you tested be substituted?'

'Yes, of course it could have been. All I have to go on was the sworn affidavit and the documented chain of custody which seemed totally in order.'

'But it is possible that Mrs. Evelyn Appleby in an effort to protect her husband supplied you with another pair of work overalls of her husband's rather than the ones actually worn by him on the day of the murder?'

'This is possible. Again, I must state that what was provided to us looked authentic and certainly the chain of custody over the item in question was as well documented as I have ever seen.'

'Fine, thank you Dr. Fiske. No further questions your honor.'

'Mr. O'Brien any redirect?'

'Yes, your honor, one final question.'

'Dr. Fiske, you work closely with the State Police Forensic Laboratory, did they ever inform you of the existence of any other sample of clothing of Mr. Frank Appleby's that they were forensically testing?'

'No, they didn't and therefore I seriously doubt that any other sample of clothing was involved in forensic testing from Mr. Frank Appleby. They were of course testing the clothing of Mr. Wilbur Cosgrove.'

'Thank you Dr. Fiske. No further questions your honor but the defense would like to reserve this witness for recall if necessary.'

'Alright, Dr. Fiske, you are dismissed unless notified of a recall. Mr. O'Brien please call your next witness.'

'Thank you your honor. The defense calls Dr. Raymond Rey to the stand.'

After being sworn the questioning commenced.

'Dr. Rey, can you state for the court your full name?'

'Raymond William Rey.'

'And what is your occupation?'

'Forensic Scientist and Criminologist.'

'And for whom do you work?'

'I am in partnership with two other forensic scientists and we trade under the name of Altos, Rey and Wallace Forensic Scientists and Criminologists.'

'And where do you personally reside?'

'2410 Foxcroft Lane, Falls Church, Virginia.'

'And your business address?'

'Park Lane Building I, Lee Highway, Tyson's Corner, Virginia.'

'And can you outline your education for us?'

'Yes, I have a Bachelor of Science degree in Human Biology from Catholic University, a Master of Forensic Science and Criminology from American University, a Juris Doctor degree from the University of Virginia and a

PhD in Forensic Science and Criminology from Pittsburg University.'

'I note you graduated from law school, are you a member of any state bars?'

'Yes, I am an active member of the Virginia State Bar and the District of Columbia Bar.'

Mr. Brandywell was on his feet.

'Your honor, the prosecution will stipulate Dr. Rey as an expert witness.'

'Fine, Mr. O'Brien you may commence your examination of this witness.'

'Thank you your honor. Dr. Rey, did you have an opportunity to examine the murder scene and also review the police photographs of the murder scene?'

'I did.'

'Further, did you have occasion to study the police and autopsy reports regarding the murder of Mr. Wilbur Cosgrove?'

'I did.'

'Further, have you had an opportunity to study the testimony of Dr. Panski, the prosecution's forensic expert?'

'I have.'

'What is your opinion as to the cause of death of Mr. Wilbur Cosgrove?'

'Mr. Cosgrove died from the effects of one shotgun blast to his chest fired at point blank range. My findings would be consistent with the cause of death as stated in the coroner's and police reports.'

'So there is little or no controversy as to the cause of Mr. Cosgrove's death?'

'I would think not, all relevant parties agree as to the cause of death.'

'What in your opinion would have been the resultant blood spray caused by the shotgun blast?'

'First, it should be noted that the shotgun pellets in almost every case did not exit the body but became lodged in the flesh. There are a few exceptions and these occurred on the outer parts of both the left and right arms where a very few pellets would have created an exit wound. The result of this point blank shotgun blast would be the creation of a huge and almost instantaneous blood spray backwards toward the shooter. This would have been accentuated by the size of the subject and also by his corpulence.'

'How far might the blood spray back travel?'

'In my calculations I would estimate up to twelve to fifteen feet away.'

'And how large or wide would this blood spray be at its maximum travelling distance of twelve to fifteen feet?'

'I estimate it would have fanned out to cover an area ten feet tall, which was two feet beyond the height of the ceiling and twelve feet wide.'

'Would that mean two feet of the ceiling was also covered with blood spray as well as the eight feet height of the walls in the room?'

'That is correct.'

'How far away from the murdered man do you estimate the killer would have been when the shot was fired?'

'Approximately three feet away.'

'What would be the result on the killer in regard to the blood spray?'

'The killer would have been covered from head to toe with fine blood droplets.'

'What about the possibility the killer fired from behind a wall or partition?'

'My examination of the room where Mr. Cosgrove was murdered would rule this out as a possibility.'

'Why is that?'

'The room where the murder took place is about ten feet wide and twelve feet long. There were no partitions in the room only the four walls. Additionally, my calculations place Mr. Cosgrove and his killer near the center of the room when the shot was fired. I can tell this with some degree of certainty by the position Mr. Cosgrove was found on the floor, by the ambulance crew's statements and the trajectory of the blood spray.'

'What about the shield theory proposed by the prosecution witness, Dr. Panski?'

'This theory is not borne out by the blood spray pattern. While a shield could conceivably stop the blood spray reaching the killer it would have to be very large and cumbersome to achieve that objective fully. It also would be more difficult for the killer to aim and fire the shotgun which would of necessity have to be held in one hand while the shield was held in the other. Then there would be the complex procedure of carrying away from the crime scene the shield and disposing of such damning evidence. No, I don't subscribe to the shield theory.'

'You mentioned the blood spray also did not support the shield theory?'

'Yes, that is correct; a large shield would have interrupted the blood spray. This was not the case. I found the blood spray only interrupted by one human form.'

'Can you estimate the size of the individual from the blood spray?'

'Yes, the individual was very slight and of an approximate height of five feet four to five feet seven inches.'

'May it please the court, would the defendant please stand up?'

'Now, as you can see Dr. Rey, the defendant, Mr. Appleby, is at least six feet tall maybe a little taller. Could a man his size be the killer?'

'In my opinion no, the blood spray confirms the killer to be much smaller.'

'Could you see any scenario that a larger individual could be the killer?'

'Oh, I suppose any good scientist could be off an inch or so but five or six inches, no, I really could not see that as being possible.'

'Thank you Dr. Rey, no further questions at this time.'

'Mr. Brandywell.'

'Dr. Rey, you state there was no partition in the room where Mr. Cosgrove was shot but certainly there was furniture or objects that would interrupt and alter the blood spray?'

'There was some furniture in the room but mostly it banned the walls leaving the center of the room empty, hence, the blood spray was not interrupted except by the killer's body.'

'And are you sure the calculation of the size of the killer is correct, certainly, there is more margin for error than you have told us?'

'No, I think not. I must admit I was somewhat shocked when the original calculations indicated such a small person so I checked the calculation four separate times. It always worked out the same.'

'What if the killer was slightly stooped, bending down or crouching, this would certainly affect the blood spray would it not?'

'Yes, that is true, it would.'

'So it is possible that a six foot tall man could crouch down making himself look like a five foot five inch man in regard to the blood spray?'

'Yes, that is a possibility.'

'No further questions your honor'.

'Mr. O'Brien redirect.'

'Dr. Rey, would it be possible to detect a person crouching down as part of the blood spray pattern?'

'Possibly, particularly if they were standing sideways, straight on it would be more difficult unless the body form was altered acutely. For instance, if the killer had been on his knees that would show-up on the blood spray pattern as his legs would be totally out of proportion with the rest of his body.'

'In you examination did you see any evidence that the killer had adopted a kneeling, stooping or crouching position?'

'No, I did not.'

'No further questions your honor.'

'Fine, we will adjourn for lunch and recommence promptly at two p.m.'

In the afternoon Liam put on the stand Ronald Davidson, Frank Appleby's landlord, who testified, much as he had done at the bail hearing, as to Frank's fine character and his record as an ideal tenant both in his payment record and his preservation of his property. He also testified most helpfully to Frank's placid non-aggressive personality and Christian attitude. Next Liam put on the stand Mr. Horace Granger. Mr. Granger, as the customer who Frank was working for on the day of the murder, testified that Frank had completed a volume of work which would have been almost impossible to complete had he left the premises for the period the prosecution had asserted. He also attested to his work ethic, his fine Christian attitude and honesty and his soft non-violent personality. John Brandywell for his part was fairly content to let this testimony in without challenge except the point that Frank had completed an amount of work that would take an experienced gardener a full eight hours of work. Brandywell contended he could have easily speeded up his work or cut his lunch hour short or both to achieve the work output noted.

Liam had used Ronald Davidson as a time filler as he hadn't wanted to put Dr. Ralph Johnson on in the late afternoon when the jurors were tired. He had purposely put Horace Granger on in the late afternoon to set the stage for the testimony of Dr. Johnson. Horace Granger's testimony had been very helpful. He had verified the exact time that he and his wife had been present with Frank at their property. Now he would be looking to Dr. Ralph Johnson to testify to

Frank's presence during the hours the Granger's were away, thus making it a physical impossibility that Frank Appleby could have murdered Wilbur Cosgrove on Wednesday twenty-eight June the date in question.

# Thirty-three

ON the seventh day of the trial Judge Philip Draper seemed in extremely good humor. He smiled widely at the jurors and thanked them again for their patience and their fulfilling their civic duty. Obviously, no infractions of trial procedural rules had been uncovered and the report from the bailiff in regard to small talk in the jury room had been positive.

'Mr. O'Brien, would you call your first witness?'

'Thank you your honor, the defense calls to the stand Dr. Ralph Johnson.'

No sooner had the name of Dr. Ralph Johnson been mentioned than a ripple of excitement went through the courtroom. People turned towards each other and brief words or glances passed between them. Those who had no idea who Dr. Ralph Johnson was, like many newcomers and members of the national press questioned Dr. Johnson's identity.

The door to the courtroom swung open and ever so slowly but in a determined manner, Dr. Ralph Johnson, with the aid of his cane shuffled in. It was then an amazing happening took place. As he passed each row all the persons in that row stood up. Row after row lifted themselves up to mark his presence. When he reached the bar and entered the three prosecutors and the two defense counsels stood erect as did all the jurors and alternates. The bailiff rushed to assist Dr. Johnson to the witness stand. Everyone now standing looked at Judge Draper. As Dr. Johnson passed Judge Draper stood and bowed. When Dr. Johnson reached the stand and was seated with the assistance of the bailiff an ear deafening and sustained applause erupted and lasted a full three minutes. The members of the national press who had seen it all and were normally totally jaded, even if professional, knew they had their lead story.

Finally, after the sustained applause and the courtroom audience had re-seated themselves there was dead silence.

Dr. Johnson was sworn and then Liam carefully and deliberately started the questioning.

'Could you tell the court your full name?'

'Ralph Ian Johnson.'

'Where do you reside Dr. Johnson?'

'I live with my daughter and son-in-law at 21 West Cornwall Street.'

'How long have you lived in Leesburg?'

'I was born here in Leesburg and have lived here all my life save the time I went away to university and medical school.'

'And how old are you now sir?'

'Eighty-nine.'

'I would imagine you are retired?'

'Yes, I retired about eight years ago.'

'And how do you spend your time now?'

'I am fortunate I can see quite well so I do a good deal of reading and I enjoy T.V., particularly the sports.'

'Do you recall where you were on Wednesday June twenty-eighth of this year?'

'Yes I do, I was in my apartment in my daughter and son-in-laws home on West Cornwall Street. My apartment is on the second floor of their house.'

'And do you recall what you were doing that day?'

'Yes I do. I didn't read and I didn't watch T.V. and I didn't go out in the garden. I sat in my favorite chair and looked out my window.'

'Why did you sit looking out Dr. Johnson?'

'June twenty-eighth is the day I lost my wife five years ago. I thought about her all day and our happy and loving years together.'

'What do you see from your window?'

'My window looks out over the back garden of our neighbors, the Granger's.'

'Mr. and Mrs. Horace Granger?'

'Yes.'

'And what did you see?'

'Mr. Frank Appleby was working in the Granger's back garden. I watched Frank, he is a wonderful worker you know.'

'Do you know Frank fairly well?'

'I should, I was his mother's doctor and delivered Frank.'

'Did Frank ever leave the garden on the day in question?'

'Frank arrived about nine a.m. I had been looking out since about seven-thirty a.m. He set all his tools out and began to cultivate and water bushes and shrubs. He worked there all day.'

'Did Frank ever leave the Granger's back garden?'

'Not until about three-thirty p.m. after the Granger's came home and Mrs. Granger called him into the house. He came out and ran around and picked-up his tools in a hurry and left straight away.'

'But didn't he leave for lunch around two p.m.?'

'No, Frank had brought his lunch and ate it under a large apple tree, the one with the stone wall built around it.'

'And Frank never left?'

'No, Frank never left until three-thirty p.m. after Mrs. Granger called him into the house.'

'Did he look upset when he left the Granger's home?'

'Yes, he looked very unsettled.'

'Dr. Johnson are you sure about the time Frank left the Granger's?'

'Oh yes, I have a large wall clock opposite my chair. It was three-thirty p.m.'

'Do you know where Frank was going?'

'No, but later I learned he rushed to the hospital to be with his son Frankie.'

'No, further questions your honor.'

'Mr. Brandywell.'

'Your honor the prosecution has only a few questions.'

'Dr. Johnson are you sure your clock was showing the correct time?'

'Yes, I am very confident it was correct. I have a radio next to my window chair. I listen each day to the twelve o'clock news. On Wednesday June twenty-eight I turned on the radio when the clock showed twelve noon and at that time it was correct.'

'When you listened to the radio did you continue to look out the window?'

'Yes, during the entire fifteen minute news program.'

'Did you leave your chair to eat or to go to the bathroom that day?'

'I went to the bathroom when I got up and I never had any food that day until the evening when I had a small snack. I just didn't have the heart John; I hope you understand I just couldn't stop thinking about my dear wife who I loved so much.'

'The prosecution has no further questions your honor.'

'Dr. Johnson, you may leave now and thank you very much for your assistance in this trial.'

Judge Draper then stood as the bailiff rushed to assist Dr. Johnson. Everyone stood and the courtroom erupted in applause again and continued until long after Dr. Johnson had left the chamber.

John Branywell huddled with the prosecution's team. When things settled down, John Brandywell stood.

'Your honor the prosecution will not continue to prosecute Frank Appleby for the murder of Wilbur Cosgrove.

If my learned colleague Liam O'Brien will make a motion to dismiss based on physical impossibility the prosecution will join in that motion. The testimony of Dr. Ralph Johnson, an impeccable source is irrefutable.'

'Mr. Brandywell, it is with great pleasure that I make the motion to dismiss which you suggest based on the eyewitness testimony of Dr. Ralph Johnson and the irrefutable nature of his honesty and powers of observation proving beyond all reasonable doubt the physical impossibility that the defendant Mr. Frank Appleby killed Mr. Wilbur Cosgrove on Wednesday June twenty-eight as charged.'

'The prosecution gladly joins in this motion your honor to avert any chance of a miscarriage of justice. To proceed could lead to a totally unsafe judgement which we cannot risk.'

Judge Draper took a long moment to consider the gravity of what had happened today in his courtroom. Then in a most dramatic manner Judge Draper held his gavel high and brought it down with a thunderous blow.

'Case dismissed.'

Camera flashes ignited as if firecrackers wired to produce a chain reaction. Patrick reached Frank first and hugged him. Then Liam piled-in, seconds later Kelly and Irving Johnson joined the scrum. Finally, Roland Alberts, one arm in a sling arrived from where he had been seated in the back of the courtroom. Roland completed the circle by wrapping his one good arm around Patrick and Liam. Frank was in the center of the pile looking happy but stunned. Only Heather who was back at the office and Jim Brogan who was still in hospital weren't there to celebrate the victory.

The most admired man in Loudoun County history had set Frank free and Jim Brogan had found him through basic hard grafting police work.

The hour belonged to the defense but as John Brandywell, Eugene Harrison and Bruce Rodgers packed-up, both Liam and Patrick rushed to their table to congratulate them. Liam spoke first.

'Thank you John, you and your team set a new standard of legal honor today.'

'Thanks Liam, there was no way I was going to continue to prosecute Frank after Dr. Ralph Johnson's testimony. Every old Loudoun family has a tale to tell about Dr. Johnson. Dr. Johnson came to my home in a blizzard on the night my mother died. He stayed with her all night. He gave her an injection to ease her pain. He held her hand until nearly sun-up when she passed away quietly with her angel still there comforting her. If Dr. Johnson said Frank worked in Mr. and Mrs. Horace Granger's back-garden until that emergency telephone call came in from his wife at three-thirty p.m. then he did.'

Patrick spoke next.

'Thank you John and team, your honorable action saved me from making a fool of myself with a not so good closing statement.'

Eugene Harrison spoke.

'Nonsense Patrick, you and Liam are great attorneys. We have the utmost respect for you both. It was a pleasure to share the same courtroom with you.'

'Thanks Gene, you're too kind, if there are any legal heroes in this courtroom today it is you three.'

This duty done Patrick and Liam returned to Frank who was now surrounded by well wishers and the press. A T.V. journalist from Channel 9 asked if we would agree to a press conference outside on the courtroom steps. He indicated all the microphones would be placed together so we only had to do it once and all the media would get the story. Frank, Liam and Patrick agreed. Patrick decided Frank should go first then Liam and last Patrick himself would say a word or two. Once outside Frank made his statement.

'I want to thank everyone who believed in me and stuck by me through the dark hours. I want to thank my lawyers; Patrick Hurst and Liam O'Brien. Additionally, I want to thank my wife and family who know the truth that I never hurt anyone. I also want to thank from the bottom of my heart Dr. Ralph Johnson. He not only delivered me once, but twice.'

'Are you happy to be free?'

'To say I am happy is a gross understatement, delirious is more like it. Now here are my attorneys, Liam O'Brien to be followed by Patrick Hurst.'

'The entire defense team wants to also thank Dr. Johnson and Jim Brogan our private investigator who realized the relevance to the trial of the information Dr. Johnson possessed. We would also like to thank the Commonwealth Attorney, Mr. John Brandywell and Assistant Commonwealth Attorneys, Mr. Eugene Harrison and Mr. Bruce Rodgers for joining us in the motion to dismiss. They are the real heroes. They struck a mighty blow today for justice.'

'Would you have won the case if it had been allowed to go to the jury?'

'We will never know for sure, but yes, I think we would have won, we had truth on our side.'

'If Frank Appleby didn't murder Wilbur Cosgrove, who did?'

'I don't know. Now I will turn you over to Patrick Hurst.'

'Thanks Liam, for my part I want to thank our client, Frank Appleby. His innocence kept us going even on the darkest of days. I also want to thank our entire defense team; Jim Brogan, Roland Alberts, Kelly Madison, Heather Thompson, Irving Johnson and of course my distinguished co-counsel Liam O'Brien. Not only did Dr. Johnson's remarkable testimony end the trial but it saved the defense from putting Frank Appleby Jr. on the stand. Frankie has been through enough. He is only a nine year old child. I am happy he could avoid the added trauma.'

'Will you take another murder defense?'

'Oh, I would have to think carefully about that, maybe some day. We all need a little reflection time now.'

'Were you surprised the way the trial ended?'

'Yes, I was. I don't think any of us could have anticipated the way the trial ended.'

'Did the testimony of Dr. Johnson seal the case?'

'Yes, absolutely. His testimony was mighty. Now if you will agree, we will start to celebrate properly with our client.'

After the press conference was over Frank invited the entire defense team to his house that evening. He and Evelyn had already agreed that if he was freed they would have a big party. Evelyn had shown her faith in Frank's innocence by buying all the food and drinks in advance of the end of the trial. As it worked out the trial had ended about one and one-half days before schedule. Liam had planned to seek testimony from Frank Appleby, Jr. (Frankie). Deputy Wayne Broomfield, the Reverend Donald Weeks, Frank's pastor, Jim Abbot, the owner of the local garden center and Helen Wright, owner of the local hardware store. Other than Frankie and Deputy Broomfield, they were the same witnesses who had been so effective and persuasive at Frank's bail hearing. Frankie would have testified that he was the one who transported the shotgun to Wilbur Cosgrove's outbuilding and after showing it to Mr. Cosgrove placed it in a corner. Strangely, Wilbur Cosgrove never touched the gun; hence, his fingerprints were never on the shotgun. However, as Frankie bolted and ran home the shotgun was left there for use by the real murderer.'

When the appointed time arrived the entire defense team and their spouses or boyfriends/girlfriends arrived. Liam was there with wife Fiona, Roland with wife Terri, Pritch and Sarah, Irving Johnson and his wife Carole, Heather and her husband Brad and of course Patrick and Kelly. Deputy Wayne Broomfield had been invited and arrived alone. There was great eating, drinking and toasting. The highlight of the evening occurred about nine-thirty when Jim Brogan entered in a wheel chair carefully watched over by his wife Kathleen. Jim's head wound had healed nicely while he was in the coma. All he needed was to wakeup and start to eat and move. The Appleby children were running around helter-skelter in the happiest of moods. Even Frankie, who had returned home in late July, traumatized after the attack and almost a month in hospital looked happy and well adjusted. Evelyn looked radiant and held hands most of the evening with Frank except when she had to play hostess and deal with the food. All in all, it was a joyous occasion. At eleven p.m. Evelyn served coffee and tea with cake and Frank and Evelyn kissed as if they were newly-weds. Liam told Frank that he could take a lie-in tomorrow but Frank said that after the trial wells wishers had offered him three new gardening jobs and he was eager to be outside after his confining experience. He said he might just start one of the jobs in the morning. With that signal the crowd started to disburse. Patrick and Kelly were the last to leave. As they were leaving Frank grabbed Patrick and gave him a big kiss on the forehead which under the circumstances seemed quite O.K.

When they got in the car and started in towards Leesburg on Route 15 Kelly broke the silence by telling Patrick that Evelyn Appleby had made a strange remark to her during the evening. She couldn't remember the exact words but it sounded to Kelly like a halfway admission that she had killed Wilbur Cosgrove. She didn't come right out and admit it but she had come close. Patrick thought about what Kelly had told him for a minute or so and then confided; Liam and I came to that conclusion some time ago. We were sure Frank didn't do it and when the sheriff and the FBI hadn't been able to break the two would-be assassins, Evelyn moved into first place as a suspect.

'What will happen to her Patrick?'

'I don't honestly know. We could be wrong, but if we came to that conclusion it is probable Sheriff Dunn will come to the same conclusion, particularly now that the case against Frank has collapsed.'

'I hope if she did it they don't catch her.'

'Well, we aren't going to turn her in anyway, particularly only based on a hunch.'

'Would you defend her if she was ever charged?'

'I doubt it, what with a new wife to support.'

'We'll see about that!'

Patrick knew one fact Kelly did not. He had spent his entire eight-thousand dollar fee defending Frank and of the twenty-five thousand dollar defense fund given to Patrick by Sarah Foster, only one hundred dollars remained. Another state appointed murder defense would almost certainly have to be rejected. How many defense teams' had a Sarah Foster to stave off bankruptcy? Besides, there was no way he was going to lose another wife.

# Thirty-Four

THE trial of Frank Appleby started on a beautiful September day and ended on an even more glorious one. November was approaching which would mark one year to go to the election of governor of the Commonwealth. The general had already been criss-crossing the State looking for votes. Today, he had already been in Hanover, Green, Culpepper and Orange counties. Tonight he was scheduled to speak to the faithful in Shenandoah, Front Royal and Winchester. The next day he had a seven a.m. prayer breakfast in Fredericksburg and then he would spend the balance of his day in Arlington and Fairfax with late evening engagements in Warrenton and Manassas before returning to Richmond. He was setting a frantic pace and the early opinion polls had him slightly ahead. He had told Pritch to stay in Leesburg and mop-up all details until after the election and then return to Richmond to take-up his new duties. This would mean that Pritch would be stationed in Leesburg for one additional year which pleased both Sarah and Patrick immensely. While he wouldn't be the attorney general after the election he assured Pritch that his new position would be safe.

About two months after the acquittal of Frank Appleby Patrick called the board of directors together for a post mortem meeting. Everyone was present including; Jim, Roland, Liam, Irving, Kelly, Heather and of course Patrick. They discussed the trial and the areas they thought they had done well in and other areas in which they felt they had failed. Jim Brogan felt he had let the team down badly by allowing himself to be suckered into the meeting with the child pornography ring thugs at White's Ferry and subsequently being taken out of action. Liam apologized for what he described as his weak cross-examination. He cited the fact that his cross of Roy Harris, one of Frank's card-playing buddies, was not his greatest hour. He felt he had failed to breakdown Harris' damning testimony. Patrick felt his inexperience had really shown throughout the trial and he was slow to anticipate the necessary stages during their preparation. He cited the fact that he had to be told by Liam to hire a forensic scientist as an expert witness as only one example.

Finally, the review shifted to an analysis of who killed Wilbur Cosgrove. The team was split over this issue. Some members felt that securing the acquittal of Frank Appleby was the main goal and that had been accomplished. Enough said, success had been secured. Others felt great disquiet that they had not helped to find the real killer. They indicated this denied the team real closure in the case, so once again, and not for the first time, they revisited the possible suspects. The two Dutch child pornography ring thugs had all but been ruled out by the FBI and the sheriff's department but were still a minor possibility. Particularly, since they had admitted to meeting with Wilbur Cosgrove prior to his death. Evelyn Appleby and Marion Cosgrove were suspects. There was a general feeling among the team members that of the two women, Evelyn Appleby was the better suspect since she had a motive, after all it was her son who was molested. However, most of the team members clung to the view that there was another parent out there who had avenged the molestation of their child. A final possibility but one that there was little support for and no real evidence to back-up was that Wilbur Cosgrove had been involved with a client in some kind of business deal that had gone sour and the client had exacted revenge.

In the end, the team was no closer to solving the murder but they agreed to meet from time to time to discuss any new developments in the case. The truth of the matter was they had all grown so close during the Appleby trial they needed some reason to stay in touch.

Pritch finally proposed to Sarah, she accepted and he was now eager to take her to Richmond to start their new life together as man and wife after the election. He made a suggestion to Patrick that they organize a double wedding on election day. When Patrick mentioned Pritch's suggestion to Kelly she readily agreed. Two problems still existed. First, there was the little problem of the divorce from Cindy which would not be signed by the judge for several more months. Second, Pritch and Patrick were the best of friends but in a double wedding ceremony they would of necessity have to select other best men. Fortunately, Pritch had gotten very close to the entire defense team and selected Roland Alberts, who was now fully recovered, as his best man. Roland was thrilled at the prospect. Patrick asked Liam to serve as his best man, Liam's partners Mick Kelly and John Jo Sullivan agreed to act as ushers. Kelly selected Heather as her matron of honor and Sarah selected her sister Mary to act as her maid of honor. Jim Brogan, Harry Dean, Irving Johnson, Ralph Harrington and wives were asked if they would be honoured guests and sit in the front row with family members. They all accept with great pleasure.

With all the major players in place the details of really organizing the weddings were placed in the capable hands of Sarah's and Kelly's mums. Over the ensuing months they helped select the dresses and invitations, supplied the necessary lists of relatives and family friends. The local country club was booked for the reception and the mothers' hovered over every last detail. Sarah's father was deceased but a favorite uncle agreed to act in his place and give away the bride. Kelly's father, Dr. Ron, was very much alive but taking a low profile; stating; 'my only function is to lift my wallet'. The costs were split equally with one exception, Sarah's mother planned to have oceans of fresh orchids flown in from Hawaii to adorn every dinner table. The wedding was in the evening scheduled for seven p.m. with arrival at the country club to occur about nine p.m. after the compulsory hour of official photographs. The divorce a vinculo matrimonii (final divorce decree) arrived well before the planned wedding date. Patrick was now free to remarry and this time he vowed it would be forever.

When the wedding date finally arrived, Patrick was very excited because his brother, Robert, had travelled all the way from Baku, Azerbaijan to be present. When Sarah and Kelly walked down the aisle they were so beautiful they sucked the breath out of the assembled congregation. The wedding went like clockwork and the couples arrived at the country club almost exactly at nine p.m. as scheduled. Everyone was welcomed by a champagne reception followed by a sit-down dinner served with military precision. The quality of the food was exceptional. Sarah's mother who had entertained at the highest levels insured the result. After dinner the focus changed slightly as the best men and the parents had their say. The best men's speeches were heavily rehearsed in an effort to milk maximum laughter and were delivered by obviously outstanding public speakers who had honed their skills in numerous courtrooms around Virginia. At eleven p.m. the dancing commenced.

Deputy Wayne Broomfield asked Kelly for a dance. She happily accepted. Wayne told Kelly there had been an arrest in the Wilbur Cosgrove murder case. Once Frank had been acquitted Sheriff Dunn honed in on Evelyn Appleby and Marion Cosgrove. He had interviewed both women at great length. During the interview with Marion Cosgrove she had broken-down and admitted she had murdered her husband. Evidently, she had gone to the back garden building to tell Wilbur lunch was ready. She saw Wilbur raping Frankie. She had literally caught Wilbur with his pants down and a full erection. A huge fight ensued. She screamed at him concerning his evil act with the Appleby child and told him she knew about his computer in the basement with the filthy pictures. She told him she wasn't going to let him continue to hurt innocent children and grabbed the shotgun from the corner and shot Wilbur once in the chest. She then ran to bottom of the garden and threw the shotgun in the creek. Then she ran to the house and called for an ambulance. She quickly washed her face and hands and changed clothes. This only took a total of three minutes. She then threw the blood-stained dress in the washing machine and started it. The next day she burned the blood-splattered dress. When she returned to the outbuilding she had sincerely tried to help Wilbur as she loved him but knew he had to be stopped as he was destroying too many young lives. She was genuinely hysterical by the time the sheriff and ambulance arrived.

John Brandywell's theory that it was Frank Appleby who threw the shotgun in the creek after he had murdered Wilbur Cosgrove had therefore been totally wrong.

Kelly was amazed at Wayne's news and couldn't wait to tell Patrick, Liam and the other members of the team what had transpired but first she had some questions for Wayne.

'How come Marion Cosgrove's fingerprints weren't on the shotgun?'

'Mrs. Cosgrove was working in the kitchen and was wearing rubber gloves. When she went to the outbuilding she still had the rubber gloves on.'

'How come Sheriff Dunn didn't find the bloodstained clothing in the washing machine when he questioned Marion Cosgrove?'

'Sheriff Dunn questioned Marion Cosgrove in the outbuilding. This is recommended police practice as it is felt keeping the witness at the crime scene will help them focus better on what had occurred and aid them to describe details with more clarity. Sheriff Dunn indicated he had carefully observed Mrs. Cosgrove's clothing. There was no blood splatter consistent with a high-speed splash-back.' Rather, there was a large bloodstain on the dress consistent with the fact when Sheriff Dunn had entered the outbuilding he found Mrs. Cosgrove sitting on the floor cradling her husband. Blood from his chest wound was saturating her dress in an ever-expanding circle.'

'But I thought the sheriff's department had carefully searched the Cosgrove's home?'

'True, later on the day of Wilbur Cosgrove's murder, the sheriff's department deputies had carefully searched the house for evidence of child pornography but were oblivious to the fact that Mrs. Cosgrove was now washing the blood-splattered dress worn during the murder for the third consecutive time.'

When the conversation with Wayne ended, Kelly pulled Patrick off the dance floor and out onto a club house balcony. When she told Patrick the story at first he was shocked but after he thought about it for awhile he came to terms with the reality of the situation. Even he and Liam, as close as they had been to the case, never for one instant really suspected Marion Cosgrove of the murder of her husband.

The music was in full swing when Roland Alberts cut it off abruptly at one a.m.

'Ladies and gentlemen, I have an important announcement to make. Word has just reached me that our Attorney General, Dan Rivers, has won the Virginia gubernatorial race in a landslide. Out of almost three million votes cast, Mr. Rivers has received one million eight hundred ninety-five thousand four hundred one votes while his opponent Mr. Earl Robinson has received one million one hundred one thousand two hundred ninety-six votes. This is with ninety-eight percent of the precincts reporting. It is fair to say that Loudoun County has a great new friend in the Governor's office.

The wedding guests burst into sustained applause; Patrick congratulated Pritch, 'well my old friend, your boss has pulled it off in grand style.'

'Yes counsellor, now you and I have many things to be grateful for.'

'Amen, Pritch, amen.'

After returning from their honeymoon in Barbados, Patrick received a note from Cindy. It held a simple but powerful message.

'Dear Patrick, I have learned of your marriage to Kelly. I most sincerely wish you both unending happiness. I too have remarried and I hope you can find it in your heart to wish Giles and me happiness. Thank you for all the kindness, friendship, love and devotion you gave me during our time together. Your friend forever, Cindy'

Patrick was stunned to receive such a note particularly since he had not seen or talked to Cindy in over one year. He debated whether he should show the note to Kelly. Finally, he decided he wanted his new marriage to be open and without secrets. After reading it, Kelly said, ' I am not jealous, it is better this way, it was brave of Cindy to write that note. We can now start our marriage with a clean slate without recriminations or bitterness.'

For Patrick, it was a catharsis; he felt the last remnants of pent-up pain caused by his failed first-marriage leave his body. As his father use to say, 'God was in his heaven and all was right with the World.'

Epilogue

# Epilogue

Five years after the trial of Frank Appleby ended.

Evelyn Appleby is happy with her five children and her country existence. She still tends her kitchen garden and bakes wonderful apple pies.

Frank Appleby is happily gardening in and around Leesburg.

Jonathan Pritchard has distinguished himself in the attorney general's office and is now assistant attorney general of the Commonwealth.

Sarah Foster-Pritchard gave birth to twins and is happily at home with her children.

Roland Alberts, fully recovered, is still handling divorce cases and where appropriate is using Jim Brogan as his investigator. Roland went on a diet and lost eighty pounds. He now looks marvellous at six four and two hundred forty pounds.

Jim Brogan, fully recovered, is still working hard but has promised Kathleen he will retire for a second time in two more years, she doesn't believe him.

Heather Thompson is still working for Patrick full-time. She and Brad now have a second child, a little boy, named Patrick.

Liam O'Brien defended in two additional murder trials, one in Fairfax and one in Manassas. His reputation as one of the best criminal lawyers in the Commonwealth is now secure.

Dan Rivers was re-elected to a second term as governor of Virginia. He is still crusading hard against child pornography. Larry King often has him as a guest on his show on CNN.

Sheriff Stanley Dunn was also re-elected and has recently accepted an award as one of America's ten best sheriffs.

Deputy Wayne Broomfield, disappointed at losing his chance with Kelly, is now happily married to a gym teacher at Loudoun Valley High School named Irene.

Frank Appleby Jr. (Frankie) now fourteen seems a well adjusted teenager. He has grown very tall and is now on the Loudoun County High School junior varsity basketball team as a forward.

Judge Philip Draper is still the senior circuit court judge in Virginia's 33rd circuit. Fortunately, there have been no further murders in the county since that of Wilbur Cosgrove.

Harry Dean has gone from strength to strength and now owns no fewer than eighteen separate commercial properties in downtown Leesburg.

John Brandywell, Commonwealth Attorney of Loudoun

County, was re-elected and is still prosecuting wrongdoers with vigor. He prosecuted the two Dutch would be assassins successfully. They each received twenty-five years.

Irving Johnson, now 77, is still conducting his funeral business but stops by the law offices for coffee, doughnuts and chat at least twice per week.

Dr. Ralph Johnson sadly passed away at age ninety three. Five thousand Loudoun County citizens attended his funeral which due to the numbers had to be held outdoors, it was the largest funeral in the history of the county. Frank Appleby read one of the prayers.

Cindy Hurst married Giles Burnette who was successful in his third bid for public office and is currently the congressman from the seventh congressional district of Virginia.

Marion Cosgrove was represented on a fee paying basis by Mick Kelly, Liam's partner. She was acquitted of murder on the basis of justifiable homicide. She was found guilty of the lesser offense of obstruction of justice and was given a two year suspended sentence. Virginia had a criminal statute that made homicide justifiable if an individual found their spouse having sex with another person. Mick Kelly convinced the jury that the other person need not be a man or woman but could in fact be a child. It was a landmark case in the Commonwealth.

Kelly Madison-Hurst graduated from George Mason University, School of Law and is now practicing in Leesburg with her husband in the firm of Hurst & Hurst, Attorneys-at-Law.

Patrick J. Hurst (The Counsellor) no longer a solo-practitioner now refers to himself as a 'country attorney'. He enjoys nothing more than holding conversations standing on the street corners around the courthouse and waving to passers-by. He takes great satisfaction in the fact that most everyone who passes by knows him and waves back.

The yellow sofa-bed is still in Patrick's office, a little worn but still pressed into use on rare occasions.

The Cottage at Neersville still stands but has returned to a guest cottage as Patrick and Kelly built a new two storey house just outside Hillsboro.

Roland's oversized chair was ordered by Patrick from a firm in High Point, North Carolina. It had to be specially constructed. Patrick insisted on a small brass plaque which said simply, 'Roland's Chair'. The furniture manufacturer was a little confused but complied.